The Life of
Charlie Burrell

Breaking the
Color Barrier in
Classical Music

By
Charlie Burrell
and
Mitch Handelsman
Foreword by Dianne Reeves

Proudly Published in the USA by
Books to Believe In
17011 Lincoln Ave. #408
Parker, CO 80134

Phone: (303)-794-8888

Find us on Facebook at
www.facebook.com/Books2BelieveIn

Follow us on Twitter at
@books2believein
#BooksToBelieveIn

Follow our blog at
bookstobelievein.wordpress.com
BooksToBelieveIn.com

ISBN: 1502896451

Cover Design: Capri Brock
DesignsByCapri.com

Charlie Bussel

Acknowledgements

Of course, this project could not have been done without the contributions of all the members of the Burrell family. Thanks especially to Purnell Steen for urging us to start the project in the first place, and for sending us good vibes and energy throughout. Thanks also to Syd Harriet and EJ Thornton.

Thanks to the University of Colorado Denver for a small grant and a large sabbatical to the second author. Thanks also to April Jacobs and Amada Smith for their help and input.

Dedications

To my mother.

—Charlie

To my mother and father,
who gave me music and education,
among countless other gifts.

—Mitch

This was at the City Park Jazz Festival in Denver

Table of Contents

Foreword   by Dianne Reeves   9

Prologue   17

Part I: 21

Childhood & Youth in Detroit
Mother, Family, and
School are the Foundations

Part II: 59

High School
Gonna Play Them Funky Blues
(and The Classics)

Part III: 99

Navy & College
Teaching Doors Slam Shut,
and Jazz Doors Open

Part IV: 123

Denver
A Meeting in the Back of the Streetcar
was the Beginning of Charlie's
History-Making Classical Career

Part V: 197

San Francisco
More Barriers Come Down

Part VI: 221

Denver Redux
Professional, Personal,
and Political Developments

Epilogue   291

Foreword

By Dianne Reeves

One of the things that used to happen: I had this one great aunt who was an amazing pianist, and sang all of these really wonderful songs from the early 1900's. These double-entendres. She played the piano beautifully. Her name was Katie Howard. First of all, she was this amazing cook, and you could see any number of our family over there eating some of the prime food. And every night she made a formal table for her husband. And when she had parties she had theme parties. It was just so much energy. I remember many, many times she would play the piano and my Uncle Charles would stand by her and play the bass. And she would sing these songs that the adults would be laughin' at. And we kids just loved it—we'd be laughin' because they would be laughing, and never knew what the songs were about. And she would teach me some of those lyrics; sometimes I'd have the opportunity to sing with her and Charlie Brown (we all call my uncle Charlie Brown!). At a very young age. And, you know, I would sing those lyrics. And it took me maybe 'til I was 21 to know what those words were really about! But that was even before anybody was really conscious that I could sing. I just would do it—that was just a kid thing.

I've known Charlie all my life, since I was conscious! I don't even remember the first time I ever saw him. It just seems like he was always there. In the very beginning, I remember when we moved here to Denver, Colorado. I was very young, three years old. And he was this figure that I was a little afraid of, because he had this very, very, very, strong voice. And when he would tell you what to do, you better do it! 'Cause he had this kind of command.

I could look at an orchestra and I could see, wow, for a long time it was just him. You know, one Black man in this orchestra of all White people. I thought that was a very triumphant thing, because here's a generation that busted through walls to have their intellect and their abilities accepted and viewed as equals, whether people wanted to or not. And I knew that in order for him to be there he had to work harder than anybody else.

When I looked at my uncle in the orchestra and I would listen to that music I didn't really understand it, but I would get a little bit of it. I remember, my mother bought "Longines Symphonettes" so that you could hear, you know, the popular Beethoven, the popular Bach, the popular pieces of the time. So I had a little bit of it. But to see him in an orchestra like that, you know, playin' this music, and then at the same time comin' into a little intimate jazz spot. When you stand in an orchestra it's like this, very, you know, upright thing. And then he took the bass and just played it any kinda way when he would be in a jazz setting. Still with the same mastery, but showing me that music exists in all sorts of ways. And you address it where you are, and what the music asks you to do with it. And I can appreciate all of this in retrospect: That was like a major, major bit of education for me. That was the thing that allowed me to love so many different kinds of music. At my core, I'm a jazz singer, but I love all kinds of music.

I remember when I got into junior high school and I did finally find my voice, he was right there to guide me, and really thought, "Wow, you have somethin'," and just started to expose me to a lot of different things in and around Denver. He exposed me to the great pianist Louise Duncan. I had an opportunity to work with both of them. When he would do certain parties I would do those with him. He taught me to learn the melodies of the music, to communicate with musicians. He really, really, encouraged me to learn all kinds of songs, and he gave me all kinds of records to listen to. Instrumentalists, vocalists, you know. Just kept bringin' 'em over and just sayin', "Listen to this." And then come later and ask me, you know, "What did you listen to?" and, "What did you think?" And tell me what songs to learn, and I basically had to tell him why I liked each singer, what they brought to me. I remember I was not at that time crazy about Billie Holliday, I just didn't get her. But I loved Sarah, you know. And I loved Dakota Staton—he brought Dakota Staton albums, and Dinah Washington. And so these were the first records that really grabbed my ear and really helped me to understand just how vast this art form, music, is.

One of the things that he said: You could listen to any musician and after the first two notes, any singer or any instrumentalist, you would know who it was immediately. So that was saying to me that you have to find your own thing. Without saying, "Be your own thing" when I would be doing somebody else's thing, he would steer me back to where I was.

I remember when I got into high school, into my junior year, bein' with the high school jazz band. And that was what led me to meet Clark Terry, who was also a good friend of his. So when Clark Terry found out that I was Charles Burrell's niece, that was more weight, and he was just right there for me. Because of Clark Terry I was invited to go to Dick Gibson's party. And I'll never forget the first one that I went to at the Broadmoor. And Grady Tate was on drums. I believe it was Roland Hanna at piano, Eddie Lockjaw Davis, Carl Fontana, and George Duvivier was on bass. And I remember not knowing who any of these people were, but I knew that they were somebody. And I knew that Clark knew that if he asked me to do this, then my Uncle Charlie would have prepared me well to be able to stand in front of that caliber of musician.

We drove up to the Broadmoor, to Colorado Springs, and the whole way up there, you know, he was tellin' me all these things. And I was listening, some goin' in one ear and out the other, but I think I retained a lot. But it didn't really have an effect on me until much later. He was always tellin' me things. And in the true tradition of jazz music, tellin' me jazz stories. So when I got there I had my songs that I knew that I could sing, that I had practiced. And it was perfect, you know. I could tell Clark Terry what I wanted to do. I could count it off to the band because my uncle taught me how. And I was very young! I was 15 years old. It was a really wonderful experience.

Right after that, at another gathering that Dick Gibson gave, he put Clark Terry with the Denver Symphony, which was my first symphony experience. And of course, my uncle was in it. And he helped me to understand the role of the symphony in acoustic music and what it was that I would experience. And, you know, still very shell-shocked, I think my confidence came in his belief that I could do it.

And, you know, when I would veer too much from the melody he would always say, "Just really learn the melody. The first thing you should learn is how to phrase, more than tryin' to change the melody." Like, a lot of the Sarah Vaughn I would learn verbatim. And he would say, "'At's really wonderful, but I'm sure that on the next take she sang it a totally different way." So he helped me understand that. But he also didn't break my spirit, because he knew I had the potential to develop and create in an improvisatory kind of way.

Everything for him was in the moment. He taught me in the moment. In other words, he told me to learn my scales and all that kind of stuff. And I would do that. But it was all when it was being applied that he would guide my course. And I could hear him when he would do it like that. We would play at the Unitarian Church, all kinds of different places. And after a show, he would just simply say a word or two, but I knew what he was talking about because I really had a very deep understanding of what it was I wanted to do and what it was I was listening to, and what was needed. So when he would guide me in the way that he would, he was never harsh. But strong. And in a way so that I could hear it, you know. And he never really had to tell me too many things, too many times.

The things that I remember most fondly: He was always, in a lot of ways, different from some of the other people in the family, in that he was very worldly, you know. You could kind of hear it in the way he spoke and the way he carried himself. Having access to the classical world was something as well as having access to the jazz world. They were two totally different sides of music at that time. In retrospect, I think those were the kind of things that made him seem bigger than life.

Charlie has the gift of gab, and he's very witty. He just has this "Burrell" kind of quality. Some people in the family have it. I always used to love to hear him say really hip things, you know. He had this broad vocabulary, but at the same time, he'd put a little street in it. It was just like, wow, you know, I'd never heard anything like that. He seemed to be different than anybody I knew. Bigger, yeah, and more knowledgeable. You know, he had a Mercedes! We didn't have Mercedes! That was like, wow! That's a Mercedes! He had one. He just carried himself in a way, dressed in a way, and held his cigar in a way, and moved in a way, and spoke in a way that was just like nobody else I'd ever experienced.

In a lot of ways it's like a village with my Uncle having the power of music and understanding of things in the world. But my whole family is a family of strong people, with the other ones making other contributions to all of our lives—rich contributions. You know, you could go to each one of 'em for something different. And it's that, I think more than anything, is that power in the family. Everybody in the family has somethin' different to give. And no problem givin' it. Some could be harsh, some could be soft. Whatever. But you could definitely navigate your way through this world from the elders in our family.

Everybody in the family are amazing story tellers. My mother, my uncles, all of 'em. They can tell stories about their childhood, they remember things verbatim, and they can go back to three and four years old. It's just amazing. And the stories, they're like the most important thing in my life. They've really been the glue that holds the family together.

I mean all the way down to Grandmother (Charlie's mother) makin' pancakes. You got the number of the age that you were. My Aunt Mary Beth was little but she could eat a lot and she only got, like, four. And she was cryin', you know. And when they tell it, you can see it, you know. So many stories. And it happened just this Sunday when we went to have breakfast. I know how to start it: I just say one thing, and woop! They all *just start goin'; I just sit there. And they can remember! Just little stories, and everybody tells the story in the voice and the mannerisms that the person was. And so we can see them, you know? They're still there.*

I love listening to the stories of their lives and how they came up. I remember one time, I asked my mother, "How was your house furnished?" 'Cause it just sounded like their lives were so rich!

And she said, "Furniture?? What is that? We had a rug wit' a hole in it! We danced a hole in it." And it just changed my whole thing, because the richness of their lives, the richness of their stories, that was the thing that moved me to hear these stories. And still to this day, when I hear these stories, over and over—I've heard 'em so many times it's not funny—but I still feel the same way when I hear 'em. And that richness comes from the life that you lead.

I think Charlie's story is relevant for all kinds of people, because it's a story of triumph. It's a story of someone who made a way out of no way. Not only that: When he made the way he opened it for others to come through. To me, that is the power of the story, that in so doing he found personal peace, mental peace. While he didn't garner the celebrity of a lot of people, he really, really, was able to do a job well done. He mastered his life, and his understanding of this music, and what it took to do something that he loved, not based on how much money you made or how much celebrity or any of that. But just for the art, for the passion, for the love. And I feel that same way about music, that it is something that is given to you. It's a journey. You don't know if there's gonna be a lot of icing on the cake or not. You just know that this is what makes your heart beat. That is, for me, why people from any walk of life shouldn't have any problem reading a story like this. It's relevant to everything. You want it, you see it, you work very very hard to get it.

When you read this book, listen to the voices in our family. Listen to my Uncle Charles. I don't think you would miss that he is a man of great integrity. I don't think you would miss that he is a giver. I don't think you would miss that he loves life. But I think with all the things that you see about him—with all the things that I saw about him that made him bigger than life—realize that at his core he is still eight years old, just like the rest of the family. There is a very youthful spirit that is always ready at whatever time to come out and play. That's at his core; that's what keeps 'em all young. They all have that child still very much a part of their spirit. It keeps them young, it keeps them vibrant. Anybody, to me, who can go back to when they were five years old and remember and anybody like my uncle who decides he's gonna walk eight miles today and he's over eighty years old—there's somethin' in him that propels him. And I think it's his youthful spirit. And if you tried to, like, have a race with him or anything you'd be surprised, because he might just leave you in the dust!

There's my mother at the top right, along with her siblings (clockwise): Aunt Ida, Uncle Willie, Aunt Mary, and Aunt Kay,

Voices in the Family

Joe Burrell: Charlie's Brother

Melanie Burrell: Charlie's Wife; former cellist with the Denver/Colorado Symphony Orchestra

Sharon Hill: Charlie's Niece; Dianne Reeves's Sister; Vada's Daughter

Mary Beth Mitchell: Charlie's Younger Sister

Dianne Reeves: Charlie's Niece; Vada's Daughter; 4-time Grammy-Award-winning jazz singer

Purnell Steen: Charlie's Cousin

Vada Swanson: Charlie's Younger Sister; Dianne Reeves's Mother

Katie White: Charlie's Oldest Sister

Prologue

This is just a simple story of a simple fellow, okay. But I realize that other people would like to know how this thing happened. I can sum up most of what I was doing in life in a very few words. It was a matter of love for the profession and love for the people. And that's about how simple it was. Everything after that was just an addendum to the facts.

When I was in the 7th grade, one Friday afternoon—ready to get out for that 2-day vacation, you know—Mr. Harrington, who was the music teacher, came in at 2:30 and said they had an opening for musicians and who wanted to come in. And no one raised their hands except me. And I raised my hand and went into the room, there. He looked into the corner and says, "Well, Charlie, all we have left here is a bass fiddle." He called it a bass fiddle, okay, a big aluminum bass fiddle.

I said, "I'll take it." And I started right then.

I hauled it home the first day, Monday. And Mom said, "I think maybe we need something to haul that in." So I got a little red wagon; she bought it for 25 cents from Goodwill. And I started hauling the bass in that wagon—every day, you know, to and from school. And the kids looked at me like I was crazy. I didn't care, you know.

I started right off the bat just liking the bass tremendously, so every day I would practice an hour, two hours. And my mother used to look at me. In the interim, I had heard—on our crystal set radio, which a lot of people don't know about nowadays but it was one of the first homemade sets—I heard this phenomenal sound of an orchestra on it. I finally found something. And I discovered it was the San Francisco Symphony. And the conductor was Pierre Monteux, and I didn't even know how to pronounce it in those days. But I told my mother, I said, "Hey, Mom, I'd like to perform with the San Francisco Symphony."

And she was smart beyond her years. She didn't look down her nose. She said, "Well Son, you can do anything you want to do. Just be honest to your cause and do it every day of your life. Let nothing get in your way." I thought they were great words of wisdom.

So I started right then, when I was just 12, and I got a teacher right away and started getting lessons on the bass. In retrospect I realize that that was the most difficult thing that ever happened in my life because I didn't have the fundamentals of piano behind me, which is what other kids had in back of them for a foundation to start building on—a piano or something connected with music. I had none of that—I just started cold turkey on the bass, which was the most difficult thing to hear because of the low vibrations. But I stuck with it. I said, "Well, this is it; I'm going to stick with this through thick and thin, and make my way."

When I was maybe twelve or thirteen I saw the Detroit Symphony play. And when they came out on stage I was so impressed with these elegant men with these *looooonnnng* coats and white ties. And I didn't know what they called the white thing they had on their vest, but it's a waistcoat, you know.

And I said to myself, That's what I want to look like! That's what I want to do! With these elegant classical musicians on stage—looking like nothing but pure elegance—that helped to cement what I wanted to do in life. I like to look good. And all my life I liked to dress. People ask me now, "Why do you dress up?" Hey! Every day is Christmas. And it always has been.

My life, I feel, has been in two worlds. The Negro world and the Anglo world. I was always a quasi-member of both races. When I was only 12 years old I was beginning to be exposed intimately with the White race, because I was studying music. And that was my big in. I met people along the way—especially Anglos—who helped make my life possible. And I met a lot of Blacks who almost tried to put a monkey wrench in my educational machine. They used to call me everything—I can't name what they *didn't* call me. They accused me of being everything from the bad to the worst and all this, being an Uncle Tom. I didn't have any problem with that; my mother taught me how to handle that. One Sunday at the table she said, "Look, son, let's figure this out." She says, "You know, uh, here's how we look at that. Now, Chunky," She used to call me Chunky. "Jesus Christ was the first. He was the first token. He did quite well, didn't he?" And that said it all to me. "People that normally say those things are people who are looking at you, and they have admiration for you, but they have disgust for you because you represent something that they would like to be." So I never had a problem with tokenism. A coupla fights, but no problem....

If you look close, you can see the sign for
Boyer's Haunted Shack, where I worked.

Part I:

Childhood & Youth in Detroit

Mother, Family, and School are the Foundations

*"When people know your history,
you put pieces in your life together."*

—Dianne Reeves

Chapter 1

The Burrell family: Seven kids and a worthless father and a dedicated, respected, revered, loving mother who kept the family together and intact. She was the most important element of my whole life, but especially my early life. She gave us a pattern to look forward to in life, a pattern of honesty, integrity, self-respect, love, and no racial hang-ups. Plus learning how to use the English language correctly, rather than what we called ghetto style, which is dese, dats, and doze.

My mother was born in Denver, Colorado, in 1896, when it was called Arapahoe County and not Denver County. My mother was very unusual; she came from an unusually well-versed family. Her father was a reverend and traveled over the southern United States, which is what reverends did in those days. Like a different church almost every Sunday. Little small church. And he was a Methodist, so my mother was brought up under the Methodist tradition. Her father was also one of the first ministers at the Shorter A.M.E. Church.

My father was from a place called Shepherd, Texas, which was about 55 miles outside of Houston. And my father had a little incident in Shepherd, where he had to leave in a hurry because he had committed an unsavory act—murder. But it was in self-defense. Anyhow, they got him out of town and he got on the railroad as a hobo and came to Denver, and whisked my mother off her feet and married her right away and took her back to Texas momentarily. My oldest sister was born in Texas. From there they went immediately to Toledo, Ohio, where four of the Burrells were born. From there, we came on the "Inter-Urban" from Toledo to Detroit, and that's where my young life began.

There were seven kids. Katie was the oldest. Then came Ruben, Jr., me, and my brother under me, Joe J.P. Burrell, who was named after my grandfather, who was Rev. J. P. Burrell. And then Vada, who later became a nurse and her big thing was that she had one of the greatest children in the world whose name was Dianne Reeves, who we all know now in terms of what she has contributed and has been in terms of music. After her came my youngest brother, Allen, who was a tap dancer, and a junkie. After him came my youngest sister, Mary Beth, who was one of the first Blacks to work at Bell Telephone Company in Detroit.

VADA: *There were 7 Burrells—pretty busy household. Mother (Denverado) was in control at all times. I have nothin' to say about my father, except there was a divorce when I was 10, 11 years old and we were all very happy and in agreement with our mother. We had no problems.*

We moved, first of all, into a Polish neighborhood—a place called Tillman Street. And I went to the kindergarten at that school—I can't even remember the name. But we were not there very long because of racial incidents there, you know. We had to get out of the neighborhood; my father realized that the pressure was too much for the family. And only one family. In other words, there was nothin' good on the block, you know, to be called, "Nigger, nigger, nigger" and all that kind of shit. And my father was smart enough to realize we had to move away from that because it was just too much.

JOE: *I grew up in Detroit. And we thought we were rich. Our mother was very positive about things. And our father was gone all the time. We didn't know what he was doing. But we had a rich childhood. We had a lot of fun. We never knew we were poor. We were destitute, but we never knew we were poor.*

I remember that when I was younger I used to go in the beer joints there, and dance, okay, a little dance and get free food there. They used to have free cheese and salami and things. And I would stock up on that, and get a nickel or 10 cents for doing the Buck dance in those days. It wasn't humiliating, it was just a matter of making out—you know, learning how to get along.

We moved on a street called Humboldt. And Humboldt Street was what I call a quasi-ghetto, which was only 2 and a half blocks for the Negroes. Actually, we lived in the lower part of that 2-block ghetto, which was called "Down in the Hole." Down in the Hole was the lower rung of the social strata for the Blacks there, which were not that many. We lived there for about a year. And then we moved up the next block, which was like being moved uptown!

MARY BETH: *I'm the youngest of the seven children, born and raised in Detroit during the Depression. I attended school up until high school, until I was fifteen. And then I had an onset of asthma, and my mother sent me to Denver, because we had a family here in Denver.*

Chapter 2

My mother was the greatest influence on our family, because she kept us honest, for one thing, and kept us from hating, and that was the other thing. So she was the big boss. She had more sense than all of us put together. And it took me a long while to realize that Mom was the most intelligent thing around. She had her Ph.D. in life at the age of 8, and none of us ever caught up with her, you know.

There's nothing more exciting than to walk in after school and smell a pot on the stove. That to me is the most stimulating thing in the world. You get to the heart of a man (and a woman) through their stomachs. Heh heh. That to me was graciously beautiful.

Yeah, cookin' like a son of a gun for all the family. And that's one reason why I think the whole family survived. The fact that she cooked good food. And we never could figure out how she made a way where there was no way. But she made it. Her big pride and joy early in life was tellin' all of us that not a one of us were goin' on welfare. She says, "I wouldn't accept welfare if it killed me." She says, "I have more pride than that." And that always stuck with me, you know, the appreciation I had for respecting yourself as a person. She says, "'Cause you don't know what's happening, but the White's keepin' ya' down."

My mother was a firm believer that you can do whatever you want to do. And I saw around in the ghetto that families had been on welfare two or three generations. What is this? That means no ambition. In other words, you gotta *fight* for something and be aware of the fact that everything is not free. The only thing that's free is the air. And you have to appreciate and go forward in terms of what you contribute to the social structure.

MARY BETH: *My mother was extremely nurturing to all of us, and to the neighborhood. And encouraging. The one thing I remember most about home—we all enjoyed each other very much. As a child, sitting around the table eating dinner—every day the one thing we had to do was eat dinner together. At the table she would say the blessing, and then each of us would have to say a bible verse. And it was always a hysterical moment. Everybody at the neighborhood wanted to come to our house. Or they did come.*

All of our sisters and brothers, we all went to church, every Sunday. I don't care what church you went to—you went to a church every Sunday. And after church y'all came home and you had a family gathering, a social gathering, which lasted from right after church 'til five, maybe six o'clock. We all ate every Sunday at the table, barring none except my father. There were seven children at the table, and Mom. My father was *never, never* at that table. He was always gone, doing his thing at his social club. The average person can understand what a social club is. It's a matter of getting away from home and getting out and doing your thing. Doing all the bad things that you wanna do, like drinking and carousing and all that. So that was his thing.

On Sunday, sometimes we would have meat, but most of the time we would probably have chicken. That was the main dish because that was pretty cheap at that time, and it was about all we could afford. Once a week, every Sunday, we had dessert. She had to cook up not one cobbler but two cobblers, because the Burrell family could chow—they were a bunch of eating machines. Of course, none of 'em ever had any weight problem because we always ran so much. As soon as you got through eating you went out and played for three, four, five hours, running and just doing things that youngsters do.

What happened at the roundtable for the Burrells on Sunday was a monumental thing, a big part of my life and the Burrell family life. Learning how to cope with life. It was our Sunday meeting thing, okay, where we aired all our experiences. You got seven kids at the table (eight including our niece Delores), airing our things. It was hilarious. We never had a dinner under four hours. Normally it was five hours. We'd come right from church and we'd all sit down. Mom would have us wash our hands, and we'd be clean. Then she'd go around and start. She'd say, "What did you do?" Such and such and such. You tell your little story. And if it wasn't quite right, someone would say, "No, that wasn't quite the way it happened."

I look back and think how important that was. We had a chance to experience with each other what we had done in terms of the week; our experiences—bad, good, indifferent, funny, and not so funny. My mother was always the judge, the supreme judge. If ever we got out of line with a subject, she would stop us and say, "Now wait. Let's think this through." And she would teach us how to think and use our minds. And I was so delighted that we never had television or the other little distractions that they have today.

My mother taught us so much in terms of how to prepare ourselves for life. We used to discuss everything from soup to nuts. In those days, there was no such thing as an ego. I didn't know what an ego was until I was maybe 16 years old. And an attitude? An attitude was not allowed. At the table of the Burrells, if someone (as they call it today) copped at attitude, the rest of the family would right away pounce upon 'em and say, "Look, now, you're out of order. You're wrong. That doesn't happen that way. Let's be realistic." And that was a good feature of that dinner. She always peddled realistic things, and things of this world. In other words, things that you're gonna be faced with in life and how to handle these things. And she always taught us to have a good sense of humor. And I think all of the Burrells really had a sense of humor. Of course, a couple of 'em were not the greatest sense of humor—they were kinda crazy. That was alright, they still had a sense of humor.

I remember her always saying, "Here's the way this goes, in terms of life. Always remember that you are no better than anyone else. But, *you are as good*. Don't forget those words." And they've stuck with me through my entire life. That little speech.

Plus, she explained to us about the need for religion and what part religion played. What it all boiled down to was having something in your life that was bigger than you to rely upon and thank. Not only in terms of when you were deprived and when you were down, but in terms of when you were happy. Give thanks for the better things in life as well as the worse. And figure that tomorrow is gonna be better because you're gonna make it be better.

And, of course, education was foremost at the dinner table on Sunday. The big thing was that if you want to get ahead in life, the big way to get ahead is education. And she preached that religiously. *ED—U—CA—TION*. You can get out of the quasi-ghetto and anything else by education.

We always had word games between the family. In other words, we would all have a word that we thought we could stump the rest of the family on. And we would go into that word and see what the word was and we always had a big dictionary and a set of encyclopedias, which Mom couldn't afford but we got 'em anyhow. She had them for our education. I'll never forget. Complete volumes, A to Z, of these marvelous books. So we also learned from that.

My mother said, "Carry a dictionary." I carried a dictionary for maybe twenty-five years with me—a little pocket dictionary. Being in the quasi-ghetto (That was not the first-class ghetto; there was a ghetto lower than that, okay, which I knew about.), she told us to learn both sides. When you go out, put your best foot forward. So I learned the ghetto talk, you know, how to split infinitives, and all these sort of things, from my people—Black people. Dese, doze, and dats, you know. And my mother taught us how to separate that kind of language from the normal language.

My mother also told me, "Don't talk so much. Listen." And I'll learn something, okay. I would always listen to people. I went to lectures, okay? And later, of course, I played in all the joints, and I heard all the foul stuff that was coming through, and the action of the people, okay. And I always took great pride in learning how to express myself.

And I just associated with people, which would make a big difference. Not only high-brow, but low-brow. I could go in and talk with the average musician, I could talk with the pimps, the whores, you know. And I had no problem because I knew how to talk. I knew the language that they were expected to use. Especially musicians, because back when I was coming up in the thirties, there was a special lingo going with the musicians. And you had to learn that—and I learned it. But I didn't overuse it because that was not my forte in life. My forte was a little higher in terms of how to express what you were doing and what you were about.

My mother taught us to respect people and to try to avoid physical encounter. By the same token, when a butterfly is cornered, it is prone to fight a little. Those were her words. Of course, when she said fight a little she didn't mean to get out there like we did, whippin' ass, you know. That was what the Burrells were famous for, you know. The whole family. We had nice tempers. All of us had good tempers except my youngest sister Mary Beth. And I later discovered she had a worse temper than all of us, but at those times she hid it because she was the youngest. She didn't say much, but she was thinking.

Anyhow, we learned to get along with ourselves, with our family, and with the community. And teachers. At our table, if we ever came up with the idea that we didn't like a teacher, my mother would say, "Okay, now let's discuss this." And we would go into our little critique of why we didn't, and she said, "Look. Let me tell ya' the facts, Dearie. The teacher *has* the education, and you have it to *get*. So, until you come to the stage and age where you can get a college degree or two, then what am I saying, kids?"

And we'd all say, "Don't criticize!" And that was the end of that.

She said, further, "*If* you come home and tell me about something derogatory about the teacher, I'm gonna whip your ass." She'd just tell ya' like it was. And that's just how she said it. "I'm gonna whip your little ass. Okay?" And so we never did. We learned that the teacher was right. And 99% of the time they were right. That's how simple that was.

DIANNE: *My grandmother was really something, because she was open to a lot of things. She had all of these kids that did all of these different things, and she encouraged their spirits. And as grandchildren, she encouraged ours, you know. She just had a way of being able to speak to each individual child in a different way, the way that they needed to be spoken to. What you needed to hear. And there were so many things that she wanted for me.*

She could just say a coupla words, and it would be right to your soul. I mean, you really understood, because it was said in a moment she knew you could hear it. It was very, very strong.

MARY BETH: *She was very vocal and very articulate. She always told stories. She always entertained us. We would sit at the dinner table and she'd just tell us stories about her family. And the way she related stories to us is, she didn't embellish anything in her childhood, about the glamour or nothing. The one thing we got was her real love for her father. The way she talked about her father, we remember as if he were living. I mean, he's just always like a person that was alive, because he was so kind. And that's what I remember. And she also had this unconditional love of her children. Probably why we are as close as we are today is that we were close as children and we had to look out for each other. I don't care what happened—if anything happened to one of the children, we were always there. Each of us looked out after each other. That was her MO. She was about caring for her children, against all odds. So we had this unconditional love for my mother. Also, she made sure that we did everything. Everything that was available, we were involved in it. And she made a way. She was a person that always made a way out of no way. And she had the extreme responsibility of not having any support in raising children. She raised us by herself. Even though my father lived with us, he wasn't home half the time. She was also very protective and made sure that nothing happened to us. We could probably write a book just about her, and the way she was in our maturation.*

Chapter 3

I never remember a day that any one of the Burrell kids was not in school. I don't care whether it rained, snowed, sleeted, anything, we did not miss one day of school. Except my brother Joe. He skipped one day and for years he regretted it, because Mom caught him and that was the end of that. The rest of 'em were always in school. I never missed a day from kindergarten through high school. Not *one... single... day* did I miss. That was because I was always so involved and interested in school. I loved school. I just loved to learn—to learn about different cultures, to see how they lived in different places. And I always had a book or books around me. Plus I always carried my little dictionary so I could enhance words and be more knowledgeable on how to describe and explain the things that I saw and enjoyed in my life.

The important things in my younger life all began when I was in Chaney Elementary School. We were fortunate because we were only about three blocks from Chaney School. I went all through Chaney School with my sisters and brothers, you know. There were only ten, maybe fifteen Blacks in there, if that many. But all the ones that were in there—their families made sure that they were there to learn and not play games, okay. So we had the best education and the best teachers because we were in a predominantly White school. I look back now and realize that I was extremely fortunate that I did come up this way because I was exposed to two things. One was the best schooling, and the second was a balance between Whites and Blacks. So we had no big problem there, alright.

My school days were magnificent—a well-rounded education which most kids today are not afforded. One of the most valuable things in my life in that period was goin' to the lunch room every day to get *good food.* In those days it was not McDonald's and all this. In the kitchen you had mothers working, okay, and it was all volunteer. And they cooked, good, good, meals. So you looked forward to lunch. I said, "Boy, that's enough to keep me going for a while." In the afternoon, say about two o'clock, the kindergarten students would all get a cold glass of Sealtest milk and graham crackers. They had no pop machines; the only beverage you got was milk. Okay. This was a beautiful thing because you got free milk, see. You got your good lunch, and free milk, you can go ahead and do something constructive with your life— tryin' to learn, *learn,* okay—because your stomach is settled.

One of the other things we learned was how to get along with other children. Even in Chaney, they didn't tolerate kids being bullied and things of this character. They just would not tolerate it. We had a very clean school.

$$\text{\Large 𝄞 𝄢 𝄞}$$

VADA: *We had an advantage. What we were taught is to discuss our culture and background. And that was really, really, rewarding.*

In my classroom there was an Armenian girl, Lillian. And she taught us how to say good mornin' in Armenian. We had a Turk in the class, and a Greek. And I found out the Turks didn't like the Greeks. Then there was a German girl there, and she was arrogant. She probably had more money, her parents had money; you could tell by the way she dressed and everything else. And Ewing Zimmerman, he was German. He was a bright kid. Then we had a lot of Polish children in the class, and English was not good, because their parents had just come from Poland, that generation. So they didn't speak good English. With Italians, same way. Then we had some Hungarian Gypsies that had come into the neighborhood. So it was a real melting pot, and we learned a lot about their foods, and they learned a lot about us, and what have you.

It was good for us because it really taught me a lot about how prejudiced people were, and sometimes why. I found out that the Irish Protestants didn't like the Catholic Irish. People hated on the basis of religion, color, and ethnic background. But the children were taught all this at home. And they'd tell it. And, of course, I would, too. And then I'd tell my stories. And the teacher, sometimes I noticed her eyes would be watery.

We had a teacher who was Native American, who committed suicide, and that was a sad time in my life. We always liked her, but there was always a sadness about her. She just never seemed happy. But she would always tell us things that we would never have known about Native Americans. I recall when she told us that she didn't know her mother and father, because she was taken away as a child. In later years I found out that this government did take children away from their parents and teach 'em to be White. I think that's what happened to her. She used to talk about the Ottawa Indians, I believe. It was a sad day when we lost her, when they told us that she committed suicide. That's the first time I had ever known of suicide.

CHARLIE: One of my marvelous memories of a teacher was a real old teacher who was almost 80 years old then, her name was Mahoney. Little, short, and she taught English. And I must say God bless her because I had a difficult time with English. And she would keep me after school fifteen, twenty minutes every day, and explain to me this, and explain to me that. She would teach me how to compose, which I was pretty poor in. She was one of my real remarkable, striking influences in terms of teaching.

VADA: *We had another teacher, Jewish teacher. German Jew. Eisenberg. Now, she always stayed by herself, and I never knew why. The* guy named Ewing Zimmerman was German, and he was racist. And Miss Bacon, that was the principal, put him out of school; he was expelled because he had said derogatory things to Miss Eisenberg, about her heritage.

We found out what Germany was doin'. When I got to Condon Junior High, we had a social studies teacher, Miss King. She brought up a lot of issues for us. She taught us how to think about where that war was going, to write letters to state that this country should stop Germany. And they didn't do anything. And she'd tell us this. Then she would bring clippings from different magazines from the Jews in Germany. It was never part of the curriculum. And then, that kind of really got us thinkin'. Of course, we had a prejudice too, against Germany. And then they was walkin' through Poland and Czechoslovakia, and those smaller countries. And this government still didn't do anything. I did recall her sayin' that there was a big influx of Jews comin' into the United States at that time, but I couldn't put all that together until I got older. Then I found out a whole lot of stuff about the war. And I could put things in perspective. I still think about it.

History-wise, we were taught European and Medieval history. I didn't even know about a Mexican when I moved here. I was taught about the Aztecs.

CHARLIE: We were never taught about Blacks. I never knew.

VADA: My mother taught us our history. That's what I was able to share at school.

CHARLIE: In Chaney School, the big thing for the Negroes was something about a tiger with pancakes and shit. Little Black Sambo. Hey! Give me a break. Of course, we survived it because we talked to our mother and she said, "Look, uh, there are some things in education you're not gonna like. But you get your big education, and weed out."

VADA: She would come down to school, too.

CHARLIE: Oh, she would come down all the time.

VADA: *There was a Lutheran church and school, just off the edge of the playground. And I remember they were havin' a play, Snow White and the Seven Dwarfs. Well, I knew I wasn't gonna be Snow White! But I wanted to be a dwarf. And they didn't pick me to be a dwarf. So I was cryin', and the minister over at that Lutheran school—it was his daughter who ran the auditorium class. He would always come over and visit his daughter. So he come over that day and he asked me why I was cryin'. And I told him because I wanted to be in the play and they didn't choose me. He asked me some questions, and I told him they didn't choose me because I was colored.*

CHARLIE: Oh, boy, heh, heh, heh.

VADA: *I got to play a dwarf. I got the part. It was good, because it kinda stimulated me to do other things I could do, like— The other kids were poor in English, especially the Poles and the Czechs, and Italians, too. Then I could make all the speeches in the auditorium. I would be picked, along with Ella May the German. And there was always a competition—she would never say it, but I could feel it—with each other. 'Cause that's the way she was taught.*

And then the Armenian, we were friendly. And I was friendly with the Turks, and the Greeks. But then, I always kept stuff goin', too. Like I could handle any pressure on me racially with the students in the class, because I would keep the Irish goin' by asking the protestant if they ever heard of a Orange Irish. Then you got a fight! Who said that? Then I would look stupid—but I knew what I was doin'! So I'd get them fightin' and get off of me.

The Greek—her dad owned a bakery. And she brought some bread to school one day, and they ignored Leo. And when I found that out, when they come to serve me I didn't take it. And they asked me why, and I said, "Because you didn't give Leo any." Well, that got it off of me right away.

CHARLIE: She was manipulative, honey! She knew how. That was just her make-up.

VADA: *They taught me to be! And I was sensitive too. I always knew they didn't like Miss Eisenberg but I didn't know why, because she was nice to us. And I noticed that she never went in the teacher's lounge. And then I began to find out why she was like she was. 'Course, I was nice in her class all the time, 'cause I liked her, you see.*

And then, too, the hall guards were always White, most time blond if they could get 'em. I found out how to be a hall guard, and I put myself in the position— I was a hall guard in the sixth grade. So, what I did was to tell all the Blacks, or colored as we called 'em then, what we were gonna do so you can be the hall guard when I leave.

I wanted to be a hall guard because number one, it meant that you were good. It meant that you had good grades. It meant that you were as good as the White ones. We were taught that you had to be better than them to get ahead. So that gave me that feelin', too.

CHARLIE: High prestige, very prestigious.

VADA: *That meant we were clean people, and all this good stuff. So I had a lot of reasons for wantin' to be a hall guard. And I felt that I could make as good a hall guard as the blonds, you know, them other ones.*

VADA: *One day I was called into the principal's office, I was about ten years old. Never shall forget. And as I walked into the principal's office there was a White girl in there who told the principal, "She's the one. She's the one." And I didn't know what was goin' on! So the principal said, "C'mon, I want to talk with you." And she told the White girl to sit down. And the White girl's mother was there with her. And they were told to wait outside. And Miss Bacon, the principal, took me into her private office and asked me what happened.*

I was confused. I didn't know what they were talkin' about. Then Miss Bacon told me that the girl said I had hit her and beat her up and I ran away. And she saw me running away. And I told her I hadn't been in a fight. I didn't hit anyone. And at that point I began cryin' and was really upset. Then I asked Miss Bacon if I could go get my mother, because I didn't fight anyone, and I didn't fight on the playground. I never fought on the playground. And I recited these little different things. So Miss Bacon said, "You just wait here, I'll be back." And I thought, Well, I'm doomed. I'm hung.

She called the girl in without the girl's mother. And she asked the girl some questions. And finally the girl told her she didn't really know who hit her but that she saw me running. In the meantime, she asked her what color dress I had on. And she had asked me what I had worn to school the day before. And the colors were different.

Miss Bacon still had me sittin' there and she called in the girl's mother and asked her to sit down. And she said, "Your child is lying." And that was a term you didn't use. You didn't call anyone a liar. She said, "Your daughter is lyin', and it makes for bad relations in the school. And you are upholding her. I believe what Ida Louise (they called me Ida) said." She stated the colors of the dresses, and they were different. And the rules, I had recited the school rules. She told the mother that, "Your child had broken the rule." She had investigated and found out really what had happened. She said that I was to go back to my class. And about that time the girl was cryin' all over the place. I was, too.

I just felt so vindicated by that. It kinda gave me a little more trust in some certain White people. It's traumatic to be lied on like that.

𝄞 𝄢 𝄞

I'll never forget the table with all the seven kids around the dinner table on Sunday, "Now look. Let's discuss the word *nigger*." And we looked it up in the dictionary, and the word was not a color of a person, it was the action of the person, their attitude. "That was a niggerly attitude," okay? And it was described as being self-centered, ignorant, and all of those things. She said, "That is what a nigger is all about." She says, "You can be White and be a nigger. You can be Chinese and be a nigger." And she went on and on. "You can be Greek and be a nigger." She says, "Don't forget that." She said, "When they use the word, don't get all upset about it. *Unless*, the tonality is so that you feel that you have to make some kind of reaction to what they're talking about."

My mother taught us to evaluate not races, but people, an individual. She taught us that early in life. And she wouldn't allow us to get excited about being a racist son-of-a-gun, because she'd take ya' to task. If you called a Polish person a Pollack, she's slap you 'side your face. Said, "Now, you don't do that. How would you like them to call you a nigger?" And that ended that. You learned how to respect people as individuals, okay. You didn't have time for it, for one thing, because you were too busy tryin' to scratch out a living. Get food, Baby. You didn't have time for no small things like being a racist. Racist to what? What were you better than, you know? Your dog? Heh, heh. Shit.

VADA: *I come home one day and I had been in a fight, and she wanted to know why, what happened. She would try to teach me to express myself verbally. Young ladies and girls didn't fight. And so, I said they called me a nigger. "Who called you a nigger?" And I told her, that Italian girl. "What did you call her?" And I called her a derogatory name, too. I don't know what I called her, but it was a dirty name. Mother said, "Well, why did you have to fight about it? Didn't get your just do?" I wanted to fight, 'cause she figured I had picked it anyway. Which I had! So, she was right. But it was a lesson to be learned, you know, expressin' yourself. How to take care of yourself. Find out their weak points!*

Chapter 4

From Chaney, we moved on to Condon Intermediate School, which was maybe two miles from where we lived. We had different kinds of ethnic backgrounds there too, of course. We had, to my knowledge, German, French, Jewish, Negro, Italian. A cross-section of all kind of people. There was a good, good, relationship there, to teach them how to get along with the social structure. And to me, that was very important. When I went to high school, which was the famous Cass Tech High School, I was given a gift with having gone to Chaney and Condon school, because it prepared me for a lot of social integration that otherwise I probably never would have had.

Another interesting aspect of my days in Condon was the principal of our school. He was a Frenchman, okay, and he was a very respectable looking man. He dressed like an elegant statesman. He had those funny-looking glasses they had in those days. Plus he would dress in marvelous, beautiful suits every day—well-groomed, you know. Our favorite thing was going to the assembly affairs, and he would sing the French song, "Alluetta, Jaunté Alluetta." It was just like yesterday that he was up there, a proud man like you could never believe. Very proud. That helped the image for the kids; something to look forward to rather than ratter-tatter. That was a pretty straightforward thing that he was doing, inadvertently, I think.

In those days, the teachers dressed. All of 'em were ladies. They dressed in gingham, you know, nice, cotton gingham dresses. And they always smelled good. We used to follow some of the teachers down the hall just to smell!

Condon's where I started my education in music. By the time I was in the 8th grade I played my first jazz job—with a fellow whose name was Simon Morris, and he played drums. White, Jewish. His father was a rag man. Had a horse and a buggy. Five-piece band. Piano, and a sax player who couldn't play (neither could I!). But we played, we started playing little tunes, you know. And we made our first big outing at one of the what they called "Friday programs" after school, a little dance for the school kids. And I'll never forget because I made my first 25 cents playing my first job there with Simon Morris. Boy! You're talking about rich. I went home and told Mom, "Look what I made Mom! I made a quarter!" And I gave her twenty cents and I kept five. And it all seemed to develop from that, little by little, you know. We started playing in garages, and so forth.

When I first started, I didn't know who Duke Ellington was. I thought Duke Ellington was royalty. And I thought Count Basie was the Count of Basie. Aaay! I had a rude awakening when the kids from the ghetto told me. They just put my boots on, said, "Look, hey Daahling, here's who Count Basie is...." And here's who all the other musicians were, you know, Duke Ellington, so forth. And we started having sessions in the garage every Friday, Saturday, and Sunday. We would play in the garage, learning how to play jazz. From that thing came such people as Lucky Thompson, Billy

Horner, and so many others who came through that same school. That's the way we learned to play; every Friday, Saturday, and Sunday we'd have "barn dances." So we learned from that.

I was just enamored of the bass—it just got hold of me, you know. That was my Linus blanket. Whenever I had little problems that cropped up I'd go and grab the bass. And in an hour or two it was all over—I had forgotten what the problem was. One of my most trying times in life was when I was about 17, and I fell in love with a girl from Texas. I was working in the B & C Club, okay. I fell in love with her and all this sort of thing. And I was going with her for maybe six or eight months I guess. And finally somebody told me, "Well, don't you know what she's doing?"

I said, "No, what do you mean, 'what's she doing'?"

He says, "You're not the main man in her life. Her main man in her life is her PIMP!"

OOPS! That scared me half to death! And I looked up and I said, My MY my my! I finally discovered she was buying his car, and all this sort of thing. Way back in the thirties, you know. And I said, What is all of this noise? And I asked her. She said, "Oh, yeah. You're my number two!" Aaaaaaah! That put the biggest thing on me in the world. I mean, that momentarily made me contemplate suicide—for five minutes. And I went and picked up the bass and played it out, baby! The next day I forgot who she even was.

The bass brought me through a lot of trials and tribulations, you know. Not only did I practice when I was having trials. I just practiced every day because I wanted to be somebody, and I wanted to succeed. So it was nothing for me to practice six and eight hours a day. NOTHING.

I learned early in life from one of my teachers, you know, how to prepare yourself physically and emotionally for what you were doing. And that was to respect the bass for what the bass could do. That was my premise even early in life, was to learn how to develop a good solid bass tone. A foundation where the other instruments could build on that. And I got thrills out of just playing a note but playing it with such intensity that it helped to set the stage for someone else to build. I've always done that. I have a firm belief that the bass is the foundation, was the foundation, and will always be the foundation, and if you don't have that you don't have much to go on.

KATIE: *Well, now. Charles had the determination of whatever he was gonna do he was gonna do it like nobody else could do it. But he was determined. I guess I might have helped him through the music end of it. Because, I love music. And I loved to dance. And I could see it in him and I said, Now I'm not gonna see him be no dern honky-tonker out there. He gonna do what he has to do. And that's where I was with him and the music. Am I right, Charles?*

CHARLIE: Yeah. And many a time when I was coming up—In those days, that was way back in Detroit days, I was only paying 25 cents for a lesson. And Katie was working like a dog, all kinda jobs all over the place. House jobs, mostly. And every now and then I'd have to borrow a nickel or a dime from her to pay for my lessons. A nickel, a dime was big money. And she was supportive, you know. She looked at me, she said, "Now don't squander this!" A dime! Don't squander this, you know. Don't be ridiculous; I always used it for my music lessons. And Katie was right there to help me.

VADA: *Charles used to practice all the time. Whenever he got a chance. He'd go in the dining room and practice. One day my brother Ruben and I were out. We got home, and steam was comin' from under the basement door. And Ruben said, "Quick. Slowly turn on the faucets up and down." He said, "I gotta run down here and get the steam." Because* we had a steam furnace. Charles was in the dinin' room, practicin' his bass. And we got everything under control, and my brother Ruben went in there and said, "Damn!" He said, "Lookit this! Nero fiddled while Rome burned! Look at 'im. He doesn't even know that we were about to blow up!" And he didn't! He just kept on playin' and ignored us.

Chapter 5

A friend of mine's name was Bud Kennedy, in Detroit. This was way back in 1932. He was Anglo, and was a real dominant influence on my life in those days because he helped me to be a better person, by not only doin' the good things but the bad things. Bud Kennedy lived on the fringes, three blocks from what we called the mini-ghetto where I lived. He lived with his grandmother whom I had never—to this day—seen. Just three blocks away. He told me that she was kind of funny, you know, she doesn't like Blacks. I said, OK.

Anyhow, Bud Kennedy and I became very good friends. He used to hang around; he was the only White person that ever hung around with any of the Black kids, and my only friend in those days was Bud Kennedy, who was Anglo. For maybe 5-6 years.

Bud taught me a lot about how to hustle. Every morning at 5 o'clock he would get up and sell the *Detroit Free Press* paper and I would get up and help 'im. And every morning I'd make as much as 10, 15 cents, and that was big money.

Of course, it wasn't all legitimate. We had an illegitimate side. In the winters, when it was freezing, one of our favorite games was to go around and collect the top, the cream, off of the milk bottles. In those days, the milk bottles were glass. When it got cold, the cream used to jump up about an inch and a half or two, with the top on it. And we would come along and cut off, with our little knives, about a quarter of an inch or half inch of the frozen cream and have a *good* time, you know!

He was one of the mainstays in helping our gang activity. By gang, I don't mean the gang like today. Gang activity was only three or four, because there were only about three, four, or five of us that ever stole. But Bud was smart, because he was our lookout. He would stay back about a block away, and whenever *fuuuzzz* would encroach, he would whistle. And he had a hell of a good whistle. He could do some kind of whistle, and we could hear him a block away and that would give us the alarm. Then we'd run on from there and go. And he would be right next to the line of demarcation where he would jump right back over to the White side and they wouldn't think he was even connected with what was going on on the other side.

He taught me another good lesson, indirectly, about tryin' to be a better person. And that was involved in the crap games. I played a little craps, you know, shootin' dice as they called it. And Bud was my backer. He had a little money; I don't know where he got it. Didn't care. But he had a little money—he always had a dollar or two, change and stuff. So this one day we went into the alley and started shooting craps. I was on a roll! I was hot! So Bud kept eggin' me on— he was a funny fellow. Saying, "OK, do what you can. Get 'em, Baby, get 'em." So there were about 10 people in the crap game. Bud was on the fringes, he was not in the game per se— he was on the side feeding me, okay. So after about an hour or two I had just about won all the money in the game, and I said, "I think I've had enough." And the other fellas, who were all men—I was the only boy there, really, said, "No, you don't quit now. You play on!" And I got the message! How am I gonna' get out of this, you know?

So Bud was standin' on the sideline there, and all of a sudden, he had a whole handful of change, he threw it out in the middle of the pot and said, "Here, fellas!" And as they dove for it, we ran!

I was thirteen or fourteen. That was a learning experience. I said to myself, That was not too cool. I lucked out, because I could have gotten seriously maimed for life, or even killed by these big, burly, Black dudes in that game. But because of Bud, and his wisdom and ingenuity, we played it smart. When he threw out that whole bunch of nickels, dimes, quarters, and half-dollars, everyone jumped out there, and I can see it today like it happened yesterday, you know. As they jumped one way, we ran the other! And for a second there, they didn't realize what had happened. By the time they did, they couldn't catch us. We were swift. Like you can't believe. Yes, sir.

In that crap game, I won one of the fellow's welfare checks. And that was a big no-no. His name was John, and I think he lived two or three doors from us, you know. So John was crying like a baby, came over, and had his father come over to my mother and ask her to return that welfare check because that's all they had to live on. And my mother was so cool. She said, "Look, I'm gonna' return this check, but I'm also gonna' put the fear of God in ya'. If you ever let my son get in a crap game again, I will have you hung up!" After that, for about a month, I really couldn't come out the house! Because all these fellows were laying for me, gettin' ready to get Charlie, you know. So that taught me a lesson, like I think that's enough of gambling. To this day I've never had a pair of dice in my hand. Every little bit helps in terms of forming the kind of person that you want to be.

We always ate a dinner meal every day with the whole family. To my recollection, only one time was anyone ever absent from that dinner meal, and that was me and my brother. That was the time we ran away from home. You know how youngsters are; you think you're being put upon, you think you're being used, you know. It wasn't being used or abused, it was just that we thought we were. We were beginning to feel our oats. We were maybe about 13, 14 maybe. We thought we could do better outside. We both jumped to the conclusion that we just needed to run away from home and get away from all this *pressure*. We thought we were being subjugated with inhumane treatment, because we had little obligations to do around the house, and so forth.

We went up to the railroad tracks and caught a train— not a passenger train, of course, just a local freight—and we got maybe about 7, 8 miles away from home. We looked up and it was about 3 o'clock in the afternoon. And we hadn't had anything to eat since that morning. So we said, Look, maybe we'd better head on back to the household. So we did get back, and of course we were late for dinner. And, of course, we didn't have any dinner! My mother said, "If you go into the ice box, you have had it." And we knew what she was talking about so we didn't. But after being hungry—"*hongry,*" as you used to call it—we learnt a lesson in life. Hey, there's no place like home.

Mom never questioned us about it—she knew what we did—until we were grown. She says, "I know what you did. You jumped out the bedroom window, you and your brother, and you were going to leave home." She says, "You know how I know?"

We says, "No."

She says, "'Cause Vada told us." Boy! God, dern! "Vada told us you were runnin' away from home." Okay. So the line of communication was strong in that family.

Chapter 6

MARY BETH: *I remember this vividly: All of my brothers worked, all of 'em made money, but Charles always had everything. Like he had the first roller skates. He had the first sled. He had the first car, the first bicycle, in the neighborhood. He worked, and got it. And it was always surprising.*

JOE: *Charles was so busy working. He had the first bicycle in the neighborhood—the first Black to own a bicycle. And he was paying fifty cent a week for that. He worked for Boyer's Haunted Shack, and he bought a car for about twenty dollars. And he fixed it—ran like a top. That car was somethn' else, Model A. And I worked at the Apple House, before I could drive, for two dollars a week, but that was big money. And then they'd give me food to take home—it was a fruit place.*

CHARLIE: My mother, she was a hustler, too. By hustler, I mean she would get out and make a few coins. For I think three or four or five years there. She had seven kids, okay, plus my niece who happened to come there then, so it was almost eight. And she would go out and sell something called "Fashion Frocks." That was a company which sold dresses and things. She would go out and sell Fashion Frocks and she made quite a nice little comfortable monetary intake at that. When she sold a dress she would get a commission. She had maybe a half a dozen of her friends that would buy dresses from her. That helped to bring in the money to support our family.

JOE: *So we ate good and we lived good—we thought. And my mother was right on top of us about everything, and she was our savior. My father wasn't shit. My mother was just fantastic. She taught us to love people. Not to kiss anybody's ass. At that time, light-skinned Blacks had all the advantages of the system. So the darker skinned Blacks would cater to the light-skinned Blacks. They had all the good jobs. They had the little bit of money that Blacks had, and all the advantages. So the darker-skinned Blacks would cater to them, and still to this day a lot of that goes on in the Black community. Maybe conscious, maybe unconscious.*

CHARLIE: In those days, people didn't have much of an opportunity to get ahead, because there were no jobs, almost no jobs open to the Blacks in those days—janitor jobs, and some elevator jobs, IF (now listen to this carefully), IF you were yaller, and a woman, and had good hair, they would hire you as elevator operators, ok. I remember this in a place called J. L. Hudson's in Detroit, which was on Woodward Avenue. Every time I'd go in there I'd be flabbergasted at these beautiful Black, Creole women on the elevators. But there were no Black ones in there, no dark ones. All yaller, as we used to call it, with the good hair.

Consequently, from the ghetto, all they could do was janitor jobs and in the middle thirties they started hiring Blacks at Henry Ford's factory. And you had a few Blacks who were workin' in the post office, who we called the elite. Because they had a salary. And you had a few workin' in other government activities, but not many. They didn't have much to do.

VADA: *I remember Charles went to work at Boyer's Haunted Shack. It was a bicycle outlet on Grand River in Detroit. And he worked*

there as a young guy, still in elementary and junior high school, and he got his first bike.

CHARLIE: Bud Kennedy helped me buy my first car, which was a 1930 Model A rumble-seat car. And he bought it with his money, for 17 dollars. And I promised to pay half of that because it would be half my car. But he was so nice, he put the title in my name. And I was just turning 16 then. I paid Bud Kennedy his half of the money for the car and got the car.

And that led me to another phase of my life, which was working for Boyer's Haunted Shack. I was blessed in the fact that they let me clean up, and be a sub-handy man, I call it. I worked under a good friend of mine, whose name was Clifford Madison. He was a mechanic, Black dude, at Boyer's Haunted Shack. He took care of changing tires and spark plugs, fixing cars, so forth. And he taught me a lot about how to change tires. In those days, they didn't change tires with pneumatic, pressurized equipment; they had tire irons that you changed these with. And I learned how to change tires, and I learned how to work on cars. He taught me how to rebuild an engine. I rebuilt my first engine, and the last, with the supervision of Clifford Madison. Every two or three hours I would go to him for instructions as to what I do. I think it took me about two months, if not more than that, to rebuild the motor. But I got it rebuilt and it ran like a charm. If it hadn't been for Bud Kennedy, I wouldn't have been in a position to even have had my first car.

For people like Bud Kennedy, who was gracious enough to help me, I will be forever thankful. Bud was a little strange, though. He loved to be around where the excitement was, you know. And there was no excitement with his grandmother. He was a youngster, in his teens. And he was the only real friend that I had who was Anglo, for four or five years, maybe, and it helped me to make better decisions about people.

In back of us, there was a big field, probably half a block long. In the winter time, the firemen would flood that field so we could have a place to ice skate! That would help to take the kids off the streets. We'd have great fun up there, and that's where I learned how to drive a car on ice—my two-door Model A Ford. We used to take it out there on the ice and four fellas would lift up the back end and we would try to go. We had all kind of games and sports.

Down there was a place called H. E. Woods, which was a construction company, and that was part of my little stealing episode. We'd steal from them and go out and sell it to the rag men. They were right across the street from the Humboldt area, and they never had any Blacks there, never! No janitor, no nothin'. Lily White. We had all kinds of things going, you know. We would hustle milk bottles, 'cause you could get a penny for a milk bottle. Rags, iron, copper, zinc, and so forth. We'd collect these things, go around with our little bags and sell 'em to the rag men. We did errands for people, and washed their floors, worked at anything we could just to make ends meet.

Also, I worked in a store called C. E. F. Smith, which was right down on Buchanan, one block from our place. Another way we helped sustain life for the family was that I worked for him bagging potatoes and taking care of the produce, and so forth. But when the potatoes got a little spot on them, or other things, I would cut that off and take it home. And that was nourishment for the family. Plus, we went to the Western Market, which was about ten, twelve blocks from where we lived. We'd go down there and hustle fruits and vegetables that had spots on them, cut the spots off, and bring them back home. We had plenty of good vegetables and fruits to help sustain the family. That was our thing every Saturday morning, if we could. My mother was always magnificent—she always knew how to make a way out of no way.

Down the other end of the street was the junk yard where we made a lot of our money. We would go around the back of the junk yard and steal the rags and the junk and so forth, and come back around to the main office and sell it to 'em! Sold them their own things.

One time, I was about 13 or 14, there was a big rag yard down there at the end of Humboldt street and one block over. We collected a lot of rags, bottles, and things, and took them down to this junk yard which was at the end of 18th St. And this fella cheated us out of what we thought we should be getting. Our way of getting back at him was to set the rag yard on fire. Must have been smoldering for months. But that was our way of getting back at him. This was not a proud thing, but just a thing that happened.

MARY BETH: *One time he was riding me on his bicycle and I got my foot caught in the spokes of his bicycle. And at that time my mom was working. What he did was just kept me on the bicycle, made me hold my feet out, and just biked me on down to the hospital, which was about five miles. This is probably what makes them more like men than boys, because he just naturally took care of this. He took me on to the hospital. It's always nice, though, when you're from a big family, to be sick, to be the sick one, because you get all the attention. And somehow or another somebody comes up, as poor as we were, with cookies and even ice cream. So enjoying poor health at that time was a good thing!*

Chapter 7

My father was a scoundrel, and he used to get the three boys up in the morning—we were only about maybe 8, 9, and 10—he would get us up at four o'clock in the morning to go out and hustle—that's the word they used instead of "steal"—hustle coal from the railroad tracks so we'd have fuel for our coal stove. We had an old pot-belly coal stove which was outlandish; it had cracks all over the place. We would go on the railroad track every morning at 4 o'clock. We were about a block and a half from the railroad track.

We had a good time, but it was also dangerous. What we would do is wait for a slow freight train to come through with coal cars on it and we'd walk down 2 or 3 blocks below where we wanted to get off, and stack coal on the side. And when we got near our home, where we wanted to get it off, we'd kick the coal off. And that was called *coal hustling*. I was hustling coal from the time I was 7 or 8 years old. By the time I was 9 or 10 I was a pro. That helped us to make a living.

But we later learned that that was really not the way to go because it was pretty dangerous. The railroad detectives were always up there and they didn't shoot blanks—they shot real bullets. My mother didn't know about that. But it was very, very dangerous.

MARY BETH: *In the neighborhood we lived in there was a train track right in back of us, and this is where we played. We played on the tracks, and we played on the sand pile. I remember, I used to see my brothers run and hop on a train, a moving train. And they did it with such finesse, I thought, Ooooh, this is great! So I tried doing it. And I did do it. And I almost got hooked under the wheels. And then finally I caught on. All three of my older brothers told me if they ever caught me on the train track, what would happen to me. That was the only threat that any of them had ever fostered on me.*

The big thing that helped me get out of coal stealing was the fact that I got greedy, okay. One evening it was getting good and Joe was picking up pieces of coal. Now, he was pretty strong—he would carry two bushels of coal on his back, and I could only carry one. He later suffered from that—it was one of those debilitating things that happens to you later on in life because of what you did before in life.

Anyhow, we picked up this coal, and I picked up a lump of coal which was a pretty big sized lump and I looked over and I saw another lump which was even bigger! When I reached over and grabbed that big lump of coal I smashed my finger. My index finger, right hand. And I thought surely my bass playing days were over.

I had to go to the receiving hospital and the intern there told me to turn my head away from him, and if I couldn't feel a needle going in my finger, they would probably have to amputate. Well, I was pretty slick. I looked out of the corner of my eye—a peripheral thing—and every time he touched it I said, "Oooh!" I wasn't feeling a thing. And he said, "Okay, we'll treat it." So they put in a draining tube. For almost six months they drained that finger. And it took me about a year and a half of massaging my finger gently—every day—to get the mobility back in the finger.

Crushing my finger was one of the incidents that helped break me up from a *worse way of life*. It helped me to realize that the only good way was the honest way. But the other thing that really helped was the fact that me and my brother Joe were on the railroad tracks at maybe six o'clock in the morning. And he was a fast runner; I wasn't quite as fast as he. We saw this one train coming down with coal on it and he decided to catch the train. In the interim, another train was coming in the other direction which caught us in the middle of these two trains. One was going east and one was going west. So there we were! And all of a sudden we heard a "BING!! PING!!" It was the railroad detectives shooting at us! Joe caught the train—he could run much faster than me. So he got the train and I saw his body slam up against the railroad cars. But he held on. And he said, "Jump for it, Chuck! Run! Catch it, and hold on!!" And I did.

That was the most frightening moment of my life. We knew that if we wanted to live we'd have to hop the train. And we rode three and a half, four miles down the railroad tracks until we could get off. But when we did, that was the absolute end of my railroad days. I said there'd be no more of this, and I stopped that. And I never looked back. Since then I have been nothin' but a model student and a model person, because I respected myself and I respected people.

After this little incident on that railroad track, up there, I became very straight-laced. And I did nothing but practice on my bass every day. From the time I was in the kindergarten through high school, I didn't miss a day of school. Not ... one ... day. That's how interested I was in making sure that I went to school. But my mother was the influence in that. She said, "The only way to get out of the ghetto is by education." And she preached that to all of us, religiously. Which was the truth. Education and hard work. Her philosophy was that hard work never *killed* anybody. "Why don't you try it?" You know. So we all did, and out of the seven kids, six of them came out very well, and we had no big problems.

That's me on bass, with my friend
Billy Horner on trumpet on the left.

Part II:

High School

Gonna Play Them Funky Blues
(and the Classics)

*"They were not wicked men,—the problem of life is
not the problem of the wicked....
And ... they put their hands kindly, half sorrowfully,
on his shoulders, and said,
'Now,—of course, we—we know how you
feel about it;' but you see it is
impossible,—that is—well—it is premature. Sometime, we
trust—sincerely trust—all such distinctions will fade away;
but now the world is as it is.'"*

—W. E. B. Du Bois

Chapter 8

I got into Cass Technical High School, which was one of the most prominent high schools for the arts in that section of the country. It had the most extensive curriculum for students. And I was luckily accepted to Cass Tech—reluctantly, I'll put it that way, because I hadn't had much music experience.

I was on the bottom rung of the ladder because most of the young musicians there had had two to three to five to seven years of some piano or violin or something musical before they got to Cass Tech. So they were blessed. I didn't have anything but the bass. But they accepted me. They realized that some kids were disadvantaged and didn't have the chance to do anything but they could become decent students. So I started. I was 15. There were maybe 10-12 Black students, and no Black faculty.

You didn't have to audition, but by the time you got there you had to start proving yourself. They would not retain you in the music department if you were not making good grades and progress. And I showed such great respect for music that they kept me. I was one of the poorer musicians, obviously. But I had something that probably most of 'em didn't have; that was the ambition and the will and desire to be a musician. And I applied myself accordingly.

Cass Tech taught me more in music than I have since learned. It had a program which was designed to make you a good, professional musician. I started learning from the grass roots and I had four years of piano. Four years of piano! And I practiced every day. I made room for all this practicing. I never knew how I did it. I had started on piano, and with the piano they gave us solfège, which was voice training. And then they started orchestration—learning how to write for orchestras. It was the beginning of a college course for music. I didn't realize that until later. And it was a four-year course.

I started learning about how to be a part of the world that I wanted, which was the classical world. I didn't recognize any of these names, but I was going to be very knowledgeable with some of my peer groups. They were talking about Rimsky-Korsakov, and I made the mistake of saying, "Yeah, those brothers were twins, er—" And they straightened me out on that! And from that I learned: Keep your mouth shut and your ears open and learn. And when you know something, then say something.

When I got good enough, which was in the tenth grade, every Saturday I went to what they called All-City High School Orchestra, which was probably 150 musicians on stage—*at* Cass Tech. Every Saturday. We started at 9 o'clock and weren't through 'til 4 o'clock in the afternoon. That was when we had *rehearsals*, OK? At rehearsals you would have a teacher from the Detroit Symphony come there and give you section lessons. You'd have one hour or an hour and a half of playing with the orchestra and then you'd have one hour with individual lessons or section lessons from these teachers.

We had private lessons from the people who were in the Detroit Symphony. There were at least 13-15 of the musicians from the Detroit Symphony who were teachers there. And mine happened to be the principal bass player, Gaston Brohan, and I got a lesson every week. Every Friday we had a free lesson. All the bass players were White except me. And he told me when I first started studying with him that he would teach me conditionally. What's this condition routine, you know? He said, "If you don't try to play the classics, I'll teach you."

I said, "Oh fine!" You know, you do the old ghetto routine: "Yeah, boss! I ain't playin' no classics! I wanna play *jazz*! Gonna play them funky *blues*!" Of course, I was lying out of my teeth, because I wanted to learn how to play the bass, period, as best I could. My ambition was to play with the symphony but he didn't have to know that! So I kept that within me. And I got him over on my side, but said to myself, "I'll fix you!" And he taught me, although he taught me *wrong*. He didn't do it intentionally (he taught everybody wrong), he just didn't know any better. It took me three or four years to get over a lot of the bad habits that he had taught me. Mostly about how to hold the bow.

Coincidently, he was very famous for making the best bass rosin in the world! No one has ever duplicated the rosin that he made. And I still have a cake of his rosin called OAK. He gave me 12 cakes of rosin in 1939 when I graduated from high school, and I still have one cake of his rosin left. It was the best bass rosin. Scientists and chemists have tried to reproduce it. They can't. They never have, and they probably never will. It was called OAK Rosin by Gaston Brohan. That was his contribution.

High school was one of the most valuable times in my life; I felt sincerely that I had a chance to start making my way in the profession which I wanted to be in, which was the classical profession. Of course, I knew that it would be tough. It didn't matter, because I said I'm still going to go on.

I used to go out to Belle Isle every morning with my car at 5 o'clock and practice from 5 until eight—when it was warm, obviously—with the mosquitoes and all that sort of thing. And the policemen used to bring their horses over to listen. Because that's the only "noise" (they called it) they had ever heard that they didn't hear otherwise. They'd get the horses accustomed to this noise. And every now and then they'd bring me a sandwich, or a piece of watermelon. I'd thank 'em. That was for 3-4 years, I would go out there every morning at 5 o'clock and practice my bass 5-8 and then go to school and go through all the high school things and study my books in the free study periods.

I was always busy, busy as a bee. I *never* had any grass growing under my feet. I was always busy trying to get ahead. I remember the words of my mother, "The way to get out of the ghetto is through education." That always stuck in my mind—education. Education. And by getting a musical education and a legitimate education, that was a way of getting out of the ghetto. And so our whole family did—all of our family got out of the ghetto with education.

Every Saturday in the summer we could go to the Institute of Art, on Woodward Avenue and Kirby, and see the biggest name musicians in the world. I remember seeing Andre Segovia there, Heifetz, Piatigorsky, and dozens of others, for 10 cents. That was all part of the education, too. You heard these famous musicians. One of the most memorable events in my life was seeing the greatest pianist of that time, Ignacy Paderewski, play in our little hall, for the musical class. That was the most, because he was also the former Prime Minister of Poland. That was a real enlightening thing to me.

My real jazz thing started then, too. Every Friday we would have a neighborhood jazz band, maybe 10-12 musicians in that age group. We'd get in the garages and learn how to read jazz charts, jazz music. We listened to all the jazz artists of that time—Count Basic, Duke Ellington, and Jimmy Lunceford. And of course Louis Armstrong. We listened to these and we tried to duplicate or see how close we could come to what they were doing. And that's how I started with my jazz along with taking classical lessons.

In Detroit, when I was maybe 16, I wanted to become, like all kids, another Joe Louis. So I got into the Golden Gloves, which was an organization which promoted young fighters. That was one of the things that really steered me onto music, was the fact that I got into the semi-finals. I'll never forget it. I got into the semi-finals of the Golden Gloves and I thought I was pretty hot stuff. I went in there and the fellow who was my opponent was Anglo, and a southpaw, a left-hander. They put me in the ring, and it was the most gruesome two minutes of my entire life. He beat me so badly I thought there must have been three or four fellows in there beating on me, because he hit me places I had never been hit in my life.

After the first round, which was only a two-minute round, I came out into the corner and my trainer said, "Oh, he didn't hit you."

I said, "Wha, w-w-w-what did he use in there?" Heh heh. And my trainer laughed. And I said, That was it! I threw up my hands and took off the gloves, and I haven't looked back. I got my experience from being whipped, and I mean thoroughly whipped. Boy, that little fellow whipped me something *terrible*! And that changed my mind. And I didn't want to go to the Golden Gloves so I got away from the Golden Gloves and immediately got back on my bass like I was supposed to. And that was my little episode with wanting to be a boxer.

Chapter 9

VADA: *As we got older, my mother remarried and we moved into this lovely home. With the stepfather we had, it was a whole different life style for us. And we were introduced to a lot of good things in our lives. We were introduced to foods—we would almost consider them gourmet foods, now. Our lives began to change from there.*

CHARLIE: After my mother divorced my worthless father, when I was sixteen, when we moved into what we called paradise, then we really started having a family get-together and gathering on Sundays because of the endeavors of my stepfather. Our first stepfather. He was a marvelous man—his name was William Fillings. I don't know what Mom had on 'im but she knew how to handle 'im. He was in love, you know, and he brought home his paycheck every Friday and gave it to Mom. And I never could figure that out. Our old man never did that. The maximum thing he ever did anytime was give her a quarter for the whole family to eat on. And she said, "Well, how do you expect me to feed the children on this?"

He would say, "Well, Aunt Dutch." That's what they called my mother. "You know how it is. The Good Lord says, 'Make a way where there is no way.'" Oh, he was a prick. For the first sixteen years of our lives we never had any father. We didn't think anything about it because we had great, great volumes of love from Mother. Of course, one thing she always preached was, "I know your father was worthless and all that, but don't hate the fool, just pity him." So we grew up with that attitude about the old man. It kept us from being really disturbing youngsters.

William Fillings was a janitor at Chrysler Motor Company. He looked almost like an Oriental because he had straight hair and he was rather light. We used to call him one of the "ickety" Negroes. "Ickety" was a word they used for one that looked almost like he was White. He was French, part French, from Louisiana. French and Negro. He was brought up as a strict Catholic. His mother was Catholic, and he was instilled with these Catholic things. But he knew what he wanted in life. He wanted my mother. His big happiness in life was marrying her, with seven children. How did a woman get a good man with seven children? Very lovingly! And Dutch, my mother, was unusual. What woman today could go out and get a good man, who would provide for seven children that were not his? None that I know of. But she made a way where there was no way. Besides that, not only did she have one good husband, but after Mr. Fillings died, she locked up on another one! So she had two of the finest men I've ever known.

The second one's name was Arthur Mobley. And he was as good as gold. He was a veteran. Mom got two goodies, and I never could figure that out. But she had something!

Anyhow, we moved over on Hartford and Milford. That was like paradise. We still had our Sunday dinners. Mr. Fillings, my stepfather, always allowed the family to eat without him. But he was always up in the bedroom. He would sometimes cook Creole food because he was from down there. But he would allow the family to get together and have their little Sunday séance.

I know now why he was not home on Sunday, because he was Catholic. And here were all these infidels around the table. And he had his church, which was different than all the rest of us. In those days, the Negroes who were light and had good hair went to one specific church, and he belonged to that church. Also, he worked nights. That's another reason. Consequently, he was not exposed to the Burrell "enigma," I call it, of the Sunday afternoons.

Every Sunday in the wintertime, from the old steam furnaces when there was a lot of moisture inside, the windows would frost up. You could hardly see out of 'em because there was a big film over the windows. Every now and then we used to rub our hand across the window and look out, and we'd see five to six to a dozen kids out there looking in, you know, and wantin' to come in to join the festivities. We were having so much fun they couldn't believe it! The whole neighborhood used to come up and say, "Can't we come in?"

"No, no, no. This is private. This is only family." The only thing that actually stopped us from going on any further was that we had a gospel church two doors from us, so Sunday evening they had a big prayer meeting which started at about 7 o'clock. They started congregating at about 6 or 6:30. At 7 o'clock you had to join the festivities because they were rockin'. They were really swingin' their thing over there.

My mother used to say, "You know, that is not the most gracious type of music in the world." She says, "But it's necessary. They're expressing themselves. And just have respect for them, and decide whether you want to, or you don't want to, envelop that life style." She was telling us something, training us how to think and educate ourselves in what we wanted in life.

And on Sundays, Mom didn't have to write it out—we were all given our obligations to the household for the week.

And my younger sisters had the task of washing dishes, drying dishes, and cleaning the kitchen. Me and my brothers had the task of cleaning the floors, washing the walls, cutting the grass, trimming the bushes, and washing the windows, especially on the outside. Very few kids liked to wash windows, but we as a family had no problem because Mother taught us, "Hey, that's a part of your obligation. This is a big social structure and we all do our part." And she would always ask us, "Don't we?"

And we answered, "Yes, Mom!" You know. Because we knew better. That was another facet of what she had helped to instill in us—respect, respect, respect. I look back now and sometimes I almost have a tear because I realize that she was so far ahead of her times in terms of learning. And they talk about psychology. She had her Ph.D., I still say, in life like no other person I ever met. I'm not speaking this way because she was my mother, but because the average mother didn't have that kind of relationship.

Chapter 10

From this same neighborhood came a very wonderful French horn player named Julius Watkins. He was probably the finest French horn player I've ever heard in my life—and I've heard all of them. He was just a gifted musician. And he lived only one block from where we moved, over on Hartford and Milford, after we got out of the ghetto, the quasi-ghetto. He later went to New York.

Julius Watkins was one of the most important influences in my young musical career. He was born in Detroit and his father worked at Henry Ford's. He was one of four children in the family, the only one that was really musical. He started his French horn lessons at the age of seven, with a most renowned French horn teacher who was the principal French horn player in the Detroit Symphony. His name was Francis Hellstein. Julius studied for nine years with Hellstein, and Julius Watkins became the most important of all the people that influenced me in my young life because he represented all the things that I wanted to be. He had integrity, much class, good personality. And he was an excellent musician.

He was the very first French horn player to play jazz, the very first. In about 1936 he was playing jazz with the big boys in Detroit, like Al McKibbon, J. C. Heard, and a wonderful trombone player named Smitty. He was right in there with them, playing the French horn, professionally. He left Detroit and went to New York right before the war. New York didn't treat him kindly because he was too nice, but he still managed to gain a reputation. He had the thrill of playing with some of the Broadway shows there for years, which no Negro ever played with. He also played on a couple records with Quincy Jones back in the fifties.

Julius was a part of the clan that used to come down to Cass Tech every Saturday for the All-City High School Orchestra. Not only Julius Watkins, another very outstanding musician: Bags, Milt Jackson, who was a vibraphone player, one of the finest, and the founder of the Modern Jazz Quartet. He was with that congregation in that time, every Saturday.

Al McKibbon was also there, in the bass section. Of course, he was so far ahead of us, jazz wise, it was a little beneath his dignity to appear. He only appeared when he wanted to appear. But he was also there at that time.

To this day, my favorite bass player in all the world is Al McKibbon. No one could touch him except the almighty Jimmy Blanton, who was the first. But in terms of holding a band together there was no one like Al McKibbon. He was one of my biggest teachers, although he didn't know it. I first started listening to him when I was only about seventeen, and he was playin' at a place on the west side in Detroit, called the Pine Grove, on Warren Avenue and Beechwood in Detroit. I never really got good enough to play there because I wasn't of that caliber, and I wasn't really that interested. I wanted to know about it, but I wasn't about to kill myself in terms of staying up all night partying. That was not my cup of tea. But Al was there.

Julius Watkins would also play at the Pine Grove, which was designed for the best Black musicians. That's where all the big musicians played and jammed. I wasn't allowed to play there, I wasn't that big. I think they let me play one time, about five minutes of blues, and then Al McKibbon told me to "Sit down, boy." And there was only a year's difference between Al and me chronologically, but twenty-five years professionally. He was a professional, a big gun then.

Al was with the big band named McKinney's Cotton-Pickers, at a club in Detroit called the Adams Club. I used to sneak down and listen to him play. I'd never heard a bass sound like that in my life. He had a hundred dollar bass, standard bass, which he pushed the big band with (there were 12-14 pieces in that band), and you could hear him above everybody, *without amplification.* And his bass line was the best—I never heard a bass line like that in my life. And I still haven't.

He could hold the tempo like you wouldn't believe. Drummers in those days were inclined to rush or drag, overplay. But when Al was there they didn't do it. He had a way with his musicianship, and if his musicianship didn't work, his mouth worked. He was kind of a big fellow, and he was very authoritative. And he could handle the situations. That was a part of my learning thing with Al, and all through the years I respected and still do respect him as the greatest bass player I've ever known.

The great Al McKibbon. That's where I learned the feeling of respect for the bass itself. He played the bass like no one else ever could. With the advent of amplification it's made a bunch of hypocrites out of the possible good bass players who don't know how to—what they call—play *down in the bass.*

If I had wanted to be a jazz bass player, I would pattern myself after Al McKibbon. It probably would have *killed* me, but I would want to pattern myself after Al McKibbon's style, because that was the most grand style in the world. He was with Dizzy Gillespie's first big band. He later became George Shearing's bass player for seven years. That's where he made his real name.

$$\oint \ 9: \ \oint$$

MARY BETH: *We were the only ones that had a record player in our neighborhood, and it went 24 hours a day. I always wonder how my mother put up with it. It went 24 hours a day because we were all different ages. And so, my older brother stayed out late, and if he come in at 2 o'clock in the morning he'd just turn on the record player. And by the time he was in bed, Charles was up and he had his record on. And then my younger brother had just stacks and stacks. So we had all the latest jazz records. Then Charles would come in and play all this symphony music, you know. And we couldn't do anything about it, because he was older. Vada liked blues and symphony music, so she would have Cleanhead Vinson and Lebensraum on the same stack. We would just say, "Oh, my God, what is she doing!"*

So we had this commotion always going on. We had the one record player, we didn't have a choice. But it worked out well because this is when—and this is a good thing—because this is when you learn to listen. You don't learn to, you're listening, you don't have a choice. So then it becomes a part of you. So you do have a real appreciation for all kinds of music.

CHARLIE: In those days, actually, not all Negroes liked jazz. We had Negroes who in those days were called the "uppity Negroes." You know, these were the ones that thought they were better than the lower Negroes. Racial inequality within the race! And these people thought it was demeaning to listen to jazz! Now this was in the Black race. If it hadn't been for the nice feeling of the Anglo race, jazz never would have survived in this country, because the Negroes never supported jazz.

The average Black person wasn't having jazz records in their house. They had religious records, normally, and probably "I'm Dreaming of a White Christmas" and some of these other songs, which were actually not jazz songs. And a few other things like by Paul Whiteman, and so forth. Boy, this is a hard road to hoe, because when your own people don't support you, whaddya do? But they only supported a small group of jazz musicians, normally in the corner joints. And that was about as far as they could go. The exception was the big outing in a lot of cities where they had the ballroom expressly designated for one day of the week—which was a Monday, the worst day of the week for all events because people had to go to work on Tuesday. In Detroit, they had the Graystone Ballroom, which was on Woodward Avenue. That was the only place where big bands could really play, like Duke, Cab, and all these big bands. Count Basie, Lucky Millinder, Fats Waller, would all come at this particular room, and that was the only time. On Monday, the off night—the only night the Negroes had access to this thing. And the Blacks really showed up for that. But other than that they didn't do too much in terms of helping to extend the growth of jazz per se. It was one of those things that the average person hasn't thought about but I did think about because this meant one thing to me: If your own people don't support you, where do you go from there?

Jimmy Blanton was from St. Louis and he played bass with a band called Jeter-Pillars. That was one of the tightest combos in the United States in those days. And that's where Jimmy Blanton got his start. As a matter of fact, I had a recording of him in 1937 where he played the first bass solo I had ever heard! And it was a blues break. I'll never forget, because it was at my sister's place in Detroit where she lived. And I hear this sound, and I said What is that? It was the most magnificent sound I ever heard in my life. So I spent a weekend and wore out three records listening to Jimmy Blanton play this thing. My sister said, "Jesus Christmas, Chunky, what is this?"

I said, "You have to listen to this." I knew that thing by heart. Baby, that was my bible, okay. That was when I discovered Jimmy Blanton, who started out with Jeter-Pillars in St. Louis, with one of the great tenor sax men that I have ever heard, Charlie Pillars, who was also with the Great Lakes Naval Training Band. Black band up there. And that was the beginning of the Jimmy Blanton era. No one has ever come close in my book. They can play fast and furious and that sort of thing, but for really pushin' that bass, there's no one that can come close. If you ever want to hear a true sound, get the Duke Ellington song "Cottontail." With Jimmy Blanton on bass. Not Oscar Pettiford, but Jimmy Blanton. Oscar Pettiford's a marvelous bass player too, but Jimmy Blanton on bass. And the way he starts will knock your teeth out. He starts out on a high B-flat and he runs, a-boh-boh-*boh-boh-BOM-BOM-BOM-BOM!* With a whole band, you know, a fourteen-piece band? And then you hear that sound and, my God!

Me and Al McKibbon first heard Jimmy Blanton live in 1939 in the Graystone Ballroom, playing with Duke Ellington. We both went together. He had finished high school and I was just about to finish. So we were at the Graystone Ballroom and we didn't dance. We stood right in front of the band stand, okay, to listen to what this dude was doin' with that bass. So Jimmy Blanton came up there and played a solo, a very difficult song to play, "Liza." And me and Al McKibbon looked at each other. Al said, "Oh, shoot, who's gonna blow whose brains out first? You or me?" Who could play like that? And that was the first introduction we both had to Jimmy Blanton. He played "Liza." Every musician knows that just to play the chord changes is enough to stagger one bass player.

But Jimmy Blanton was playing things like, a-boo-boo-do-bo-do-bo-do-bo-do-bo-do-bo-do-bo-do-bo-do-bo-deeee! You know. And Al looked at me and I looked at him and I said, "Wha'? What is that?" We both went out of there thoroughly, not disgusted, but just thrilled at the fact that we had seen him. But we were realistic, knowing that that's the daddy of all bass playing. And he was. Jimmy Blanton was without a doubt the father of modern bass playing. The father! That was '39; he was seventy years ahead of his time! There's been nothin' to come near him even today, nothing on the bass. Honestly. Nobody has come close to *the* Jimmy Blanton. He started all of this thing called the bass solo.

I met a fellow named Milt Hinton, okay. And he was the big man of that day. He was the bass player with Cab Calloway. I met him down at the Michigan Theater in Detroit. He was playing the stage show then with Cab Calloway's band. The "Hi-De-Hi-De-Ho Man," alright? And they used to do four or five shows a day. In those days you could go in the theater, and come out in intermission and go backstage and meet the musicians and go back in, or the musicians would come and bring you back in. And Milt Hinton was doing one of those shows and I went backstage. And I'll never forget, I smelled something from the door. I smelled this food, you know, and I said, My, my! He was *cooking* backstage. It was a T-bone steak! I didn't know what a T-bone steak was. In those days you couldn't really go out and get a good meal because the average restaurant was still a little segregated. You knew that you were not welcome there.

So I went backstage and there was Milt Hinton, you know, and he said, "Come on, Baby! Come on up the room, here, I'm cookin' a little somethin' here."

And I said, "Hi Milt..." Such and Such. "Charlie Burrell...."

"Yeah, OK, babe, what's goin' on! Oh, you want to be a bass player? Yeah! Well look, sit down, here, let me tell you the facts of life!" And he sat down and talked to me. Pulled no punches. He always told me to stay clean, don't ever get hooked. He says, "Your music should be enough to stimulate ya'." And he was never hooked on anything.

Now he was 26 and I was 16, but he was going on 50 music-wise. So he took me under his wing and started to teach me. Every time he'd come to Detroit he'd give me a lesson. He was giving me a lesson in *life*, okay, not only about being a musician, but in life. He told me one thing: "If you want to play in the profession learn all facets of the bass. And by the same token, learn how to play everything that's in the bass register. Learn to play tuba, and learn string bass, learn everything. The classics, and jazz, everything that comes along you learn it so that you would be available. Learn how to read, learn how to fake. And learn how to smile!" And I did. He was my teacher and my mentor. He taught me more about bass in five minutes than I learned in five years. Bass, plus the psychology of how to live. Being — a — person. Every time he came to town I would get with Milt, and he'd say, "How're you coming? What're you doing? You OK?" He was keeping close tabs on me.

I didn't know how close he was keepin' tabs 'til years later. One of my friends, the piano player Albert Holmes, told me, "You know, one night Milt Hinton was in this club."

"Milt Hinton?"

"Yeah, just checking up on ya." He kept tabs. And so I kept in good contact with Milt all through the years.

Years and years and years and years later, maybe 15-20 years ago, my younger brother Joe was at a dance in Detroit and he went up and told Milt Hinton, "You know, you're the only bass player I've ever heard that sounded good. My brother sounds just like you."

And Milt stood there and said, "Well who's your brother?"

He says, "Charlie Burrell."

Milt Hinton told him, "Well, that's one of my students, fool!"

"Oooh! No wonder he sounds good."

And I played tuba. I had learned from Milt Hinton that the way to be a good bass player was to know how to play all bass instruments. So I started studying tuba with one of the greatest teachers, probably, of that time. His name was Robert Burns, Sr. He was the head of the music department at Cass Tech. I studied tuba with him for four years. And I was selected to be one of the three or four that was destined to audition for Curtis Institute. Of course, if I had made it I couldn't have gone, because I was so poor. But just the thought of being selected was enough for me. Anyhow, that's where I learned to play tuba. I was a decent tuba player.

Speaking of Robert Burns, Sr., he had a son whose name was Robert Burns, Jr. And Robert Burns, Jr. had what we called a territorial band, which used to play around all over Michigan, and so forth. My good friend Billy Horner played with them. Billy was the only Black dude that ever played, and the reason he did was because he was a little lighter than most of them, and they didn't notice the fact that they had a Black man in there. Consequently, he got away with that. I have more to say about Billy later.

VADA: *Charlie played tuba, in the church band. Sounded pretty good! And Moses Wooten was on the piano, and Rose Crawford played trombone, Dorothy played trumpet. We had rousing good times. That's how I think we got our start in music and music appreciation.*

We were also fortunate in that in the school system that we were in, they encouraged the arts and appreciation for music, and we would get to see the Detroit Symphony. They would charter a coach for the school, and we got a chance to go to the Masonic Temple in Detroit and watch the Symphony. We all were in music classes in school—choirs and plays and what have you.

We were surrounded by a lot of jazz in Detroit. Every week there was always a new musician comin', so every week we got to see everybody. Ella Fitzgerald, Count Basie, Earl Fatha Hines, Duke, everybody. Moms Mabley. We saw the comedians. There was always a long show. Every week we managed to get enough money to go.

How I got my first bass was in 1938, in Detroit. I was one year from graduating from Cass Tech. I couldn't afford a bass so I was still usin' a school bass. And my cousin, my mother's uncle, came there. He was then a bishop in Waco, Texas, and his name was J. P. Howard. He came to Detroit and talked to me, and he said, "I'm goin' to do something for you." We went down on Woodward Avenue to Grinnell's Music Store, and he bought my first bass for me. It cost one hundred dollars, and he said to me, "Charlie, you can pay that back, when you will." And I paid him back five dollars a week. Five dollars a week. You know how long that took. And after I made the last payment he sent me a check for one hundred dollars. That was my cousin, J. P. Howard, who was a bishop in the Methodist Church. That taught me that people do care, you know.

How We all joined the union in Detroit about the same time: Julius Watkins, Billy Horner, me, and Fathead Eugene Johnson who played marvelous alto saxophone. We were about 17 or 18. And I learned a lesson in life, about unionism, at the age of 19, from a very wonderful piano player, Albert Holmes. At that time I was playing at a club down at Paradise Valley in Detroit, at a club called the Old B & C Club, on St. Antoine Street and Beacon. The reason it's called B & C was 'cause it was on Beacon, you know, Beacon Club. We had a four-piece group down there which played the shows. We worked seven nights a week! And made more money and had more fun than I ever had in my life.

Anyhow, Albert Holmes taught me a lesson about respecting the unions. I had joined the union. And one day something came along, a better job, for one appearance. And I didn't tell Albert Holmes about not making the job that night. So I didn't, I skipped the job and had that other important job, you know. And that was the biggest no-no of my life but it taught me a lesson. Because Albert Holmes was my true friend, he proffered charges against me to the union. And they had me up in front of the board of directors; it cost me fifty dollars. And fifty dollars back in 1939 was a big chunk of money! It took me 6-8 months to pay that fifty dollars off. But it taught me a lesson: to be faithful to the union. Because the union was the only thing we had in terms of prestige and clout. Outside the union we had nothing. In those times, it was very important to be a part of this union structure.

He was a gentleman, and he taught me the ropes. He taught me self-respect, and the respect for the union. He told me to my face, he says, "Look, Charlie, the reason I'm fining you is because I love you." I couldn't figure that out for a while, 'til it dawned upon me. And ever since then I've been enamored of the union because in terms of the musician, that was the only strength we had, and support. We almost had no clout in those days. Later, in Denver, I spent seventeen years on the union board of directors.

Chapter 11

I was scuffling in trying to make a living in those early days. I was an apprentice plumber to a fellow whose name was Mr. Slaughter. I'll never forget him. Black plumbers in those days couldn't belong to the union. That was another one of those things which you just didn't fight; you just had to go along with the program and accept it for what it was.

Of course, I learned how to work with toilets, obviously, and snakes. Those were the old fashioned snakes; before the advent of the motorized thing, so I had to do all those by hand. But I learned that, learned how to put in faucets and just about every little thing. I used to put furnaces together. And that was with asbestos in those days—they used asbestos for the base of the furnace. I was a master at all that stuff. That didn't last but a couple years, but that was enough because that helped me, too. That was in 1935. I was only 15 when I first started with him, and I stayed with him for two or three years.

His wife was a marvelous lady, but she was quite a bit younger than him. And I think she got sweet on me so I didn't get too close to them because I felt, Noooo, you don't do that. Respect. Mama always taught me, respect who and what you're working for, okay, and your job. Never get entangled in your job on something that is not "kosher" (as they called it). So I left that alone.

The way she dressed—she'd be in her nightgown, you know, with a very slim robe. You could almost see through it. I said, Oops, you know. And she used to invite me in for lunch and so forth while her husband—who's twenty years older than her—was working his butt off, you know. He was the boss. And then, too, his son was a friend of mine. He tried to play tenor saxophone. So it all grew into the fact that I was almost like a part of the family, with the exception that his wife was a little sweet—I do believe—on me and I was determined not to let that happen. And I didn't. Like Mom said, respect what you're doing. And I did.

Another segment of my wonderful life back in the old days in Detroit was being a painter. Me and my good friend Billy Horner, the trumpet player, were real big hustlers. We used to paint houses, inside and out. We did that for maybe three years. What broke me of that was one little incident. One Saturday afternoon we were painting the eaves of a house, and it was two and a half stories high. We had these ladders hooked up there; they were not the best ladders in the world. And Billy Horner was holding the ladder down on the ground and I was up painting the eaves. And Billy forgot the fact that I needed all of his support! So he moved off to get something and in that interim the ladder slipped from under me and I fell. I grabbed the gutters and held on for dear life. I screamed at Billy, and it was only a matter of 5, maybe 10 seconds before he had the ladder back up there. But after I managed to get myself back on the ladder and get down, I said, "Billy. That's it." I haven't been up on a ladder since—not to that height. From then on we painted inside, you know, cabinets and things. Still scuffling, tryin' to make it.

When I was in high school, I was still working at Boyer's Haunted Shack on Grand River and 15th or 16th Street, right across from St. Leo's Church. And I worked there for a (White) fellow named Carl. That was another facet of how my life seemed to turn around. Because I was working there and he had trusted me, okay. And I was a little thief, so I stole some things in there. He happened to catch me, and he said to me, "Charlie, I have faith in you." He says, "Now, you made a mistake. Okay. Now, I want you to get through high school, with the best grades. And when you do you come back and talk to me and we'll discuss this." He didn't turn me over to the police or anything, but he did something for me that made me realize that it was all worthwhile—he had faith in me. From that time on I was pretty straight for a ghetto kid, you know? Very straight, as a matter of fact. I stole nothing. That changed my whole philosophy in terms of what to do with your life. And I'll never forget, because that just made it possible for me to think positively about the good side of people in the world. He had belief, and when I did graduate from high school, he was there! At my graduation! And that to me was the most phenomenal thing in the world, to have a man who had so much faith in me.

The ice man. The ice man was one of the most charmed people in the world, because he was getting, as we used to say, spaghetti that no one else was getting. He would deliver ice and would have a piece of sex in three minutes, and go on and do his little ice thing. Because people didn't have money to pay for ice. And he took it out in what he called trade, you know. It was all a part of a big social structure and a big social survival.

I was an ice man, once. Yeah. I delivered ice for a fellow named J. B. Parker, for almost three years. Maybe a little more than that. From the time I was sixteen to about nineteen, I think. He had a 1930 Model A quarter-ton pick-up which he put the ice in, and I was the one who was his driver and deliverer, because he weighed five hundred pounds. And this truck was funny, because when it would go down the street, it would go down the street half-mast, I used to call it. When I was driving, it would go down to that side of the street, and when he got behind the wheel it went that way. You always knew where he was sitting. I was his little driver. I made money, and it taught me about life. And in the winter time I was a coal man, delivering coal. After stealing coal from the railroad tracks I was delivering coal, legitimately. I would go to the coal yard for J. B. and pick up the coal and bring it back to his little shack where he lived, which was on Vinewood Street and Kirby. A little shack. In those days, you know, Black people didn't have too much. And he had this little coal shack, and that's where he lived for quite a while, until he moved to the basement of a friend of mine whose name was Miss Bryant. He lived in their basement for maybe two or three years.

When he passed away, at age 25, they had to bring a hoist in there from the moving van to get him out, because there was no other way they could get him out. A hoist from a moving van, to get him out of the basement. Anyhow, I worked for him for about three years, got the experience of being an ice and coal man. That was all helpful in terms of me making a living in those days.

I had other little odd jobs, you know, here and there. Nothing too heavy, but I was always working at some little odd job. Music is beautiful but don't give up your day job! I learned from the voice of experience in the neighborhood that you always keep your day job; musicians who were successful always had a day job. Of course, they were janitors and things, but they had a day job. And they never let that day job go, so they always kept—like the boys said—beans, on the table.

I didn't realize how emotional I was until I was maybe nineteen years old and I had just finished high school. And I'll never forget, coming down Woodward Avenue was a big Michigan State Band. And they got down to the heart of the Negro neighborhood, which was around Canfield, and they started playing the "Stars and Stripes." And when I heard this it was the first time I realized I was emotional because I cried. I cried for people. And I knew what the country was. I cried because I had allegiance to the country, which to me was sacred. To me, it meant you don't start racism and all that bullshit. You start thinking of sacred things. And I did. And I put my hand on my chest, I'll never forget. And I can still cry now because this to me represented something which was bigger than all of us, okay. It was a camaraderie between peoples and races. And I knew it would get better. Now this was way back in 1939. But anytime I hear the "Stars and Stripes" it brings a tear to my eye because this is the way it's supposed to be.

In terms of civics, they've forgot about teaching in schools. They forgot and left out the civics, just like they forgot and demolished music education and appreciation for the arts, which helps all people to live a much, much better life. It broadens your scope and you are appreciating what's out there in life. There's not only one thing, there are a combination of many things out there which help you to become a better person and to become a more understanding person—tolerant—and knowing how to give to life without just being selfish.

Chapter 12

By the time you came out of Cass Tech you could play professionally. And that's what happened because most of the kids, they were all White, they went to studios like WWJ and WXYZ. In those days they had orchestras with the radio stations. So they went to these stations. Of course, I didn't go anyplace but to the joints, the corner joints. That's as far as I could go, but I was happy because it all tied together and started my life as a musician.

I started playing in a place in Detroit, one of my first real jobs, at Henry's Bar. That was down in Black Bottom; a corner bar. And that's about as far as you could get, in those days, being a Black musician. And of course, you know why they call it Black Bottom: because it was the real super-ghetto of ghettos. That was the lowest you got in life in Detroit. That was goin' out east off of Gratiot Avenue, about a half a mile off of Gratiot Avenue. That's where I started really getting into jazz heavily. It was all a learning experience. There was no animosity there to speak of. Either you could do it or you couldn't. Now if you were real bad, they would let you know. Like this fellow from Detroit who changed his name. Yusef Lateef. His real name was Bill Evans. He was later known as one of the—has been for years, I guess—one of the finer musicians around. But in those days he was not accepted. He played tenor saxophone, and he was barred from these joints because he couldn't play in tune! The fellow who had the band there would say, "Uh, no. Ah, Baby, don't pull that horn out tonight, because you have to learn that you're flat. And until you can play up to the pitch, don't even worry with it." Now, that was way back in '36, '37. So he came out and went to the Vanguard thing in New York where everything went. In other words, it was open field day on intonation and so forth. And he changed his name and made it for all those years.

Make no mistake, it was not a vicious thing. Just said, "No, Baby, you can't play your horn tonight because you have to go home and see if you can't come up. Here's the pitch, you know." But they were nice about it, you know.

There was another place in west Detroit where they used to go and jam; I think it was called the House of Joy, on McGraw and Warren Avenue. Now, when you had a jam session, you had a real learning experience. You didn't just come up and honk your horn! If you didn't know what you were doing, you know, the musicians were adamant about telling you, "No, get off the stand!" And if you didn't get off they would kick you off the stand. They had no qualms to give you the reality of what you did do and what you didn't do. At this club they used to get the real jam sessions going. And I had the pleasure of hearing Al McKibbon, the trombone player named Smitty, and all the other big musicians who used to come in there. That's where you got your experience.

Of course, I was fortunate enough not to ever be on that bandstand! Because I had more sense than that. I said, "No no no no, I'm not ready for these big-timers." But that was my education in terms of learning what to do and how to do, you know. And also, in being a social being, I learned something then that my mother taught me, too—how to be a person.

I never played with Fats Waller, for the same reason. John Simmons, who was the bass player with Fats then, was at this after-hour club where they were playing. Of course, I was there, a youngster, nineteen years old. Fats was playing. And John Simmons said, "Hey, Baby! You wanna play?" I said, "Oh, nooo! You have to be kidding! No no no! Please!" I was smarter than that! I'm not that stupid. I didn't have that kind of *ego*. Cause I couldn't play "Come to Jesus" in those days. And I knew it, I wasn't that crazy. I just listened to them play.

My first real job playing classical music was at Ebenezer Church in Detroit. The first thing I did was the Messiah. Handel's Messiah. That was the first legitimate job I had had playing by myself. I mean, on bass. I had a feeling that was most gratifying and satisfying. I couldn't believe that this was old Charlie. Young Charlie! Playing this thing—Handel's Messiah. But that was my first association with becoming a classical musician. I was 19—I had just gotten out of high school. I did that for Christmas. That was my first big job. I've had quite a few on top of that!

The National Youth Orchestra was an offshoot of the WPA. It was designed to help the young people of that era get work and to sustain themselves. I played in that orchestra, along with Milt Jackson ("Bags"), Julius Watkins, and Billy Horner. And we all more or less succeeded in the musical field after that. The little orchestra was all Black—it was designed to help the Blacks, because Blacks still didn't integrate with Whites. In terms of working, there were no working integrated units in that era.

We were getting seventeen dollars a month. And we were real high class! That was in 1940; we were the real elite of the musical thing. I had a car! I had a 1939 Ford. And Bags had a car. And Billy Horner had a 1940 Ford. We were real first-class musicians at that time. All of them became successful in the music field, mostly in jazz. No one else pursued the classics except me. It was a helpful thing, because if we hadn't had that we might have gone into drugs, or stealing or something.

That was a period when I was learning how to be a professional musician. But I had all the opportunity in the world jazz-wise because I was working. I was one of the very few that was working, because I was a little more educated than the average one and they respected me more because I wasn't on drugs or anything. And I was aspiring and trying. But I think the reason most of the jazz musicians respected me was because I was trying to get somewhere in the classical field, which they thought was an impossible field to ever break into for a Black dude. So they humored me, you know. Said, "Oh, yeah, you're gonna be alright, honey." All this sort of thing. It was humoring but that's okay. That was alright because it all helped, you know.

I moved out of my house when I was nineteen, because my mother told us that—all of us—as soon as we finished high school we had to go. Don't get crazy, just go. And that was all of us, so when each one respectively reached nineteen we left. No big problems, you know. When I graduated from high school, when I was nineteen, I came home like on graduation day, Friday or something, and that Monday I had my clothes packed and was leaving. And Mom said, "Well, Son, keep in touch!" She was smart! We all did the same thing. When you got to be nineteen, that was it: you left, baby! There was no ifs, ands, and buts about it.

She said to me, "Look, you know you can always come back home for a meal." That helped me because I realized I had to make my own living, and I did. I got me a room right away, for 5 dollars a week. Big money! You know, 20 dollars a month. I got a room in a Black person's home where they rented out rooms, until I was able to work up to getting into a small, 10-12-15-unit apartments that they had on the East Side of Detroit.

After a few years of living on the East Side I moved across town. And we had talent on the West Side too, which people don't remember but I do. One fellow whose name was Moon Mullins was a heck of a tenor sax player. And another fellow was Lamont Hamilton; he was a superb tenor sax player. What happened with these two fellows, they both were into narcotics, drugs, heroin. They were fabulous players. And Moon had one other flaw: he beat his wife. He liked to whip, beat his wife religiously, beat her every day. He beat her, and after three or four years of insult and humiliation and beating, one day we heard the news that she got up in his chest with a .45. Sat up over him and blew him away. And that was the end of Moon Mullins.

Lamont went off and did his little thing in New York with a few of the big people. But they couldn't use him because he was too heavy on heroin. Back in those days, they didn't have much dope, I'll tell ya' that first of all. They didn't have much dope in the jazz scene back in those days, Black or White. The big dope was marijuana. That was the heaviest dope. When I came up all they did was smoke "weed." And among the first few fellows who got into that bag were Lamont and Moon, and they didn't last very long.

And right along with that group came, a little later, my youngest brother, Allen, who was a heroin addict at 14. And a hell of a dancer, one of the finest dancers I've ever met in my life. But he got hooked on heroin when he was 14. And as he came along he became one of the most popular people in

Detroit because he was a good dancer. He had more talent in his little finger than I had in my whole body. It's a God-given talent to be a tap dancer. He became part of a good team there—he joined Baby Lawrence, who was another addict but the finest tap dancer, probably, in the country at that time. He and my brother Allen were a team but they couldn't use 'em because they were both junkies. So that ended that right off the bat.

I guess I'd sound like some of the politicians today who say they took a puff of marijuana but didn't inhale? I took a puff and it damn near choked me. I was, I think 17, and I let that go. And I never did anything else after that. For the rest of my life I got high off of my music. And still do. I just finished this morning practicing one of these Strauss things—very difficult thing called "Ein Helden Leben." Pardon my French, but it's kicked my ass all these years and kept me very humble. I realize you really can't play it like the cello players do, but you try. And I'm still trying on that.

As far as the alcohol was concerned, that same year I wanted to experience, you know, just having a good time drinking. I was playing a place called Brewster Center in Detroit, with the back-up band, ghost bass player, okay, for this little show they had there. And I was backstage and I was sippin' on some Rittenhouse Rye Whiskey. By the end of the show I was completely *plastered*, you know. I think it took me two weeks to recuperate from that. I was just 17 then. I never took another drink 'til I was 35, OK. That helped me to learn the pros and cons of what you do and what you don't do. The main thing is that I learned a lesson in life, and that was this: To be yourself, you know. I learned to stay away from things, which never bothered me because I was always high on my music.

Chapter 13

Billy Horner, my friend who played trumpet, was one of my real mentors in my early days in music because he had had education, lessons, and so forth, long before I even got in the field. He was the first Negro that really broke the barrier, to be accepted, actually, into the White man's world of the classics. Actually, Billy—indirectly—had a big influence on me getting my job with the Denver Symphony ten years later.

Billy was 17 or 18 years old when he was chosen to go abroad with the Leopold Stokowski All-Youth Orchestra. And the fella' who chose him was Saul Caston, the principal trumpeter in Philadelphia in those days, under Stokowski. Caston auditioned Billy and he made it possible so that Billy could be accepted. And Billy was accepted. But he never went abroad with the orchestra. They were gettin' ready to go on their state tour overseas, and they called Billy and told him he couldn't go because he was Black. The only reason they couldn't do it was because: RACE. Once again. They said, No, he's Black, he can't go. That was devastating, another one of those devastating blows, in terms of race relationships. But it also was an inspiration for me to go along the path, to realize there was a possibility there. A few years later Billy played with Jimmy Lunceford. Second trumpet. He later was a trumpet player for Motown. And ten years later, Saul Caston would be the conductor of the Denver Symphony.

I knew a young bass player in Detroit whose name was Flournoy Hocker. Hocker lived one block from me when we moved out of the ghetto to Milford and Hartford, which was like moving to the boulevard, you know, compared to where we were. He was an excellent bass player, very young. He was only about 2 or 3 years older than me. But he had studied violin from the time he was about seven or something like that. His parents were affluent, because his dad had a good job, I think in the post office. He was scheduled to take an audition with the Detroit Symphony—this was way back in the thirties. He was such a good bass player he could play head and shoulders over most of the bass players in the Symphony.

He went down to take an audition with the Symphony in Detroit, and he played rings around everyone. But the conductor told him, the time isn't right. Okay? Go back and wait for a while. And Flournoy couldn't take that pressure, and couldn't take the outcome of that, and went home and, uh, blew his brains out with a gun, a rifle, or some shit. He blew his brains out.

That put a serious thing on not only me but Al McKibbon, who was coming up at the same time. It was a tragic loss for us because the race thing was the reason for him committing suicide. That helped me to become more strengthened in terms of: they were not going to make me commit suicide if I got to that point. There would be no question about committing suicide because I learned that lesson years ago, about committing suicide. Blacks used to have a saying about committing suicide: You don't do that, because it *hurts*. And that was the end of that. I left that alone.

Chapter 14

I went to New York in 1939 with Billy Horner. The reason we did was because a fellow named Al Hayes, who was from Detroit and came right from my neighborhood, was playing trombone with Lionel Hampton's Band. So he told us to come on up because they would be on 52nd Street, where they had all the music in the world that you wanted to hear in one block. Billy and I went there and we stayed at the Braddock Hotel. Oh, God, it was the worst hotel I ever stayed at in my life. It was a bedbug- and roach-infested hotel. It was a Black hotel, obviously, and Billy and I went in there, and *whew*, that was an experience. So Billy was kind of an aggressive son-of-a-gun. He would talk, you know. So we got ready to check out, and the guy said You owe such and such. And Billy said, "No, we don't owe you a thing. You owe *us* for staying with those cockroaches and bedbugs." So we just walked out, and nothin' was ever said.

The night before that we were out on 52nd Street. In one block you could hear all of jazz. We heard Oscar Peterson, Art Tatum, Duke Ellington's Band, Red Allen and his band, and Erroll Garner was there with his group. Slam Stewart was with Erroll Garner and his group then. This was all in a radius of one block! So we spent from eight o'clock 'til three o'clock in the morning listening to nothin' but the very finest in music. Oh, yeah, Teddy Wilson was there with his little band. And we listened to all this magnificent music up and down the strip. That was an eye-opening experience for me—it taught me that these magnificent musicians could hardly make it in jazz. And that made me think more and more about being a classical musician. It helped me come to the fact that, look, like the boys say, you have a day job. Which for me was being a classical musician. And don't ever abuse that. And I never did in fifty years of my playing with the major orchestras. But I'm getting' ahead of myself. More about that later!

Another one of our little episodes was we were the first Blacks to play for the Detroit Lions football team. Now that was way back in the thirties, too. That was at the old Navin Field, that's where they used to play, on Trumbull and Michigan Avenue. That was another one of those big affairs, because Blacks had never played with 'em before. Billy was playing trumpet and I was playing sousaphone. And our fee was five free tickets, all the hot dogs you could eat, and ten dollars. And that was pretty big remuneration for what we did, in those days. In those days I could eat anywhere from 7 to 10 hot dogs, you know, and they had good hot dogs with good chili, you know. And Coca-Cola. So we had a good time.

Me and Billy Horner, first again, had the pleasure of playing for the University of Detroit Marching Band. Out on Six Mile Road and Livernois in Detroit. That was a short-lived thing, because the winters back in Detroit could be vicious. I think I played one season with 'em, and after freezing my lips, my feet and everything else—and the first time in my life having my lips stuck to the mouthpiece—we both said that's enough of that. So we were the first with that, again. So me and Billy had the distinction of being the first with quite a few little in-and-out bands.

After I graduated in 1939, my ambition was to go to Boston to get a good teacher. So I saved my money and in 1940 I had the pleasure of going up to Boston. I took my bass on the bus—you put it on the bottom of the bus, you know—and I went up to Boston. I did not go to Boston University, but I studied with the teacher at Boston University, who was on the second bass stand of the Boston Symphony. His name was Ludwig Juht. And he was my teacher for that summer. I call it one of my greatest adventures in life, because I ate more Boston beans and cornbread than I ever ate in my life. That was all I could afford.

While I was there I stayed about a mile and a half away from the Conservatory where my teacher taught. And I lived on the top floor of one of those three- or four-story walk-ups. The hottest place I'd ever been in my life. And the hall was so narrow, I would almost have to drag the bass up to get it up there. But I did that every day.

And I ate with a family called the Holmes's. Their son Albert, one of my great mentors, was the fella in Detroit who taught me a lesson about unionism—the one who put the fear of the union in me, and respect for the union. The one that had me fined fifty dollars for not respecting the job, not respecting the union procedure. That's where I got the connect into Boston. He said, "That's where I'm from. Get there and my sister and my father will help you out. Anyhow, I didn't stay with them, but I ate with them occasionally. I loved them dearly but the food was horrible, positively horrifying. They were the kind of family that would save food from five weeks before. And the only refrigeration then was ice box! And I was a little particular about what I put down my stomach. But I stayed right down the street from them in one of those row houses.

While I was there in Boston, my practice room was actually in what they call Fenway Park—this was a little park off the big baseball park. And I would practice there every morning at 5 o'clock, from 5 to at least 8 or 9, and then have my lesson. I had the pleasure of also hearing the first time, on the Charles River, the Boston Pops Orchestra, under the directorship of Arthur Fiedler. Twenty years later, of course, I would have a little run-in with Fiedler, before we became friends.

That was a very trying summer, but very advantageous, and I learned an awful lot. Without a doubt the best teaching experience I had ever had, with the exception of Oscar LeGasse, who came much later. But that summer helped to settle me down in terms of becoming a halfway decent bass player.

After spending that summer there I came back to Detroit and I would get jobs here and there, kicking around. I worked at Henry Ford's for two weeks, Henry Ford's plant. I went there and applied for a job at Henry Ford's and told them I had a high school education. I was proud that I had graduated from high school! They said, "Boy, you're overly qualified."

I didn't figure it out for a couple o' weeks and I talked to some friends of mine and they said, "Well, look, Darling, you don't do it that way. You go out there and you tell them you had an eighth-grade education. And they'll hire you." So I did. I went back in and I talked the language they wanted to hear. "Yessa'. I didn't graduate but I got to eight' grade, and I want's ta woke fo' *Fode's!* Henry *Fode's!* 'Cause I like that business." You know. See, that's the way you had to play your game. I played the game and got the job. And I worked for two or three weeks, in the foundry, punchin' nails, ten penny nails, in sand blocks for the motors of the car. And I discovered that this was not for me! So that was the end of that job. And it took me six months to get over the pleurisy that I had from all that congestion in my chest after that—six months of good eating, good soul food: beans, greens, and things of that nature; pig feet and crap, to get over that Henry Ford affair.

I had another job working at nights on the weekend running an elevator down in the square in Detroit. And that lasted very shortly. After a couple weeks I said I don't think I can stand it because I couldn't stay *awake*. Running this elevator up and down from I think it was 2 o'clock in the morning after my job at the B & C until 10. And boy, about 5 o'clock I was dead asleep some of the time.

When I was at the B & C Club in Detroit, working, right around the corner was an after-hour club named the Frog's After Hours Club. Al McKibbon was there, playing with Kelly Martin, a drummer who later became one of the drummers with Erroll Garner for many years. He was one of my big influences in life too, because he represented something I always adored, and that was he dressed beautifully, he smelled good, and he could play his ass off. And a personality like you can't believe. He was just too cute to be around! That was my pride and joy, because almost every weekend I would go up to listen to Al McKibbon and these boys.

Four or five nights a week, after I got through with my job at the B & C at 2 o'clock, I'd be over there at 2:15, 'til 5 and 6 in the morning listening to this magnificent Al McKibbon. Al always thought that I looked down my nose at him but I never did; I looked up to him like he was the greatest thing since hash.

I came out to Denver in about 1940 for two weeks. That's what inspired me to come to Denver nine years later. I came out here for a two-week vacation. And I met my family out here, which is aunts and uncles and so forth. And the weather was so magnificent I said when I got back to Detroit: Someday, somehow, I'm gonna' get a chance to go back to Denver and make that my home.

Guess when this was taken!

Part III:

Navy & College

Teaching Doors Slam Shut, and Jazz Doors Open

*"Clark Terry left and joined the Navy.
For a while, I was so down, I thought of joining the Navy
myself so I could play with the great Navy
band they had up there in the Great Lakes."*

—Miles Davis

Chapter 15

VADA: I recall that in 1941, when the war broke out, December 7, I was in the Michigan Theater watching Count Basie and the Ink Spots. And it came on the news. I got home, and my mother was the one who was upset. I was still in high school; Charles and Joe and my oldest brother Ruben had all graduated from high school. And there were still three of us in school.

Ruben, the oldest, couldn't join the service because he was diabetic, and it was very, very traumatic for him because he always wanted to prove that he was as much a person as anyone else and could do and accomplish as much as anyone else. He probably accomplished more because with all of his illness; he graduated from high school when he was only 16. He always had to prove that he was like us, that he was not sick. So he did a lot of things he should not have done, to be like us. And we were taught early how to take care of him. So we always walked around with candy. We knew to watch him. We knew when to call.

Then Charles come along, and he went to join the Navy. And he went just before his birthday, because at that time you were automatically put into the Army, especially if you were Black. And they didn't have many Blacks in the Navy. So Charles joined the Navy, 'cause he didn't want to be in the Army, and we were all upset. He was sent to Great Lakes, and we were relieved that he was there, not far from the family. It was a real challenge at the time. He was a musician. And he was trying to pursue his musical career.

CHARLIE: I mostly supported myself with music until I went to the service when I was 21 or 22, and then I was lucky. I got into the service and that helped sustain the rest of my life. From the service I got into college because the Navy supported my college—they had some program where they guaranteed you a college education. And I took advantage of that and got through college from the service. It all worked out beautifully. By getting to the college thing, with the help of the service, that made it possible to still study my instrument and take lessons when I could.

The war came along. They were enlisting then for the service. And you had to go. So when it came my turn, before they drafted me I said, Well, I think I would like to see if I can't beat this rap of getting in the army. So I went down and I applied to get in the U.S. Navy.

At that time they had no Blacks in the Navy except cooks, okay. I knew what the routine was. So they put me on hold. And I came back two or three times to see if I could get in. Finally, through some connections from Cass Tech, I did manage to get in the service, and I was glad because what drove me to that was this: I had a half dozen parking violations, tickets. And the *fuuuuzz*, the police, were out looking for me, okay, and I got the word. The night before I joined the Navy the police came there, at my apartment, which me and my brother lived in, and he saw them out the front door and told me and I jumped out the side window and went over and hid until the next morning. When the recruiting office opened I went down and they accepted me. And I signed my name and I was automatically in the *U.S. Navy!* When I came back the detectives picked me up on the street and took me down to the station—they were going to arrest me and so forth and such and such. And I realized that they couldn't arrest a serviceman. And I told them, I said, "I'm now a serviceman."

I'll never forget, one of 'em looked at me and said, "Aw, shit!" Just like that, like, Curses, foiled again! That was how and why I got into the service!

So I got in the Navy. And they took me up to the training camp, a place called Great Lakes Naval Training. When they drove us up there they took us in an open truck, you know, and I looked up and on the one side of the road was the main camp and on the other side was a camp being built, for the Blacks, which was called Camp Robert Small. And that's where they took us. The camp wasn't even completed. That was 1942.

We went to the camp and started our training. In the camp I was in touch with some musicians who would later be famous: Clark Terry, who is the same age as I am; Osie Johnson, the drummer; Willie Smith, who played lead alto sax with Jimmie Lunceford; Al Grey, who became one of the greatest trombone players; and many others. Being surrounded with all these musicians kind of helped to give me confidence.

Let me tell ya' a little story about Willie Smith. He looked like he was White, you couldn't tell. Smith was the lead alto with the Jimmy Lunceford Orchestra before the War. What happened was the trumpet player Harry James had a band and was playing in Las Vegas. And he wanted to get Willie Smith out, so they sent Willie Smith over to the main camp, to the Section 8 unit! Everyone knew he wasn't crazy, but this was their way of getting him out of the service. As soon he got his discharge—honorable discharge, medical honorable discharge—the next week he joined Harry James's band in Las Vegas.

I had a chance to learn how to swim, which is what I always wanted to do. So every day all we had to do in camp was raise a flag for fifteen minutes in the morning, and the rest of the day we were free. I would go swimming in the Olympic pool they had there (it was a good thing they had) for at least two hours in the morning—at least three miles every morning. And then I'd practice four to five hours a day. Me and Clark Terry would practice in the washroom, where people would wash their clothes. On one end of the washroom Clark would have his mute in his horn, and on the other end I'd have my mute on my bass and be practicing. Every day. The other cats would look at us and say, "You guys are crazy." And we said, "Well, thank you," you know, and went on doin' what we had to do.

Major Holly came in the service, maybe a year after I'd been up to Camp Robert Small. He came in—tall fella, six foot something, you know. And he wanted to play with the band, but he didn't play any band instrument—he played the violin—so he picked up an E-flat tuba. And in two weeks he was playing enough to play in the band! In the meantime, he studied bass with me, about 3 or 4 lessons, after which I realized that he was a natural. He could do things that I couldn't do and I'd been playing since I was twelve! He had had the foundation for playing the instrument through playing the violin, for six or seven years. That made him much more adept at learning how to move on a stringed instrument. I told him one day when he came in and sight-read the lesson, "Major Holly, we're good friends, but I'm not teachin' *you* any more! 'Cause you play better'n *I* play!' You're in competition, now! Every time you go out I'm gonna' try to scalp ya'!" That's the way we talked in those days. And we became friends all through life.

They had a name for Major Holly, "Mule." The reason they called him Mule was he looked like a mule! But a more delightful person you never met in your life. Just as gentle as the days are long. And he acted like a mule, but he was gentle. He was my first student, in the Navy.

Chapter 16

I was very fortunate. When I got with the Navy Band (it was a band, not an orchestra), I had the opportunity to study, because Great Lakes Training Camp was only 40 miles north of Chicago. So I immediately made contact with a fellow in the Chicago Symphony: his name was Rudolf Fashbender. I studied with him for almost four years. A lesson every week.

My first real experience with playing with a White group was playing with a community orchestra. Fashbender arranged for me to play with the community orchestra, and the fellow who I played with was one of the violin makers in that town, and his name was Voight. He was with the Voight & Geiger company downtown, and he introduced me to the real classical side. And it went from there. I met many, many, many, good, marvelous people there, in the Navy.

♪ 𝄢 ♪

At this time I did what most youngsters do—I started going out seriously with *the girls!* I found a very attractive girl up in Waukegan, the home of Jack Benny, the comedian. I met this nice little girl, Jewel Kemp, and I thought she was about my age, 21, 22. I just knew she was over age. I started courtin' her with the consent of her parents, for six, eight, months, I guess. Just being nice friends, and we'd go out and have a banana split, a malt, you know, and hold hands and all that sort of thing. And we were friends first. And I guess things got turned up a little, you know. I still thought she was 21, at least. So after we'd had a little relationship, she came and told me that she was pregnant, and scared me half to death. And I said, "Okay, so, we'll get married." And then she told me she was 17. Aaaeeeloouu! That put a big scare on me. And I remembered when my mother told me, "Look, son. If you violate a young lady, and do not marry her, *do ... not ... come ... back ... to ... my ... doorstep!*" I had some respect for womanhood. I did. And I married her. And we had an on-and-off relationship like you can't believe. Because I was not ready. It was lust—it was not really love. It didn't get any better from that because I had plans for my life, and she had designs for my life. But her designs didn't work out.

In the interim she became friends with some of the band at Great Lakes, at Robert Small. One of the most charming incidents was when I invited Clark Terry to come up to her house on Yeoman Street, and had dinner. And we went up, me and Clark Terry, went up to her house and had dinner and she had chili. We ate the chili, and for three days we were burning up! On the way back to camp Clark said, "Uh, Charlie. Was she tryin' to kill us?" Heh, heh, heh. That was Clark Terry.

The marriage lasted two years. But out of that marriage we had two girls, Joyce and Barbara. Actually, out of that relationship also came one of the greatest things in terms of relationships with relatives. Most people speak of their in-laws very disparagingly. In my case it was a godsend. Without them and their understanding I never could have become a musician. Never. Because they told me, to my face, "Charlie, our daughter is not ready for anything. She's a little crazy, and we made her crazy." That's what they told *me*. "But now, you have ambition in life and we're gonna' get behind you and see that you have help to make it possible." That freed me from having to pay child support, 'cause I couldn't pay it anyhow. So they were my friends, and I had them all through my life and helped to make my first steps into being a musician a reality.

They helped me gracefully, in terms of getting my feet on the ground and doing what I wanted to do. They realized that their daughter's ambition was for me to work in the auto plant where her father worked, up in Kenosha, Wisconsin. I talked to her father, whose name was Congress Kemp. He says, "Charlie, I don't *ever* want you to be up there working where I am. You can do better. Here's what we're going to do. We will take care of the girls." And that made all the difference in the world. And those were only the first of my in-laws that really got behind me and helped me tremendously to make a success of life. I realized that there were more people who wanted to help you than not, if they saw that you were interested in getting your education and in getting some help.

Chapter 17

In about 1944 I divorced Jewell and came back to Detroit. I was stationed in my last year in Grosse Isle, a naval base on the west side of Detroit. I was stationed there with the band. And that's where my good friend Al Grey, the trombone player, was with the band. And I had the pleasure of helping teach him how to read music. Which was a big monumental thing because he could play jazz well, but he didn't know how to read. I had a thrill teaching him how to read.

And, of course, I was still going along playing, practicing every day. Didn't miss a day. As a matter of fact, I think for the first twenty years of my life playing the bass, I never missed a day practicing. *Not — one — day.* Rain or shine, the mail went through! That was my philosophy on the bass and every day it became *necessary* that I play. I loved the sound of the bass. I loved to be on the bottom, to make a foundation. That was grand! To make a note that had *integrity*, to help the other musicians build on.

My brother Joe was with the Marines, then. If it hadn't been for the help in Hawaii of a teacher at the university there my brother Joe would have been an out and out racist and would've have been the most treacherous hatemonger of Whites in the world. But this man, who was Anglo, turned Joe around. And he's been a model citizen, ever since.

JOE: *When the war started, they had no Black Marines. So I said, well, I'll ask to get in the Marine Corps, and when they don't take me and they go to draft me, I'll go to jail. And I was serious about that. I had it all planned. So, for three or four months I went up to apply to the Marine Corps, and they kept telling me to come back in three weeks, and come back in three weeks. And I thought that I had it made. And the fourth time I went back, three months later, they said, "Boy, what do you want?"*

I said, "I want to join the Marines!"

He says, "Raise your right hand!"

I said, "Oh, SHIT!!" Because if I had joined I would've gone into the Coast Guard because I didn't want to fight. Later on I realized, the reason I had to wait those five months is they were building a camp for me. The Marine Corps was segregated and they had no Blacks and no place to put 'em. So they had to build me a camp. So I was among the first Blacks to go into the Marine Corps. And I'm the oldest Black gunnery sergeant from that era that's living; all the other gunnery sergeants were a little older and they're all passed.

I almost destroyed myself with hate in the Marine Corps. I hated all Whites. I felt like I had a watermelon in my stomach I was so full of hate. And then this professor woke me up. I realized that I grew up in a mixed neighborhood. All the people I had known were White—all my friends and enemies were White! This family in Hawaii just woke me up. And I have never let anything spoil my day since then. Not even my wife!!

CHARLIE: And like my mother always told me, you never harbor hate because hate is worse than a cancer. It will do you in quicker than anything. Bless the dear Lord that I never fell into that pitfall of hating, which is the lowest thing in the world.

MARY BETH: *In the meantime my brothers were away. Except Charles was comin' home every other weekend. So, it wasn't very thrilling to see him. I wasn't happy with him during that period, because not only would he come home— My sister and I shared a bedroom, and we had the light coming into our bedroom in the morning, 'cause it faced the east. And Charles had this thing—whatever he did, he just did. So he would come in our bedroom at 6 o'clock in the morning and start sawin' all over the bass. And, heh heh, I do not remember our running, tellin' our mother, or anything, about it. 'Cause if we did, I don't think it helped, because he didn't stop it. It was just, "I'm up at six o'clock, everybody else is supposed to be up at six o'clock!" And we were early risers, but we were not ridiculous, you know. He was practicing. He was always serious.*

So he was not my favorite person during my teenage years. His being away and coming home almost every other weekend didn't give me a chance to brag about my brother's being in service, 'cause he was always home. I could brag about Joe in the Marine Corps but Charlie's, "Eehh, here he comes again." With his bass. And his practicing. I thought he was just the most ridiculous person in the world. Heh heh. But we always had a good time.

Chapter 18

From the Navy I went into Wayne State University, where I met several other fine musicians who made it big after that. The musicians who were there and were my peers (and a little younger than me) were Tommy Flannigan, who played piano, Kenny Burrell, guitar (no relation to me), and Paul Chambers, who was a bass player who went with Miles Davis when he was seventeen. These were all the people, the young people who I had the pleasure of helping a little bit to make their road possible in life.

The big thing about my taking lessons was this: I didn't have one teacher long enough to become as astute as the White kids because it wasn't available. So I did the next best thing—I took all the lessons I could from here and there, and learned. I look back now and realize that one of my best teachers was a fellow named Oscar LaGasse, who happened to be a tuba player with the Detroit Symphony. He was also a cellist and had studied in France, at the Conservatoire! He taught me more about bass for the year or two that I studied with him at Wayne University than I've ever learned in my life. So he was big guns. He was the reason I got on the right track to learning how to play the bass.

About 1946 or 1947, Duke Ellington came to town, and he was looking for a bass player. I was naïve enough to think that I could fill the great, magnificent, Jimmy Blanton's shoes, who was the best bass player in all the world. I thought I would give it a shot. So I went down to the auditorium, which was called Paradise Theater, in the basement. They had a piano there which had never been tuned. Duke Ellington sicced his friend on me, Billy Strayhorn. He played all the songs and you couldn't tell him from Duke Ellington. Anyhow, he was playing piano. I swear, I couldn't believe—he was playing like a mass of notes. To myself, I just said, Which one of those notes do I play? Hey, I can't do a thing with this. There was no such thing as intonation on that thing—absolutely none! You couldn't hear what key you were in, or anything. But that was the audition, y'know. And of course I was turned down flat. They were expecting, I guess, a dazzler like the previous bass player who was THE Mr. Blanton, the greatest of all bass players. And I was glad, because I suddenly realized, hey, I didn't want that anyhow, because that was not what I wanted in life. Plus, the way that that audition was handled, I realized that all is not well that appears to be well in life, you know. You have to be ready for some big defeats and that was one of my biggest defeats in my life. But it helped me along the way.

As it turned out, Oscar Pettiford got the bass job with Duke. He was a good friend of mine. He came from a family up in Wisconsin, a family of musicians. We used to call him Injun, because he was part Indian. He was a hell of a good bass player. But he was not my favorite, because I felt that he was overpowering in terms of what he was trying to do. Plus, his attitude was not the best in the world. He was an evil son of a bitch, you know. If he didn't like what you said he'd do you in right there on the spot. Didn't have much couth, I'll put it that way. That was one of the reasons why I was never too enamored of him. But he played. He was the bass player with Duke after that for quite a spell.

I've known Oscar over the years; we used to work at a club in Detroit, King's, out in Inkster, Michigan, which was the other side of Dearborn. Inkster is where all the musicians used to come after they played their shows down in Detroit. And Pettiford used to come out there and jam—with Clark Terry, Al Grey, and Wardell Gray. I had the pleasure of playing with him on dozens and dozens of occasions. And Julius Watkins was in the band. Another one from Cass Tech was named Almond Rutherford, clarinet player. Used to call him "Rudy." He was a very learned musician. As a boy, he could read fly specks on the wall, as we used to say. He went to New York and made it big. He played with Nellie Lutcher on one of her records.

In those days, going on the road was not the best thing in the world. That was, in my book, a no-no, because you had to fight not only the conditions of the road but you had to fight real racial discrimination. If you left the city of Detroit, even in the suburbs, you were subject to big racial discriminations. And you had to be very careful. Dearborn, next to Detroit, was where the Ford factory was. You had to go through Dearborn to get to Inkster, and there was not a Black face in Dearborn. So what we had to do sometimes was to go through those cities very gingerly and "Yowsa boss" stuff. If you worked in that little village called Inkster—that's where the big Black joints were—then you had to go through Dearborn. And that was a trial and a tribulation.

We had good times, but they were kind of dangerous times, too. It was a big racial thing. These White thugs were out to do in Blacks. This was in the middle '40's. If they see a Black person they knew they could whip, you know, they would stop 'em or accost 'em and beat them. I was lucky enough to know how to drive beautifully. I had good driving training by being in the ghetto and learning how to manipulate a car like you wouldn't believe. We learned that, okay. So I was fortunate enough. If there were two or three Blacks in the car they wouldn't do anything because they'd feel like they might get hurt themselves. In those days, you couldn't stop at a restaurant, you couldn't eat at a restaurant if you were Black, in Dearborn. You didn't stop. You had your lunch with you in your car. Whatever you had—your beans or greens or whatever it was. And you ate it along the way or when you got past Dearborn.

Once I was going through there with my little Model A Ford, 1930 Model A Ford, and I was coming back from Inkster to Detroit. I got maybe halfway, and four White fellas accosted me with their cars, wanted to pull me over. I said, "This won't happen tonight!" and I floored my little Model A and ran all through the fields, down roads, and everything, and finally got out of that scrape. I remember a couple of times I was chased through Dearborn by white vandals. But I always managed to outrun them in my little 1930 Model A Ford. I still, as a matter of fact, have a replica out in my back yard here, which is a 1930 Model A Ford, which always reminds me of those times.

We were very careful before we went. If you went on Michigan Avenue, that was well-lighted and well-protected and you didn't have any problems, normally. But one time I thought I was gonna take a shortcut. I did, but it was a long cut! 'Cause I barely escaped with my life. That was when I decided I think I'll leave all this traveling outside of Detroit alone, because it's not worth it.

Chapter 19

My real beginnings of playing jazz with famous musicians started in Detroit in about 1948. I had the pleasure of playing with George Rhodes, who later became the conductor for the Sammy Davis show for twenty-something years.

They needed a bass player to play what they called an entr'acte show before Lionel Hampton's big band came on. So George Rhodes called me and asked me if I'd sub. (I had a modest reputation around Detroit, you know. There weren't many bass players around who could play.) I said, "Sure." I went down there, with George Rhodes on piano, Oliver Jackson on drums, and I forget who the guitar player was, and the very famous Arnett Cobb, who was the man who did the big thing of Lionel Hampton's, which was "Flying Home." That has always lasted, this particular type of song, which was like a blues song but it has riffs in there which are very, very distinctive. And everyone knows him, because for years a lot of musicians tried to—they did!—repeat these songs to get the audience in an uproar. The big connection goes something like this, "Ba-ba-ba Ba-ba-ba BUM.... WHAM!" You know! "Flying Home."

I played that week with George Rhodes, the entr'acte, at the Paradise Theater, which is on Woodward Avenue and Orchestra Place. And that same theater became the home of the Detroit Symphony later. They redid the hall. So that's where I got my real big start. And I lived right down the street from the theater. They had to go past my place to get to the Norwood Hotel, where the Negro musicians stayed.

But I must say that in that week playing with George Rhodes I never played so *fast*, so *hard*, in my *life*. When I finished that week, I knew that I never wanted to play jazz as a living. Two things: It was too difficult, and it was a thing which limited you in your scope. And my ambition then was to play with a symphony orchestra. Consequently, I kind of put that on the back burner and I knew I had to practice more on the classical repertoire.

Bass musicians today don't know how fortunate they are in having amplification. In those days, there was no amplification. It was all blood and guts; I mean, you *played*. The nearest amplifier was a microphone 25-50 feet from you. If that picked it up, fine, but if it didn't you *played*. I never played so hard in my life. I lost five pounds, and was eatin' five meals a day in between times, just to keep up my strength. That was the most rewarding, hardest job I had in my entire life, with the exception of one which happened in Denver with Fats Domino.

The Fats Domino. I played one night with him. God bless him, I never played so hard in my life on *that* job. No amplification, you know. And Fats Domino was not the most gifted musician; he was just popular at that time. He had a thing with him where if he started sometimes in the key of E-flat, you'd play and you'd look up and you'd realize you were in the key of E natural! You never knew how you got there. That's the way he did his singing and so forth; he played as he wanted to play. So to get sharp didn't mean a thing to him. Plus, he played those heavy blues, you know. It was *blood and guts*, no amplification for the bass! And the drummer—drummers were crazy. They didn't play with the tips of the drumsticks; they played with the back side of the sticks. The hardest job I ever did in my life was that one night with Fats Domino. For ten dollars.

To play hard, you had to pull the strings back, pluck the strings back. In those days, the strings were about a quarter of an inch off the finger board, which meant that you had to push them down. They used gut strings in that time. They use steel strings now, and they're down on the finger board. And you have amplification through your amp, which if you just touch a note it sound like BOOOOOM!! That's why they have so many fast young bass players today. With no amplification, you wouldn't have all these fast bass players, I have news for ya'. They would not be fast because they couldn't play that way. Blood and guts. Many a time I came home with bloody fingers, you know, on both hands. And I would soak them in salt brine.

Milt Hinton was probably one of the first musicians to slap the bass and slap it properly. Milt had calluses on his fingers which were a half inch thick from slapping the bass. But he came through the hard school, and you see where he ended up; he played 'til he was ninety years old.

$$\oint \; 9 \colon \oint$$

I had the pleasure of playing with Lionel Hampton's band for about a week or two. The bass player then had quit, and he was hard up for a bass player, so I got the job. And they were going on tour, but I didn't know then what was happening. He took me down to Cincinnati, or someplace in that area down there. I got there and what happened is we played one or two nights, on a weekend. Friday or Saturday. And the money was supposed to come in on Sunday. And the bus was supposed to leave, I think, at somethin' like 9 o'clock in the morning. So when I got to where the bus was supposed to leave they told me it had left two hours earlier. And I never heard from Lionel Hampton after that. He didn't even know my name. So that taught me a lesson, that thou shalt not go on the road. Here was another early lesson in life: Get your money up front, or don't go.

Chapter 20

Of course, I've always liked company, so not long after my divorce I married my second wife, whose name was Vivian. Whew. Now, this was love! I knew her. She lived one street over from me in Detroit. I lived on Hartford and she lived on Stanford. We started playing around, going together. And that fell into real big love. So I asked her mother for permission to marry her, okay. And the big thing about that was that I went to Birmingham, Alabama. I went down there to marry her. Her mother had sent her away, so she could be away from me, obviously, for the summer. But I talked to her mother and her mother thought that it was alright. So I took the train down to Birmingham, Alabama. And in the interim, I had forgotten all about this thing called the Mason-Dixon Line.

I took the train down there. Another big rude awakening was when I got on the train in Detroit I was with everybody. And then when we got down to Cincinnati, they went into the station there and they changed trains. And the conductor immediately told me I was on the first car in back of the engine. That's in the days when they had big, smoky engines, okay. Most of 'em were fueled by coal. So there I was in the car in back of the engine, with the pigs, chickens, foul-smelling people, and all of this smoke. And I said to myself, If I make this journey down there I don't think I'll ever return again. And I didn't.

So I went down there and got married to my second wife. And that was when I started at Wayne University. We had a good—I thought—a good relationship until I discovered that she was having more fun on the outside than the law allowed. By that I mean she was playing around a little bit. And of course, being a musician I knew what was going on. But being in love with her I was determined to let her go through her stage, you know, childish stage, and do these little things that she wasn't supposed to do, like having some men friends on the side and crap, you know. I said, Well, if she can do it I'd do it. So I did it.

About 1949, the early part, when I got real serious about what I had to do, we both decided that we would come to Denver. I always wanted to come to Denver. This was my ambition when I was a youngster, because I had been to Denver once before that for a two-week vacation when I was nineteen or something like that. And I loved it tremendously. So I came back; we both came to Denver and started our life there. After we had had two children—Andrea and Charles, Jr.—she was still playing around and almost eleven years had passed. And this wasn't gonna work, you know. So I just one day told her, "Look, that's it, I'm getting a divorce." That was about 1956.

All in all, I married three Black women before my current wife Melanie, and one twice, so that was four. The reason why they didn't work out was because I had too much ambition. The wives were good, marvelous, but they had no ambition. And that was it, you know. I loved them tremendously, but they were not out for doing anything. My second wife, after twenty years, told me why we couldn't make it. She sang, okay? She was a good singer. But she didn't have any formal training. And I was gonna back her going through Wayne University to get a college degree. And she was so goddamn lazy and unprincipled she wouldn't go. And she told me after all these years that the reason why we couldn't get along was because she resented me and my musical ability. *Whaaat?* This is shit. I said, "Oh, really." You know. She told me, and that kinda opened my eyes. I'll be God damned! I thought it was something' else I did, you know! Heh, heh!

Out of our family—that Sunday thing and so forth—of the kids, 90% of them turned out well. Only one did not turn out so well, and that was my youngest brother, Allen, who became addicted to heroin when he was fourteen. His other brothers were in the Service, and they didn't have the time to guide him properly. And my mother made the big mistake— like she said, the only mistake she ever made in her life—of trying to give him the things that we did not have, the material things. And it spoiled his little butt. So he went out looking for a thrill with the boys (it was not gangs, it was the boys). They did all the things you weren't supposed to do, and some other things.

My youngest brother was probably one of the greatest talents I have ever met in terms of being a person, intellectually, and as a tap dancer. But he was also a junkie, which meant that my brother could not go any further than the joints and the ghetto with his life style. In those days, it was a real no-no to accept anyone who was a junkie. And just about everyone knew who was and who wasn't a junkie, so that pretty well kept him in a pigeonhole.

Even though he had that big hang-up, that big monkey on his back, he was a very intelligent person and he gave to people. But make no mistake, he did like all addicts. He would do you in for a fix. And he would do everyone in except me and my mother. I remember him saying one time at the dinner table (this was after we got back, after the war), "People that have my condition, you know, that are addicted—you know they will steal. They will steal from anybody. And I'm no exception. With the exception of Mom and brother Charles." He was afraid of me, because he knew that I would do him in if he did anything to harm my mother or to take from my mother. My mother used to say, "When I let you in the house I'm gonna follow you around. And I'm gonna let you out and lock the door." He was the only one in the family that didn't amount to much. But he did amount to something.

Chapter 21

At Wayne University, the head of all the Detroit School Systems, his name was Smith. And when I was gettin' ready to graduate he just called me in and congratulated me, all that sort of thing, and told me the facts. As long as he was head of music in Detroit, he said, there'd never be a Black teacher. He told me in no uncertain terms that as long as he was alive there'd be no Blacks in the Detroit school system. That's what he told me. The very next day I got on the bus and left for Denver. Thirty years of that was enough. That was what really opened my eyes. In '49, the early part of '49, just before graduation.

As a musician, there was no way I could make it work there. At that time, there were no openings for any Black musicians in the big orchestras, obviously. And then being told that I couldn't even teach in Detroit, because they were not gonna have it, why fight it? That's when I came to Denver in 1949 and started my new life. As luck would have it, I've never looked back. I made a pretty good success of my life after coming to Denver.

I'm the last bass in the back:
Standing Up & Standing Out!

Part IV:

Denver

A Meeting in the Back of the Streetcar was the Beginning of Charlie's History-Making Classical Career

"Meanwhile, I started really getting pissed off with what they were talking about at Juilliard. It just wasn't happening for me there.... I played in the school symphony orchestra. We played about two notes every ninety bars, and that was that. I wanted and needed more. Plus, I knew that no white symphony orchestra was going to hire a little black motherfucker like me, no matter how good I was or how much music I knew"

—Miles Davis

"The worlds I longed for, and all their dazzling opportunities, were theirs, not mine. But they should not keep these prizes, I said; some, all, I would wrest from them."

—W. E. B. Du Bois

Chapter 22

I had to leave Detroit, because Detroit didn't offer me anything. After thirty years, I couldn't get a job. Only as a janitor, maybe. I saw no future in trying to stay in Detroit, so I came to Denver. But I always wanted to come to Denver because of the allure of the mountains and because it was my mother's birthplace. I'll never forget when I hit Highway 40 coming into Denver, in this old raggedy-ass car that I had, and I saw the mountains. I got a different perspective on life, because my favorite thing was from the Bible: "I look up to the mountains from whence I gain my strength." And that gave me a feeling of—there's a possibility. This is as close as you're gonna get to heaven, so enjoy it.

I think about how my mother educated us to be prepared for how to accept our aunts and uncles before we got to Denver. My mother said to me that her mother, whose name was Katie Howard, was a marvelous lady. She was cute as all dickens, you know. On the other hand, she was a little naughty. And it took me many years to realize what she was talking about. And I finally broke it down to the fact that she was naughty because what would happen was this: When my grandfather would be going out of town and all that sort of thing, she was having little affairs, there, with the iceman and all that sort of thing. Anyhow, that's neither here nor there; I respect her because she came through and she was pretty important in terms of getting me something physically and mentally in my lifetime.

I only knew my grandmother, Katie Howard, for a short time, because when I first came to Denver, which is 1949 in the spring, she was not too well. I think she was way up in her eighties, then, maybe even ninety. She lived with my Aunt Kay, and Aunt Kay used to take care of her. In those days, we didn't let families go to the poor house, and all that sort of thing, and be put in homes. That was a no-no within the Negro race. We took care of our own. We figured just like Aunt Kay did, that mother took care of me when I couldn't take care of myself. Now mother needs help and I'm gonna help mother. And she did. She took very good care of my grandmother, who was the most attractive woman I've ever met in my life, I think. She was gorgeous. Plus the fact that she loved to cook for her little grandson. So I would go over every morning and she would cook homemade rolls. Every mornin' I'd have me about a half a dozen to a dozen homemade rolls. And she would love it. But she died in that fall, if I remember correctly. And that was the only grandparent that I ever knew.

My aunts, Aunt Mary and Aunt Katherine and Aunt Ida were there at that time. Aunt Katherine was the social bug of the family. Any excuse for a party. If she stubbed her toe, she says, "Oh, let's have a party!" If there was a rain: "Oh, I think it's party time!" So we'd have a party. And always at this party Uncle Bill would play the piano and I would play the bass, and my dear, dear Aunt Ida would sing. And she had one of the finest voices I have ever heard. Musical talent was a legacy that was coming right on down. And my dad; he had one of the finest—not tenor voices—but soprano voices. I didn't know that for 45 years. I learned that this was a part of my heritage here in Denver.

My mother, as they say in the vernacular, put our boots on, and that meant to prepare you for eventualities of different people. She used to say to us, "Now, your Aunts are beautiful people, okay, up to a point." Then she would start us thinking about what was going on. She says, "But they're a little loose, morally." And I didn't know that until I got here and saw what was going on. She was putting it nicely, she was being very gentle with describing her three sisters and their social habits. She didn't want to tell me outright that they were all playing around, while they had husbands, with other men. That's what she was saying. "And don't let them influence you." That was an invaluable piece of advice that she gave to me. When I first got to Denver we stayed with my Aunt Mary, who—God love her—had a little hang-up. She was very attractive in those days—young and very sexy lookin'. Yaller, and good hair. All the qualifications for a sex thing.

We stayed with my aunt Mary for no more than two weeks, max. My aunt told my wife Vivian that with her looks and charm and so forth, she didn't have to worry about me makin' a living because she could make a living for me. "The men'll pay good money for that." And my wife came and told me the next morning what Aunt Mary had said, and we immediately moved away from her. That taught me a big lesson. And down the line there was a lot of little things that happened which were as my mother had said about my dear aunts, you know. They're pretty loose. But highly respected. They were ladies, but they had this thing, where I guess it came from both families, these unusual sex hormones. I guess it must have been indigenous of the Burrell family and also of the Howard family.

But they were marvelous, they were a product of that time, and at that time the only thing for Negro women was workin', as they say, in the households, for the great White father. Consequently, they had a different life style.

When I came to Denver I was exposed to the best cooks. Everyone in my family cooked. They all had their divine providence in the kitchen; they could go in there and make a way where there was no way. Without reservations, I could say that this was the best cookin' I ever had in my life, with the exception of my mother. They spoiled me for life! They were superb cooks.

They used to cook breakfast, and when we had breakfast sometimes it would be overwhelming it would be so magnificent. To have something like pork chops and hot biscuits and forty-weight gravy with rice. And the forty-weight gravy was always peppered with onions. And then, what we used to call down-home syrup. Not "syrup," but "*seerp*." And that was the syrup called alaga syrup. When you had some alaga syrup on this meal, that was heaven. You couldn't buy that kind of food. Plus, all of 'em always had something which would move ya', like prunes, apricots, or dried fruits. They would always have that. And you ate that.

I always looked forward to New Year's Eve. Because on New Year's Eve our tradition was what they called "pig happenings," okay. You'd cook up pig tails, pig ears, pig feet, and black-eyed peas. And most of the better families, richer families, had what they called hog head. They cooked a whole hog head! That's a little, you know, when you look up and see a hog head with the eyes starin' at you. It kind of makes you think! But anyhow, we had that tradition which was the good luck omen for the Black people in those days. Normally just pig tail, pig feet, and black-eyed peas. And cole slaw, of course. And homemade corn bread.

MARY BETH: *My youngest aunt— She loved fancy tables. And during that time, this is in the mid-forties, Black people ran on the road—a lot of the men ran on the road as cooks and waiters, porters. And then a lot of women worked in domestic service. A lot of them would have to fix all the fancy tables for the rich people, and cook all of these fancy foods. And we were the beneficiaries. Or I was at least. They would come home and fix all this fancy food and make all of these beautiful, beautiful tables. And because there wasn't the advent of television, people entertained each other. So they entertained at each other's house. So most of their houses were very beautiful, because they lived the way the people they worked for lived. They didn't have as much money but they lived probably a richer life because they had the music and they didn't have people doing it for them—they did it themselves.*

This was a very pivotal time in my life. The happiest year of my life at that time. I started going to Manuel High. And Manuel was a very integrated school, I mean extremely integrated, because there was Latinos, Blacks, Whites, and Japanese. That was when the relocation camps had just ended, and a lot of Japanese had come into our school. We had that benefit of really being a diverse school. We had a male teacher who started what he called a human relations class. And he selected a few from each of the groups to be in his class. And we did deal with racial issues, and it was very, very interesting. Very good for me.

Coming from Detroit, I probably had quite a bit to offer from the standpoint of having been to predominately White schools, but also coming from a town where the unions were so strong, and people were just naturally militant. They were not subservient at all. There was the striking, and you were used to people striking, you were used to conversations that people had that were working-class people—you know, ridin' the bus—and how they said, you know, "If I can't get double-time for overtime I'm not gonna work," and that type of stuff. Also, the race issue—Blacks, because of the need of labor, they had to form themselves into the union. So the union had to really embrace that.

When I first got to Denver I discovered that I had an uncle whose name was Willie Howard. One evening I went down on 23rd and Welton where they had a baseball diamond, and I saw this little short fella', maybe five foot two or three, maximum, playing first base. Light-skinned fella'. I was flabbergasted because I had never seen a man this small reach from first base to second base catching a ball! And I asked someone, "Who was that?"

They said, "That's Willie Howard. That's your uncle." What? I didn't know that. I later discovered that he played for one of those Kansas City teams, the Monarchs or, one of those Black teams. And all he did in life was play baseball and the piano. And I never could figure out how he got along. He never had to really work! But my aunts were takin' marvelous care of him because they respected him so much.

When my wife and I first moved we had a marvelous time because I loved Denver; it was my favorite place in all the world. We had a little tough time because the places we got to live were actually rooms with other people. With the help of people from Shorter Church we finally got a halfway decent place to stay, with one of the members of the Shorter Church whose name was Dr. Dickerson. We stayed—you won't believe this— in his garage, for maybe two or three years. For fifty dollars a month, in his garage, which was adapted, supposedly, for living, you know.

Chapter 23

When I first got to Denver, work was hard to find. Very difficult to find. But I was a good hustler. Mom taught us how to hustle. I knew I had to get a job, so I went all over. I would go out in the morning and I would walk all over Denver trying to find a job. And one morning I decided to walk to Golden. From west Denver it was fourteen miles. So I walked all the way out and on one side of the street I stopped in every business establishment trying to find a job. And no luck. Got all the way out to Golden. I had the presence of mind to have a dime—I caught the streetcar back from there and I just kept on hunting for a job.

Finally I went out to Fitzsimons Hospital and applied for a job out there and got hired as what they called a "bedpan specialist." I stayed out there for maybe five months. And the reason I stayed was security; the pay was good and the food was excellent. I had lunch out there every day, and I never had such good food except in the service, you know. Consequently, I stayed out there until I got my feet on the ground.

Now Fitzsimmons is in Aurora, and that's east of Denver, a connecting town. So, to get there in those days you had to take the streetcar to the loop in Aurora, and then it would turn around and go up and collect two more cents or something, and go on to Fitzsimmons. That's where it ended up.

One cold morning, in the winter, I was on the streetcar, which had a pot-bellied stove at each end for heat. I saw this fella get on with an unusual looking case, which looked like a pool cue case. But I knew what it was—a bass case for the bow. And I asked the fella, I said, "Pardon me, but I see you have— Is that a bass bow case?"

"Yeah." Such and such and such. And we struck up a conversation. And he said, "I'm John Van Buskirk."

And I said, "I'm Charlie Burrell." You know, blah, blah, blah, blah, blah.

And he said, "Incidentally, you know, I'm the principal bass player with the Symphony."

I said, "Really?" You know. So I told him what my aspirations and inspirations were, and I asked him if I could come over and study with him.

He says, "Sure." He lived out on Tamarac, right north of Colfax out in Aurora. So I used to go out there to have lessons. And after three or four lessons he asked me if I would be interested in playing with the Denver Symphony. And I thought, My God, yes! That's why I've been doing this practicing for eighteen years, you know. I said, "Sure." You know. Anyhow, he arranged the audition with Mr. Saul Caston. He was the principal trumpet with Leopold Stokowski in the Philadelphia Orchestra for 35 years, and he was without a doubt the most renowned trumpet player of the day. He had taken over the Denver Symphony in about 1946 or '47. He hadn't been here too long, you know.

Now, this is the same Saul Caston from the Billy Horner incident 10 years before! Remember? In 1937 or '38 Leopold Stokowski had gotten together the All-American Youth Orchestra to go to Europe, okay. It was all set to go. And Billy Horner, who had auditioned, won a seat. Saul Caston was the auditioner, okay. And Billy Horner had won the seat, but they told him he couldn't go because he was Black. And I think that rested heavily on Saul, from way back in the thirties—it rested heavily on Saul Caston's desire to do something. I think that may have been his motivation.

So I got a chance to audition with him. It was the most strange audition. I was scared to death, as a matter of fact. It was about a two-hour audition. And an hour and fifty-five minutes of that was interrogation. He asked me about my background; how much schooling I had had. Where did my mother come from? Where did my father come from? What did you think of this, and of that social structure? And what did I think of Marion Anderson? I felt he was pumping me, like a modest third degree, you know. What would you do if you got in the Symphony, and would you such and such and such, you know? Feeling me out to see, I guess, if I was articulate enough, for one thing, to express myself. Another thing, whether I had any racial hang-ups. Because make no mistake about it, the Whites were not the only ones that had prejudice. Oh, man, the Blacks had prejudice up their butt holes like you can't believe, you know. The White man was a novice when it came to that, because we had some stuff that I'd be ashamed to even admit nowadays. But he asked me questions. My family. At that time I was married, to Vivian.

In the last five minutes of that audition, I played a G scale, two octaves, in whole notes. And he said that was the most difficult thing a bass player could ever do, was play in tune. And after playing five minutes, he said, "You're hired." And that was the beginning of fifty years of a marvelous association. I guess he made a good investment. And I'm glad he did, because I feel like I made a good investment, too.

Saul Caston was a real icon. Believe me. He did things which had never been done and he brought forth a reaction in the arts which had never been done. And he did it in such grace, with such aplomb, that it took me years to realize how smooth this man had made the transition between the old time and the new time. Caston is the greatest man I think I've ever known in my life, due to the fact that he opened doors for not only me but for Black artists all over the country, all over the world. He had the vision to hire somebody, and in those days it was taking a big chance. But, see, he was secure within his own right because he had nothin' to worry about. This time they didn't mess with him and his decisions.

Now, there was another Black person who was hired by the Denver Symphony, a light-skinned Black. His name was Jack Bradley. Now, he was actually the first, period, to ever be hired, but I don't think he had a contract, I don't know for sure. But he was light, and you couldn't tell whether there was a Black man in there. His mother was a teacher or a social worker, and he came from what we called influence. Very influential. Consequently, it was no big problem for him, because she had given him piano lessons when he was four or five or six, you know, and violin lessons when he was seven. And all the crap, you know. I came from the school of hard knocks. My mother didn't give me a thing, you know. And I didn't start playing 'til I was twelve, and I bought all my own instruments, and I paid for all my own lessons; my mother never paid for one of my lessons. And I never went to her for money, to beg for money. So that's the reason why I said I was probably the first, because I was really the first to get a bona fide contract. I think he played one year under Saul Caston. He had had his master's degree by that time, so he immediately went down to Texas and started teaching at one of the Black Texas colleges down there, and that's where he stayed.

When I was hired, it was magnificent. I called my mother, in Detroit. And this is marvelous because for my first concert my mother got on the bus and came out to Denver. Now that was a hell of a thing. From Detroit to Denver. Two and a half day ride, and all that shit, on uncomfortable buses. And she came out here just to see her son play. And that was all worth it. It was all worthwhile, you know. Because that meant that, hey, the most important person in my life has just come to me and said hi. And that was it. And from that it was all downhill! Had no problems. Coupla run-ins, but no problems....

Actually, people in my family were not that enthused about me playing with the Symphony because they didn't understand it. But what they didn't realize was this: You didn't have to understand it; all you had to do was listen. My first recollection of Aunt Mary introducin' me to one of her friends was a little humiliating, but she didn't know any better. She said, "This is my nephew, Charlie Burrell, and he plays with the Denver *Sympathy*." She didn't know any better. And I was smart enough—I never straightened her out. I let it go, you know. But I realized then that no one in my family actually came to the Auditorium besides my cousin Purnell and his mother. And my mother came out here—Aunt Denver they called her—from Detroit, just to see her son. She was so proud. And that was all I needed in life because that was the inspiration to me to hold my ground and to walk tall.

Chapter 24

I remember my first day, coming into rehearsal. Oh, yes. Boy. And I had to laugh because Saul Caston came up and says, "Look, uh, ladies and gentleman. We have the pleasure, proud pleasure of having in our midst someone who has done" such and such and such. And I wondered who the hell's he talkin' about, you know. Then he said, "Mister Burrell is our newest acquisition." I damn near, I almost had a movement, I was shakin' like a leaf for a second, there. I graciously said, "Thank you," and all that sort of thing.

It was a good initial reception, but I later discovered that, only naturally, there was a lot of emotional tone in there which was still "Me White, you Black." Okay. It was like, "Me Tarzan, you Jane" shit. And I felt that right off the bat. I know because see, being a Negro I'm very observant, okay, I can see what people are thinking. I can look straight ahead and see with peripheral vision very well, because we learned to do that in the *ghet.* So I would look ahead and I'd see people whisper, with their little mouths going, and looking over, and kind of pointing, you know, and putting their bow up like, "Such and such and such."

It was a very cool reception. Very cool, you know. And it's been that way ever since, you know. Kind of a tongue in cheek thing: "Oh, he's alright. *BUT.*" You know that routine, "... but he's Black." But like my brother Joe, it didn't bother me. I didn't hate 'em because I just went ahead and practiced and practiced and practiced and got myself better.

The symphony was a no man's land for me. I wasn't accepted in the Black community, because they called me an elite, okay? And I wasn't accepted actually in the White community because I didn't fit. It was just one of those things. You know, I was charming, and so forth, but, I mean, you know, "Put him back in the box and send him back to the ghetto." In other words, I discovered that I was in no man's land. But it didn't bother me. I did the best I could with the best I had, you know.

Some of them made it very clear. A lot of them really couldn't hide their emotions, okay; they didn't know how to hide their true feelings. When you were walking by they'd give you this look, you know. Some wouldn't speak to you. I'd say good morning to somebody and they'd look at me like, you know, they'd walk by. Had that happen quite a few times. Until one day Saul Caston told the orchestra from the podium, "We will not have that. We will not have that." I'll never forget. And there was a different attitude from then; it was not as obvious, let me put it that way. But make no mistake, it was still there, you know. And it didn't bother me, because as soon as I got through with rehearsal, I was *gone*. I didn't think about socializing with these people. Because I had something else to look forward to. My family, and jazz. Which saved me, because the people that came out for jazz nightclubs, almost none of 'em were racists, because they came to hear jazz. And that was the big difference.

My jazz background helped tremendously—freed me up. For example, jazz musicians understand that there's a relationship with the audience. Classical musicians don't have to do that; they can hide behind the music. And they do. But in jazz, you don't hide behind the music. You have to be out there.

I always kept clean in terms of myself as a person. I mean really clean. Spotless clean. I didn't do anything that was offensive. And I was never illegal. I knew better than that. Don't ever get illegal, okay. I was, all my life, on a high from music. So I needed nothing else, in terms of a stimulant; my stimulant was people. My biggest stimulant when I first started was to see these little young girls. Ha ha ha. I loved to see them dancing and prancing and that was stimulating. And that was stimulating for 90% of the musicians in those days. That was all a part of the whole thing, you know. Peddling joy. Just having a good time at what you were doing. Playing jazz in night clubs is what psychologically helped me to never have a shrink in my life, okay. Because I met *people*. And I had a chance to play out my emotions and my frustrations.

It was never lonesome or lonely for me in the Symphony because I always had jazz on one hand to balance that. Which was marvelous, because I played with some of the best musicians and met some of the best people in my life in the jazz field. Consequently, that kept me on a very even plane with some of my compatriots down with the Symphony who were a little straight-laced and kind of strange.

I was so busy and so enthralled with the thrill of being with the Orchestra. Every time I stepped out on that stage it was like a new beginning, it was like an exploration, it was Christmas. When I stepped out I thought of everything that had gone heretofore in terms of what I had done to try to prepare myself for this sort of situation, and to be proud was an understatement. And that was still true, almost 50 years, every time I stepped on the stage it was a new beginning.

It was what I call the imperial dignity of what I was doing. I felt magnificent every time I stepped on that stage. Every performance. Of all those fifty years, I never went on the stage without feeling high, getting a good high, and feeling pride in what I was doing. Showin' people that here I am; this is Charlie. That always has been my thing. Even when I go and play now, jazz and things. It's the same thing. It's a certain amount of dignity and respect. The main thing was that I couldn't believe that I had done it. Like, Hey Mom, look at me! You know, with no hands, almost. And that's what, all my life, has been stimulating. And the people, I guess, saw that. And when I played I played always with such conviction. I enjoyed it, you know. Like, *hey*, I enjoy what I'm doing, you know. And I guess that came across.

PURNELL: *You had this electric warmth; I could tell you loved to play every time you were on that stage. There was something that was magical about being on that stage, you and that bass. I wish now I would have had a camera to capture your face. Your facial expressions ran the entire gamut of emotions. It was like from extreme sorrow to extreme joy and sometimes to anger. And you really identified with the music to a point where every fiber in your body was absorbed in the music. Of course, the entire orchestra should have been doing that, but my focus was on you.*

DIANNE: *My most sacred space that I stand in is the stage. That is the place. That is my most precious place. And I wanna be on, and right, and clear. Every time I open my mouth I want to know what I'm doin'. I don't wanna be up there not knowin' what I'm doin'. And I want to have my instrument intact, because I treated it right, not because I stayed up all night and now I can't sing this song.*

CHARLIE: I never went out galavantin' after the job. I went home and went to bed. They could have it, 'cause I had the next day to get up at five o'clock and start practicing again to try to play the classics, you know. So I didn't have time for that sort of thing.

One incident at a Symphony rehearsal which made them straighten up was in 1950, when they had a drummer here who was a little flaky during rehearsal. Had the nerve to use the "good word," you know. The no-no word. "He's, you know … niggers, you know…." And I heard him. So I waited very calmly until after rehearsal and I went over and I grabbed his neck, by his tie, and drug him outside. I mean, *druuug* him outside, and put the word down, calmly, "Now look, if you do that again, I'll have to crack your head." I wasn't upset, you know. Well, for the next two years or so after that he was apologetic. And he grew to be one of my best friends, one of my very dearest friends for years. He knew that he had made a blooper and it was a wrong thing. And that was the only real big thing that ever happened in the orchestra at that time; after that everything was nice. For a while….

Of all the types of people I've met, I feel the most free with jazz musicians who have an education. That's the Billy Taylor group, Clark Terry, and Wynton Marsalis and this group who are not intellectual snobs but they're way up there. Of course, the classical musicians are beautiful, but you have to realize, in my case, the classical musicians—you're not quite at home with them. I don't care who they are. Because you don't have the background that they have had. And that hurts. I'd rather have a person come up and say, "Charlie, how are ya'?" Okay? And that's it. Don't go into all the subterfuge of, "What you are because you're Black and because of this and because of history, because of slavery, because of cotton," and because of all that crap. See, you don't go into all that. I could get along but I couldn't get real close to many classical musicians because we have a different background. Extremely different.

By being a classical musician it was like being in a social atmosphere where you're in the middle. You're neither Black nor White. White society does not accept you, they tolerate you. And the Black society does not accept you because they resent you. But my mainstay is with black educated musicians. They're just *people*. That is my big thing.

I also love ghetto musicians, because I came from the ghetto. But most of my good friends were educated black musicians. Billy Horner was an educated Black. He was the first, of course, to be accepted into the White society, and he was struck down. And then Julius Watkins, who was the most magnificent French horn player I have ever heard, and I have heard all of them. Well, he was an intellectual musical giant.

$$\oint \; \mathbf{9}\mathbf{:} \; \oint$$

When I first started with the Symphony they looked at my face and they accepted me, but it was not a true acceptance. It was like, "Hallo." They tolerated me. And that didn't bother me, because I've been tolerated all my life! Tolerated and been a token. So it didn't bother me at all. I had quite a few friends in the orchestra, though, that were really sincere people. Without them it wouldn't have been possible. And one of the main people was the principal bass player, John van Buskirk. I was like his son. He taught me; I studied with him for 3 or 4 years. The assistant principal bass player was Alex Horst, Sr. His son played bass in the section—Alex Horst, Jr. Because of Alex Horst, Sr., I was lucky enough to get one of the best basses, probably, in the world. Because it was his bass that he brought here from Russia in 1920, his own personal bass. I used to drool every time I would hear it. And he gave me that bass in 1959. By "gave," I mean he sold it to me for $500, nothin'. He heard of me going to San Francisco. He called me and asked if I could afford the bass that I liked so much. I used to call it Black Beauty, 'cause it was a magnificent black bass with a magnificent sound. And I said, "Oh, yes."

Well he said, "Well, uh, can you afford five hundred dollars?"

"Heeeeey!" That was a steal in those days. In any day! Five hundred dollars for this marvelous instrument. So I immediately flew back to Denver and got that instrument. And he's the one that made it possible. Because this instrument was a rare instrument. And the extension on this instrument, which bass players and musicians know, was put on by Alex Horst in 1920, the year of my birth. And it worked flawlessly until I let it go. It worked all this time without any major overhauls or anything. Just had to put a couple new pads on. Anyhow, he was very important in helping me.

Another bass player in the section, the only female, was Helen Deidrich. She was almost next to me at the end of the section in the Denver Symphony. I must tell you a little about her. The reason we were such good friends was because she was a very nice person, and very attractive, and had a personality out of this world. And dressed beautifully. Had much class, and all the things that went with that. So we became very good friends because she treated me more humane than the average person, in those days especially.

I became attached to her and her family. Her husband, whose name was Frank Diedrich, was a school teacher and a superb jazz pianist. They used to have me over to their house quite frequently, and I became the quasi-godfather of their two children, Mary Jo and Russell. We had a marvelous relationship with Helen, because she made a lot of things possible in terms of smoothing over little incidents that would arise in those days because she was so, just ordinary plain people.

Anyway, these were the core of the people that actually were my good, good, good friends. I also had a good relation with a timpanist, whose name was Walter Light, who made the best tympanis in the world, and I think they haven't been surpassed yet. He was one of my good friends, too. Another good friend of mine was the principal flutist, Paul Hockstad. These were all my important people that really helped me with the orchestra that were sincere, I could tell. Being from where I came from, you can always read a person and tell what they're intentions are and how they are. And these people were all sincere people who helped me all along the line, you know. Not only helped me, but they didn't tolerate me, they accepted me as a person, okay. We would get together and do things together. Only these people, out of the whole orchestra down there, would come along and do that.

Out of the Symphony, the family of the Symphony, I think I can count some of my good friends, and I'm just thrilled to have had these friends, and most of 'em I still have. It wasn't all bad times; 95% of it was good times, you know. A lot of the people were decent. We didn't think alike, but we got along because we played music, and music—as you know, especially classical music—was supposed to be the international language which in this case was true, because it helped to bridge a lot of gaps.

MELANIE: *It's pretty amazing that orchestras can produce as marvelously as they do. When they go on tour, there are cliques and there are people who don't want to sit on the bus with somebody else. You put that same group of haggard people into a symphony concert situation, and they have to produce together. But most symphony players are not good friends with other symphony players. I mean, we might have two or three that you are good friends with, but basically, their friends are outside of the circle, and they work differently in their job. It's a tough job, in part, because often the personal relationships are not that good.*

It is amazing. During the concerts, we were concentrating so much on putting everything together that I think that's where we lost all of the pettiness. And that's the only way it could happen.

Chapter 25

MARY BETH: *I finally started working for the telephone company, in 1946. I was among the first Blacks hired at the telephone company.*

During that time the Blacks that worked for the telephone company— they hired us in twos. And we were switchboard operators. And I started out on a manual type board; that is, plugging in. And starting there, even though I was in Detroit, White people were just horrible. When we'd go to work, my friend and I, we would always have to psychologically prepare ourselves because it was a challenge. You needed a job, and everybody in the community thought is was "a good job." Of course, it wasn't. Then you'd sit down and the person next to you would move over and didn't want to sit by you, and then he'd bring a supervisor and say that you smelled. Most of 'em were eastern Europeans and they just reeked with garlic, so I said, Ooooh.

You had very little recourse, except we did have a union. And I did belong to the union. I always belonged to the union. Shortly after—I was there about six months—the union went on strike. You just had to go out. So we were out six weeks.

In '52, because I had six years, I had more seniority than a lot of people, even though I was only 22. And they promoted you in terms of seniority. So it was time for me to be promoted to supervisor, and this is when my fight began. They called me and said, "We don't think the time is right for you to be a supervisor." And I didn't say anything, I just went and filed a union grievance.

One of the things I didn't mention is that during the time I was in Detroit as a teenager, it was during the time the left-wing or communist-inspired stuff was going on. And I had been in parades with W. E. B. DuBois and Paul Robeson. They were very pro-union, and of course, what we would call race people. This is also the time that McCarthyism had started.

So when I filed a discriminatory grievance— that was the first one—they told the union that they were afraid, because I was pro-communist and that the FBI had a dossier on me this thick. It was a very frightening time. My supervisor called me in the office and said, "Because the FBI has a dossier on you, you're a risk."

I said, "I'm on a switchboard, and I'm a risk?" So I said, Okay. I didn't have hardly any recourse. And the union didn't really pursue it because they were afraid. At that time, the unions didn't have the wherewithal or the experience to fight.

JOE: *In 1938 the Detroit Fire Department hired two Blacks. One was the first Black architect to graduate from the University of Michigan, and the other was a college graduate from a southern university. And then thirteen years later they hired me. So I was the third Black fireman in Detroit, and I'm the oldest Black fireman living from that era now. And I had a beautiful time—makin' them miserable, makin' them follow the rules that they made. But I enjoyed it. And I can handle these things because I learned not to hate. And I laughed all the time—they thought I was crazy because I was always happy. But I made them miserable. They aren't gonna mess with me! I was happy making them miserable.*

I was injured on duty and I was on duty-disability for two years. I challenged them on every rule that was there, and I won. For example: After being off for two years, I happened to stop by the engine house and this fellow that was in the same class as me, White fellow, says, "Ah, you dumb son-of-a-bitch! If you'd have stayed you'd be a lieutenant now!"

And I said, "Aaaah." So I went upstairs and took a rule book, took it home, and studied it and studied it. And there's nowhere in the rule book that says I could not come back on duty. This had never happened before. So I went to the department doctor and got okayed and all that. They had outside-department doctors, and then they had official department doctors. But I went to this outside-department doctor. He assumed that they wanted me back on duty, so he okayed me to come back on duty. So I called the chief of the department for an appointment, and he's glad to see me, "Oh, Burrell, come on down, come on!" I went down, we talked for about ten minutes, and then I casually said, "By the way, I'm comin' back on duty, would you make arrangements?" I didn't say, "Can I come back?" I says, "I'm coming back, would you make arrangements?" And the shit hit the fan! Heh, heh! At that time I was involved in politics, and they assumed, because of my tenacity, that I was sent there by the NAACP. Everyone thought that I was a plant for the NAACP because I did everything right.

The chief of department said, "I'll get back with you." He didn't call me for two weeks, so I called him again for an appointment. I don't like to talk on the phone. I went to his office, and he says, "Well, Burrell, this has never happened before. No one has ever gone from a fire fighter to a lieutenant." See, it's all seniority: fire fighter, sergeant, lieutenant. But because of where I was on the seniority list, they had to make me a lieutenant. So this was the 1ˢᵗ of July. So he said, "Well, I'll get you an appointment with the Department doctor, but there's 75 recruits that are going through, so ...."

I said, "Oooh, this is Joe Burrell, this is no recruit! If you can't get me an appointment I'll get somebody who can." To make a long story short: On the 5ᵗʰ of July, I started back as a lieutenant, which has never happened before. And all the Whites were pissed off because it meant that everyone who was behind me was a step further behind. And, it meant that here's a Black lieutenant that didn't do this and didn't do that! And they knew where I was coming from so they didn't like it at all, and they gave me a fit about— they tried to, but I gave them a fit.

They always disliked me because I made them follow the rules. I says, "You White folks made them rules, and when it comes to Joe Burrell you're gonna stick to them!" And I made them stick to 'em. I proffered charges against a White sergeant—I was a lieutenant then. And that had never happened in the department. One of his men refused a direct order from me in front of about five or six other men. This was three o'clock in the morning. So I went back to the quarters and I called his sergeant and I told him what had happened. And he said, "Well, those were my orders!" And I said, "Ooooh!" So I got the rule book and I stayed up all night proffering charges against him and the firefighter. And when these charges went downtown they didn't do anything for a week or ten days. When I inquired about them the chief of the department says, well, the charges weren't typed up right. So I asked to come down and have the chief of the department's secretary type the charges for me.

And my chief was mad at me, everybody was mad at me, and they tried to drop it and I wouldn't let them. He wouldn't have gotten fired, he'd have just got a reprimand. But he couldn't take that, so he retired rather than take a reprimand from me.

There were times when I had officers that I didn't speak to, except "Yes, Sir," and "No, Sir." No conversation. I would be driving them, and all I would say would be "Yes, Sir," and "No, Sir." But I was never mad, and that kind of got their goat. I survived. And I had a good time. After 25 years, I retired. And I've been retired for over 30 years!

Chapter 26

The Symphony had only about a 12-14 week season in those days. Consequently, I had to get something else to augment, and I applied down at the City Auditorium for a job as janitor. And a wonderful fella named Tom Seymour was the manager of the auditoriums down there. He was very understanding and sympathetic with what I was doing and appreciated it, you know. And he was like a real influence and father figure to me because he would allow me the flexibility of being a janitor and a stage hand while playing with the Symphony. What I would do is get down there normally at 6 in the morning, at the auditorium, and practice until 8 o'clock, and work as a stage hand from 8 o'clock 'til 9:30, and then go for the rehearsal—which was right there— for the Symphony from 9:30 to 12, and come back at 12:30 and work as a janitor 'til 3 or 3:30. And I look back today and I realize that some of my greatest friends over the years were stage hands.

I would always hustle. In those times I was hustlin' because I had two child supports to pay, and that was not easily done. So what I did was hustle jobs. I approached Tommy Seymour again and told him I needed some summer work. Normally, the Symphony didn't have a summer season. So I told him I needed some work and he said, "Well, we have to linseed oil Red Rocks." Red Rocks Amphitheater, in the mountains out west of Denver.

I said, "Okay. Look, I can do it." So I had my old 1936 (this was about 1952 or 53) Dodge 4-door, green, which I think I paid a hundred dollars for. And I filled that thing up with linseed oil and I think it took me six weeks to linseed oil nine thousand seats at Red Rocks, *top and bottom*. And I did a thorough job, if I must say, in doing that! I mean, I didn't leave an inch unturned! I always believe whatever you do, do it the best you can, and I did. And of course that car—I had to get rid of it because it was nothin' but linseed oil!

I was profoundly proud of this because that was not the easiest job in the world to work out there in the sun eight hours a day doing that. But I did accomplish it—my big contribution to helping Red Rocks! I got the city wage, because I was under the auspices of the city and county. But I was grateful that Tommy Seymour helped me when I needed big help making money. It helped me through that summer tremendously.

I was busy bringing up a family and enjoying the wealth of being with the Symphony, which was my prime thing in life. And also enjoying the wealth of having lots of fun in the night clubs, 'cause I had more fun than a barrel of snakes in the night clubs, you know. I met all kinds of people. I met doctors, lawyers, CPAs, as they say, whores and pimps. You know, people in the street. But they were all my friends, and that's where I got a good cross-section of just being around people and being yourself. And learning how to associate with people, make them feel important, which to me is a very important facet of what you should feel in life.

My first jazz job in Denver was with George Morrison. *The* George Morrison, who was the big violin player of the era, the big shot of jazz music in Denver and in surrounding states. He had it all sewn up, because he had such marvelous talent for playing and getting along with people. So I started playing with George Morrison. You won't believe this, but I played up in Montana. We went all the way to Montana, and played a hoe-down thing in a barn. A square dance. I had to laugh because I realized that Milt Hinton years ago had told me to be sure and learn how to play all kinds of music so you can be available for work. And I did. It was a rousing success because I could slap the bass; they thought that was beautiful, gorgeous.

With George Morrison we went on what was called the Denver Post Cheyenne Special which was for the Cheyenne rodeo. Every year they had a special train which went. And George Morrison, for years, had the charge of the combos that played the little quasi-Dixieland *crud* (I call it) on that. So I had the pleasure of playing that a couple years.

I played the sousaphone. Now, the sousaphone, people know, is a little different from the tuba! A tuba is an upright bass instrument; the sousaphone hangs around your neck. And the reason I mention the sousaphone is because I had learned to play the sousaphone back in my high school days pretty well. And I was given a sousaphone by the then president of the Black local musician's union, whose name was Matthew Rucker. And this was one of the most pathetic sousaphones I'd ever had around my neck in my life. It was about a First World War vintage, okay. One valve was missing; I had to play everything with two valves. That was a real pain in the buttons, as they say, but I enjoyed it.

We played marches and Dixieland songs on the train up to Cheyenne. We got to Cheyenne, as far as we could go with them with the train, because there was still a little prejudice up in Cheyenne in those days. So we didn't get off the train. We stayed and had a big, thick T-bone steak, which in those days was heavenly; that was pay enough. So you did that, and you rested for 3, 4, or 5 hours, and then on the way back to Denver you played again! For all these drunken slobs, and crap, you know. Just as funny as heck, you know, 'cause I look at it now, most of them were doctors and lawyers and 17th Streeters—the *big* people. No Blacks! Except us, you know. And except Dr. Holmes, who was the only Black person on the train. He was a dentist, the only Black dentist for maybe 2000 people. And we would play on the way back to Denver. And for that excursion I think I got the big fee of 10 dollars! Well, that was big money in those days.

From then I played with George Morrison here and there. We were actually the first band that made a recording for the TV. A commercial. The first band, Black or White, in Denver, that made a recording for a TV commercial. And George had a 7-piece band. And his daughter, Marion Morrison Bailey, who was a very outstanding pianist and teacher, was on that recording session. And George made the session and we got twenty dollars for that session. But that commercial was never used. Reason why: BLACK!

By the way, people ask me now why I always wear a Cuffley cap, which is an English style cap. Here's the reason why: It was a very simple thing. I was taping one of the first TV programs I ever did. What happened was the technicians down there, the cameramen, said, "Look, we're getting a glare, a big shine from your head!" You know. What it this? And they wanted to put some shoe polish on my head. I said, "I don't think so!" So they powdered it up, and it wasn't getting it. So I put on my Cuffley cap, and that was my trademark from then on, with jazz, was Cuffley cap and cigar! I have three or four of 'em around the house now, you know. I keep a set in different colors, which is another one of my trademarks. I love 'em, because they're very classic, I think.

One of the most outstanding things I remember was when we played at a club on Broadway and 3rd Avenue, which was owned by a fellow named John Manley. And we later discovered that John Manley had been an international boxer. How we discovered that was: One evening when we were playing down there—for 7 dollars a night—some fellow, an Anglo, came in and asked John Manley, "What are you doing with those, um, '*the famous N-word,*' in this place?" And before you could bat an eye, John Manley hit him one punch, and this fellow rolled, it seemed like for half a mile! Right out the front door! And when he got on the street he was running like a son-of-a-gun. And it was an instant love affair with John Manley. Because he respected us as people and took good care of us, you know.

Chapter 27

When I first came to Denver they had two musicians unions, a White union, which was Local 20, and the Black musician's local which was Local 623. In the early fifties, the big word came down from New York, the New York 802 Local, that these unions had to merge. And with that merger came the demise of just about all the Black jobs for musicians in Denver.

Just before that merger I went in and asked the president of the Black local, "Look, if I'm gonna' be with the Denver Symphony I don't have to pay any dues to the Black local."

He says, "Oh, yeah, ok, you don't have to pay any dues."

And then I turned around and went the Local 20, which was the White local, and says, "Look. Now, uh, I'm a member of the Denver Symphony, do I have to pay both locals?"

He says, "Oh, no, you can pay the Black local." Well, I didn't pay either one! For about 2 or 3 years. So I got away Scott-free there in terms of paying dues. And that to me was a big deal, because in those days every penny amounted to something.

The reason why all the Black jobs were lost was that as they had amalgamated, Local 20 took over the Black union and all their assets and everything they had (which wasn't much but it was enough to us). It was a very simple procedure, but another true thing about racism. When they amalgamated they had no Blacks in the office down at the White union. All the calls that came into the union came into the White local, which was down on Logan Street, and the people that called in for a Black group were told that all the Black groups were busy, but they had some good White groups there! So over a period of six months to a year, almost all the jobs for the Blacks had dried up in Denver. Not only because of the union, but because of the Black musicians themselves, so I put that right where it belongs, okay, because they limited themselves.

Chapter 28

In the early fifties, the Denver Symphony, under the leadership of Saul Caston, was doing a Wagnerian thing up at Red Rocks. Part of the performance was called the immolation scene. And they had one of the big Wagnerian sopranos there; she was playing the role of Brunehilde. The reason I mention that is the fact that Brunehilde was so big, she was about six foot, 290 pounds. They had to lift her up on the rock to do this immolation scene with a derrick. That was the most hilarious thing I've ever seen in my life.

In that same performance, the immolation scene, which was a fire scene, was supposedly goin' off without a hitch. *Supposedly*. But what happened during the playing of the scene—the wind pushed the fires back on down to the pit, onto the musicians, and it was bedlam! It came in such a big hurry and flew back there. The people in the orchestra were afraid to move, they were afraid to leave. And Charlie was the first one to get out! And after I ran out—I left my bass—everyone followed me. That was a very terrifying experience, you know, but we got over it. And that was one of the most *electrifying*—I mean that!—electrifying evenings I think I've ever spent. But the house was full! There were nine thousand people there! And it was a magnificent success. That was a real high point of my events with the Denver Symphony.

My first big tour with the Denver Symphony was almost six weeks. We went on this tour, our "big tour" I call it, in '53, that Saul Caston had planned with Helen Black, the business manager. We went through Kansas and several other states, and we ended up in Carnegie Hall! So I had the thrill of playing in Carnegie Hall with the Denver Symphony. Okay. And that was the big thing. And I had to laugh, because en route we made our own reservations. We didn't have anybody making hotel reservations. And we stayed in anyplace you could find, you know. Most of the places were real fleabags and crap. I never had any problems, because of the Symphony, getting accommodations for a room or anything. The rooms we got were only a dollar, two dollars a night. Hell, they were glad to have somebody there, anybody there, okay.

When we got to New York and we played Carnegie Hall, the lady who did the write-up on that, her name was Cassidy, ooooh, she put a thing in the paper like you wouldn't believe. I think it was, "The western cowboys came to town. And the boys came up with their saddles and boots and they played like a bunch of cowboys..." You know, it was the most awful review I think I'd ever seen. Heh-heh. To me it was hilarious. It didn't matter, you know. It didn't bother Caston, either. He just went on.

That was the big tour we had in '53, and we went on up from New York; we came down through Michigan and through Detroit, and then back through Kansas and back to Denver. Quite an experience. My two daughters, who were living in Waukegan at that time, they were about 7 and 9, came with their mother to Chicago. I met them on the el in Chicago and they came to my performance with the Denver Symphony. I'll never forget—that was one of the most thrilling moments of my life to see my two daughters, Barbara and Joyce, there. Beautiful. Gingham, patent leather shoes, you know. And their little fine hats. In those days all the young little ladies wore nice straw hats, you know. And that was one of the biggest thrills I've ever had in my life, just seeing my two young daughters there.

We had two buses, and every third or fourth day somebody had to ride with Saul Caston and Helen Black in the limousine. And I had my day there. Oh, boy. It was marvelous; I just enjoyed every second of it. We were in two different leagues, you know. We had nothin' in common. They were rich and White and I was poor and Black. We had absolutely nothing in common, except the fact that we were both trying to get along and make a living. They tried to pump me, you know, and I was just as delightful as I could be. "Yes, Ma'am, yes sir." Aaaw, shit. They wanted to be overly patronizing. And I didn't need that bull, but they did it. And I realized what was going on. But they were good to me. They were good to me. Helen Black was among the best things that ever happened to me, because she stood up for me when I least expected it, you know.

I managed to get a hold of a good bass, which name was Glaesel, from a fellow in Boston who sold it to me for five hundred dollars. I just happened to save up the money, way back in the early fifties, '53-'54. And I was very, very proud of that bass. I had to drive down to Buena Vista and pick up the bass.

That's when I lived in the projects, okay? The city projects. Which was over on 10th and Osage. Me and my wife Vivian and two little kids. One day I left the bass in my old 1949 DeSoto, and left my son in the front, who was about a year and a half then, in the front seat with my bass over the length of the car. When I came back he had taken a salt shaker—this is my son, now, only son—and methodically put designs in the front part of the bass to the tune of about 150 little indentations. Of course, you take it with a grain of salt, as they say! But I was very, very, very, saddened by the fact that he had kind of ruined my bass.

The indentations, you couldn't get them out. He had knocked them in there nicely. There's a pattern all over the front part of the bass. Like every inch or two he made a nice little indentation. That was devastating.

Anyhow, things got pretty bad in the early fifties and I was destitute. I had to sell the bass. My wife was playing big games at that time, big money games like you couldn't believe, with her paramours in Detroit. Anyhow, that was her business, because I was tryin' to wait for her to grow up and be a responsible woman. She never did. That's why we got divorced. Anyhow, I went to sell this bass and I really couldn't sell it. So I ended up just about giving it away to a fellow who was a school teacher then. His name was Gilbert Johnson. He lives now in Colorado Springs—he still has the bass. I had to give it to him for two hundred dollars and that broke my heart. That put a dent (so to speak) in my whole financial structure. But I survived.

There was a restaurant right in back of the projects—it's still there—called the Buckhorn. And it was always my ambition to get enough money to go into the Buckhorn Exchange Restaurant, where they served, they said, the best steaks in the West. I think it took me forty years to get in there, before I had enough money to afford the thrill of going to that place.

Speaking of the projects there on 10th and Osage, that was predominately Chicanos and Blacks. That's where they started learning to get along together because they realized that you can't fight each other and make any progress. But make no mistake, there was a big, big, big line between the two.

Chapter 29

I was the house bass player at the Rossonian for this friend of mine, Harrington, who was the boss man. I would be on call just in case a bass player couldn't make it—I was called the house bass man. I'll use the word that he used to use describing me as his bass man, because everyone knows it: "This is my nigger man, here for the household. Bass player." You know. And I looked at him. OK, as long as you pay me. Harrington was a lovable fellow but he was out for money. His big thing was, If you were White you were right; if you were Black, get back. That was his philosophy, because he was makin' money. And you really couldn't blame him. So the Rossonian was not really meant for the Blacks. It was meant for the Whites. Anyhow, he used to pay me to be the house bass player there.

PURNELL *Quenton Harrington was a very, very light-skinned Negro. I remember once when I was a very small child my parents wanted to go to the Rossonian to see one of the headliners, and we were standing very close to the front of the line. And I remember Mr. Harrington walked behind my parents, deeper in the line, and got an Anglo couple and just took them in immediately. And he was famous, or infamous, for doing that.*

It was amazing that when the Rossonian was in its heyday in the fifties and sixties, the entertainers would entertain there but they still could not stay in the hotels downtown. I remember, before she passed, Marion Morrison Bailey mentioned the fact that her father's house, right there on the corner of 26th and Gilpin, was really the open door house for all the traveling musicians that came through town. They would stay there when they couldn't stay downtown, even though they did perform downtown.

Nellie Lutcher came through there, about '54 I guess it was, and played at the Rossonian. At that time she was very popular for the songs called, "Come on Down to My House Baby, Ain't Nobody Home But Me," and "Fine Brown Frame." Her bass player, George Duvivier, his grandmother had gotten desperately sick, or she died, one of the two. Back in New York. So he had to fly back to New York. Consequently, George couldn't make it, and Nellie was up a tree and asked Quentin Harrington if there was a bass player in town that could maybe cut this. And he said, "Oh yeah, Charlie can do it." Everyone thought Charlie could do it—it wasn't that easy!! So I stepped in and played that week with her at the Rossonian Lounge. That was a big break in terms of being recognized in the field.

In those days, the Denver Symphony didn't have a summer season. So it was just right, and this just happened in the last part of May. She liked me. So she said, "Could you go out with me and play?" And I did!

With Nellie, I went all over the place up in Canada and all over the United States. But the big thing was that she didn't fly. So she traveled by train. And that was beautiful for me because I always got a stateroom. A complete stateroom. I'd been sittin' in the chair coaches for years. But with Nellie I got this stateroom where I could practice six, eight hours between jobs. And that was a luxurious thing.

The big thrill was when I went with her to Honolulu. Of course, she had to take the boat over to Honolulu and I flew. So I had a half a dozen days in Honolulu to get acclimated, and get set up and conditioned before she got there. In the meantime, on the beach I met a marvelous pianist and singer, whose name was Carmen McRae! And we spent the whole day getting suntanned and burnt on Waikiki beach! I never asked for anything, like body or nothin'. We just had a beautiful afternoon. We were friends all through her lifetime.

After that Nellie came over there and we played at a place called the Brown Derby, which was the only place where Black musicians could play. They were not allowed in the big ones like the Royal Hawaiian Hotel. So we started playing at this place, and the small orchestra that was there was a fella named Buddy DeFranco and his jazz group. And with Buddy DeFranco was Eugene Wright, who became a friend of mine. They called him "The Senator." (He was the Senator, and Milt Hinton in New York was the Judge.) Eugene Wright and I got to be good friends, and for years he studied with me. He was the bass player who made that famous recording with Dave Brubeck. "Take Five"? That was him on that recording. So I had a *little* input into his fame and fortune!

In Hawaii, we met Doris Duke Cromwell, probably one of the richest ladies in the world, who was a dear friend of Nellie Lutcher's. She invited us over to her place, called *Shangri-La*. We went up there one weekend, and I was hooked on the better life. It was magnificent; I'd never seen anything like it, like in the movies. We went up there and had the thrill and pleasure of being on her estate and being exposed to one of the biggest swimming pools I've ever seen in my life. She had, on her staff up there, on call, one of the famous swimmers and divers of the day to give exhibition performances for her guests. His performance was outstanding, of course. And I had the thrill of tasting for the first time original, 1776 cognac. And I really got hooked—got hooked for life on that. At the same time, I got exposed to Cuban cigars! (I was a pipe smoker before that.) The Cuban cigars were about a dollar for the best cigar you could get, and it was called the "Winston Churchill" model, and it would last almost all day. The most mild cigar I have ever had! Between getting hooked on cognac (not brandy, cognac, there's a difference!) and also the cigars, which is still my trademark, I love them and still do to this day—*good* cigars!

But the most shocking thing was that, at that time, a Black girl's band from the States was over there, the Sweethearts of Rhythm. Okay. And I happened to meet one of the girls, who was the tenor sax player with the Sweethearts of Rhythm. People didn't know it, but over in Hawaii in those days, Black men didn't stand much of a chance of, as they say, makin' out with any kind of sex partner on the female side, because it was a no-no. And I didn't know that. But it didn't bother me, because I didn't go over there for sex anyhow, I went over there to play. Anyhow, I met this lady from the Sweethearts of Rhythm. Tenor sax. She was cute as a bug's ear. And we spent three or four hours together, I guess, you know. We held hands and walked all over the place and so forth.

And I thought I was making big headway. Ha ha ha ha ha. Another one of those disappointments in life: When I got ready to fall down on her, she told me, "Darling, we're both out looking for the same thing!"

I said, "WHAAAAAT!!!!" And that just about floored me. I said, Wait, now. You know. So my feathers were knocked down. And after being over there for quite a length of time I said I'm so glad to get out of Hawaii I didn't know what to do. 'Cause like the boys said, there was no action for any Black men over there. None, you know.

Nellie Lutcher and her band had the pleasure of being the main course, I put it, at one of these clubs in Ohio, where the trumpet player, White fellow, sang. Mel Torme. The best singer I've ever known. Played drums, too. He was the entr'acte, before Nellie Lutcher in this club in Ohio. And this was funny as hell. I never could figure out why he never really spoke to me decently, you know. And the reason was—I figured it out later—because we were on the same billing and what happened was Mel Torme was only the entr'acte. He was the first one on there. And the big artist was Nellie Lutcher and her trio, which at that time was very, very popular.

In my way of speaking, the greatest male singer I have ever heard in my life—the greatest, bar none—the greatest, was Mel Torme. I loved his voice better than any male voice I've ever heard. And really arrogant—of course, he had the right to be arrogant! What the hell, you're that good, you can be arrogant. Like I told a lot of people, if I could sing as well as he sings, I wouldn't speak to anybody, probably! But that was Mel Torme. I still, today, revere him. Of course, everyone knows that he wrote that famous "Christmas Song." I like to look back and say, Boy, that was quite an affair, you know, to have been mingling with them. He was on the first track, we were on the main billing. And that's what happened with him.

Another thing about Nellie Lutcher: The reason why I loved her, and loved playing with her, was because every time we came back off of an engagement we'd stop in Los Angeles and she'd have a big pile of gumbo. We would stop at her place in Los Angeles, and her sisters and the family would always have a big pot of gumbo. And she would go in there and doctor that gumbo up. I'd eat gumbo for three days— morning, noon, and night, you know. That was the best gumbo I ever had in my life. Real *gumbo*, you know. In other words, it was an elegant outing, financially and spiritually and stomach-wise. That's how she helped to keep us in line, in terms of the job. Every year for 4-5 years, in the summertime I would go out with Nellie and play throughout the United States and Canada. I had a good time with that.

Chapter 30

Nothing actually broke loose until the middle of the fifties when Al Rose got together the first integrated trio in Denver. He had in his group a marvelous drummer, Lee Arrelano, who was Chicano, Al Rose, who was Jewish, and Charlie Burrell, who was Black. And the people said it wouldn't work. But the trio went in the Playboy Club, on Race and Colfax, right across from the old Aladdin Theater. And we were there for four or five years, and we had the most outstanding array of people in there. Crowded every night. Every night we were there you almost had to wait to get in. And Saturday nights you couldn't get in. They had a marvelous thing goin' on Saturday nights. At twelve o'clock every Saturday we started playing Caravan, by Duke Ellington, and that was a real showpiece for the trio. You could really stretch out, so we developed that into our Saturday Night Exposé, you know.

The owner of the Playboy, Bob Wallach, knew how to keep me happy, with cognac—Remy Martin—and with Cuban cigars. So he would hand me a box of Cuban cigars every Saturday. So I was drinking and smoking the best in the world, and having the best time, and making one of the best salaries I've ever made in my life, because Al Rose, the piano player, was a marvelous businessman. After a year of having nothing but packed audiences at the Playboy, the owner of the club asked Al whether he would rather have a salary of $200 a week for the sidemen, or take a percentage. Al took a percentage of the club, and that was the smartest thing he ever did in his life. Way back in the fifties we were making over $200, and that was unheard of for musicians. Normal musicians were making $40 and $50. We were making close to $250-300 a week with Al Rose. And I was still with the Symphony! Makin' that $65-$75 a week!

With the Al Rose Trio, that was fascinating, because Al Rose played his *ass* off. Pardon my French. And Lee was very efficient. Plus they were both good people, they got along with people and socialized, and they clicked with me. We had a relationship. That was one of my good paying jobs. And Al's niece, his sister's child, is now a US Representative, Dianna DeGette.

Erroll Garner came in one evening after his job on Saturday, as a matter of fact, and he played 'til six o'clock that morning. Closed the doors, and Erroll Garner played his buttons off! All night. He brought his bass player along, who just happened to be one of my students, Eddie Calhoun—they called him "Gump." They played all morning long. That was the beginning of the breaking the barrier between the big musicians and the ordinary local musicians.

PURNELL *One of my absolute fondest memories is when you brought Erroll Garner over to the house when you played for Errol! You brought Erroll Garner over, and he ate us out of house and home that night! And that year you were responsible for corrupting me into jazz, which I loved. I remember, you and I were standing in the wings together and watched your former student Eugene Wright playing with Dave Brubeck. And Joe Morello did a roll and, remember, I ran out on stage and handed him his drumstick and ran right back off. You said, "Go get it!" And you told me to be sure to stand where I could watch Brubeck play. And the same thing when Erroll Garner played.*

With Al Rose, we went to Durango many times, and played at LuLu Belle's, which was in the corner of the Strater Hotel. That's where Al Rose got his biggest kick out of life because he loved Durango. By the way, he passed away at the age of 43. If he had lived he would have been the mayor of Durango, that's how popular he was. Everyone loved him. Dogs, cats, children, people, horses, anything you name. They loved Al.

After two or three years, Al Rose finally decided to move to Durango with his family because of family problems. After he left, I decided to get my own little trio together. And with the help of Mr. Bob Wallach who was the boss at the Playboy, we decided that we'd go and try another little spot up the street, which was on St. Paul and Colfax. And the place had been formerly named the Pick-A-Rib. And if I must say so, that was the best barbeque I had ever had in my life. And the reason was the fact that they hadn't begun to alter the meats with the enzymes—and outzymes, I call 'em—in those days. Plus they had people there who were all Black, and they all cooked down home cooking. And from the down home cooking came the best ribs I've ever had in my life, and the best beans. They cooked their beans from scratch. And that was a big difference. So that helped a lot of musicians, because that was the only place to go to get good ribs.

We moved into this place, and they called it the Band Box. I took my trio in there with a songstress named Helen Stuart. The trio comprised a piano player named "Rags," Leon Ragsdale, a good piano player and a swinger. And he was a little alky. That was alright—I kept him in line, I nurtured him. I picked him up and delivered him home from the job for a couple years. The drummer's name was Louie

Gater, who was working then on his degree from the University of Denver, his CPA; he was working diligently on that. So I had this group there in the old Band Box for about two years. And we had a tremendous success there; the place was always full. And that was really the beginning of the integration of Blacks and Whites as an audience. Before, the audience was 90% White.

From this came a good relationship with Louie Gater. Louie was a very up-and-coming businessman. And I think I taught him a lesson in life, about being responsible and respectful to other people, and especially if you're playing on a team. Be responsible for the rest of your team. He realized that this was not all fun and games.

After we had been there together a couple months and it was real successful, I think he began to feel his oats. So one night he didn't show up until about quarter of ten, you know. When payday came, I docked him a hundred dollars. He wasn't gettin' but a hundred and a quarter. But back in the fifties that was good money! Big Money! You see, you don't do things like this. So I was cool. And we finished the night, and got through. He said, "This is a little short?"

I said, "Oh, no! That's not short. You're lucky to even get that." And he looked at me—he knew better than to question me. I was strict. Good as gold but strict. And you didn't play games. From that time on he was a half an hour early for almost two years. That taught him a lesson. And the same fellow later became one of the first Blacks to become president of a bank, downtown. He's still around and still plugging and still making his way.

I had somebody put my boots on me, as they say, when I was only seventeen or eighteen years old. Albert Holmes, my friend in Detroit who did the same thing for me. And that straightened me up for my lifetime in terms of respecting where, and what, and what you had to do.

PURNELL *Mom loved you and she knew that you had my best interests at heart. Anything that you said let's do she, of course, endorsed. 'Cause she knew it was for the betterment of me, not only musically but as a human being. And it was learning how to prepare me to be in the world, showing me another side of how to be prepared for life. And for people. Remember when I first saw you play jazz, man, when we sneaked up at the Band Box? Hee, hee. Sneaked in, under age. I lied at the door like a big dog and said, "Yeah, that's my cousin up there. I'm old enough to drink. I want a scotch and water." And I had my last three dollars cover charge! And I think I was all of seventeen. And I saw you play jazz. That was the first time I ever saw you play live jazz, was at the Band Box.*

Rags and I played at a little joint down on 15th Street between Champa and Curtis, called the Piano Lounge. And the fella' who owned it was Morrie Bernstein. We were there for quite a spell. I didn't know anything about Morrie's accomplishments then, but he wrote something called "Israel, Oh Israel." And that was later presented to the Denver Symphony for them to make a recording, and the stupid folks down there turned it down—Board of Directors said, no it would never go—turned it down. But Morrie was very persistent, and kept going along. So the next thing we knew, the Israel Symphony was performing it with Zubin Mehta, okay. So that was a big, "Hey, hello" to the board of directors down with the Denver Symphony. In other words, I'm sayin' that they were not out for the progression, building of the Orchestra. It was a personality thing, a big club thing. I didn't know it for years after that, but that was the name o' that game.

When I played for Morrie Bernstein down at the Piano Lounge, we had a trio there at the time which was Rags Ragsdale on piano and a fellow on drums who was extremely unique because he was not only a drummer but he was a tap dancer. He was the only tap dancer I have ever seen tap dance barefoot. But if you looked at the soles of his feet, his calluses were about an inch thick. And when he tap danced—we had a little platform down there—it sounded just like regular metal taps on shoes! So that was Curly Russell. And he was also a very outstanding personality. People loved him because he could tap dance and play drums, and also tap dance bare-footed.

At the Piano Lounge I had my first real physical encounter which I had never had in my adult life. What happened was this: We were playing one night and a little girl came in—of course, I was not married then. And her name was Doris Fleisher. So we had struck up a little relationship and this particular night a fellow came there—his name was Gene Carter, okay. And I'll say in all sincerity that he's still one of my very dearest friends. But what happened was he came in, and I didn't know what was going on, but he had been involved with Doris. And I guess Doris had broken it off. But he wasn't ready for it to be called quits! So he came in this night, and it happened because he was a little full of—as we called—the "juice." A little drunk, you know. So he came in this one night and he was talking. I was never a violent person, never have been, okay. He sat there and at intermission I came over and he came to the booth where we were sitting and he started mouthing off, you know. He was getting very angry and violent. He told Doris what he was going to do to her—he was gonna' slap her and all this sort of thing, and I just laid back cool, and I said OK to myself and let this go on.

But he made the fatal mistake of saying, "After I finish with you I'm going to get on—" and pointed to me. At that time he had pulled the panic button and I had never done it before but I grabbed him by his neck and pumped at least sixty or seventy blows before they could get me off of him. I had never done that before. Anyhow, after they got me off I just went back and played! It was no big deal, you know. But I watched my back after that.

The next day he came by my sister's place, where I was staying, on Jackson and 34th, and apologized. I didn't recognize him because his face looked like a meat grinder had ran over him or something. I later learned that he was the 9th Army District boxing *champ*! And that scared me to death! I said, What! You know. Champion Boxer! It got me a little frightened, and I said, OK. But later on we patched it up and he's still one of my very dear friends. Which means that actually you don't have to use guns and weapons to settle disputes. He was wrong, and I was not really right but I was gonna' defend my honor. You didn't play games. I didn't believe in talking. They taught me in the ghetto you don't talk, you act, you know. So when he made the resolve to kick my ass, I guess he pushed the wrong button and I never knew I had that much in me, but I guess I did. I was always a little feisty when I was young, but I was never a bully. I didn't have time to be a bully because that was not in my make-up. I believe in treating you right but don't play with me, you know. You call me names and so forth, but please don't attack me. He made the mistake.

Also at that time I started playing with a small group which was headed by a wonderful fellow who was instrumental in helping to bring jazz to Denver. That was Shelley Rhym, a drummer. A very modest man. Superb fellow. And he had all the connections to the Black musicians. He had a little group which was performing around Denver, and I performed with them. We had with us a fellow named Charlie Sandborn on tenor sax; he was an excellent man. We would play in different joints in Denver.

I have to give credit to Shelley Rhym. He was a real important part of the cultural aspect of good behavior and learning in the Denver area, especially for the Chicanos and for the Blacks. He had all the contact with all the musicians of the day—the Charlie Parkers, Dizzy Gillespies, and all the young be-boppers and so forth. He was of that school, so consequently he dedicated most of his life to trying to help youngsters in terms of becoming better citizens and better musicians, and teaching them that there's a possibility that they can make it out there. But they must, they must learn how to *read* music. And that's what he was teaching most of his life. He always wanted to see the musicians get better, and better, and better.

In those days, I tried to get young Black musicians to study, to learn how to read, but a lot of them thought that it would hamper their artistic ability. I says, "No no no no. You don't mean hamper. It means that you won't be able to play anyplace else if you *don't* learn how to read, okay? Read! Learn how to read. Learn the instrument, okay?" That was a big fight, too.

I think I played with Shelley for 8 or 9 years in Denver, at the different clubs. And Shelley and I and the rest of 'em used to play at a place on Five Points (the heart of Denver's Black community) which was very, very, very, seldom heard of, which was called Benny Hooper's. In the basement. That's where all the jazz musicians—that's the only place they could play back in those days, so Shelley Rhym had charge of that, and we played down there for quite a few years. And jammed. That's where we learned. And you meet all the good musicians down there: Count Basie, Duke's people came down there, Lionel Hampton's people. All the Black musicians came down there. Sarah Vaughn 'n all of 'em. They came down there at Benny Hooper's, in the basement.

One of our big things was when we played at a place called Lil's After Hour Club, which was on 29th and Welton. And the fellow who had it built was Frank Miller. He was a scoundrel, but a marvelous guy. To call a shot a shot, I mean he was a pimp. But he gave, you know. He knew how to do it. So he had this club called Lil's After Hour Club. And Shelley had his band in there for, oh, three or four, maybe five years, I guess. I was a part of the group because we didn't start until 2 o'clock in the morning. Two to normally five, or whenever. And we had all the big names coming in there. It was the only place between Kansas City and California, Los Angeles, where they could really stop and enjoy themselves and play. At that time, there were no Black musicians in Las Vegas. You still had to go in the back door in Las Vegas; that gives you an idea of what was going on there. But at Lil's we had the pleasure of having all kind of good musicians coming in there, and people.

Out of that little clan came such nice people as Cedar Walton, who is still playing piano. He was a part of that group because he was goin' to DU then, and so was I. I had the pleasure of being, as he called me, a father figure. Heh, heh. He learned a little bit there.

Not only Cedar Walton, but another fellow named Mose Allison, who was Anglo, okay, and he came there because his father had a farm down south and they had share croppers and all that sort of thing, you know, and he always wanted to play the Black music. So he learned how to play—he was there two or three years, with his trumpet but mainly on the piano and singing. And he learned how to sing like the Blacks. He was down there stealing our music, but we didn't mind because he was just people, and we knew what he was doing. He wanted to learn and we respected what he was doing and where he was going, and his ability. He was just one of us, one of the boys. "Hey, bro'," you know.

The tragic part was after he got out of that and started playing over the country and the world, what they called the "motel syndicate," which was the Holliday Inn and all those things. A friend of mine met him and said, "Do you remember such and such in Denver?"

And he said, "Oh, no, I don't remember that." It was kind of a shock, because I tried to talk to him once and he acted like he didn't know me.

The only reason I look back on Mose Allison with disdain is the fact that when he got famous he turned, as the boys say, and that was a real no-no. He didn't have to do that, because we still loved him and people didn't give a damn where he came from. But have some respect for where you did come from, Baby, you know, your roots. And this was a part of his roots, between this and his Daddy's plantation, we knew what was goin' on, you know, we're not crazy. Well, you can't blame him, you know, he was a little afraid of himself. He was afraid that the White industry would not support him in terms of where he came from. But he was wrong, dead wrong. Actually they would have embraced him more, and given him more accolades than he could ever think of. I think he should have had more pride in how he learned. Which was no big thing! Just like me, I learned from the White folks how to play the bass. And they made it possible for me and others to break into the classical realm. Anyhow, he was there.

One of the most memorable moments in my life was when one night, after hours, the great Charlie Parker came up on the stand. And everyone was so excited that Charlie Parker, *Biiirrrd* was there! And he was gonna come up an' play! Well, I had to laugh, because Bird came up and sat in the chair in the front of the bandstand and went dead asleep for two hours! That was the only Bird I ever heard, you know! Which was nothing. That was the closest I ever got to playing with Charlie Parker! Heh-heh. We often talk about that, you know. Boy, that was a real eye opener, wasn't it? They said, "What you think of Bird?" Not much, because we didn't know him, and we didn't hear anything!

We were playing for two hours, and he slept through all of it. And Tad Dameron, who a lot of people recognize, was also one of the fellas who used to come up on the stage there and play. Thelonious Monk would come in and play. My old Navy buddies, Clark Terry and Al Grey. Ben Webster, and I could go on and on and on. Everybody that was anybody came up there to Lil's and played, you know. And the famous Dinah Washington had just appeared, I think, down at the Rossonian, you know. And she used to come around. So everyone was there. It was real big time. About as big time as you wanted to get.

I thought Dinah Washington was magnificent. She had her own style. She was a rowdy, make no mistake! The boys said Dinah could cuss like a sailor. Boy, she would cuss you out one side and down the other, you know. She was rowdy, but she could sing. Nobody could replace Dinah for what she was doing; it was Dinah's style and you knew right off the bat when she opened her mouth that was Dinah! She was top drawer. Always liked Dinah.

In those days, all of the good musicians came there. Slam Stewart used to come down there and play—he liked Denver because he could get away from the big hustle-bustle of New York. So he would come down and play at the Rossonian.

One of the most famous French horn players in all the world, and my good buddy from Detroit, came to Denver for a few years. Julius Watkins. He was the first one that played jazz, and he was doing it back in 1934 and 5, when he was 14 and 15 years old! But he had studied with Francis Hellstein. He studied nine years with him, from the time he was five or six or something. He also played with Shelley Rhym. The famous and magnificent Julius Watkins.

Chapter 31

I played for a fellow named Charlie Romolo, who had a place called Romolo's. Romolo's was unique in that it had classical opera singers there who would perform solos from opera all night. And they used to have as much as six or eight singers down there. And one of these singers was one of my good friends, Helen Diedrich. I didn't know that she could sing, and I went in one night and I discovered that she was one of the finest singers I had ever heard! Her daughter, who was then 17 or 18 or 19, was singing also at Romolo's, which was then the place to go after the theater.

By the way, another fine restaurant up on 17th Street was called Lou's Awful Coffee Steak House. This was owned by two brothers. They had the best prime ribs; the musicians used to go there, if they could afford it, on Sunday, and take their family for an outing. You know, 2 or 3 dollars, you could have the best prime rib in town. If they had a gig on Saturday night, they'd go. If they didn't have a gig on Saturday night, they stayed home and had beans.

Anyway, Romolo had a night club, the Club Algiers, right north of the Brown Palace, right across the street, upstairs. And that was where I met one of my idols of all my lifetime, whose name was Billie Holliday. Billie Holliday, as most people know, was *the* singer in those days. But she had a little problem. She was addicted, you know. She was on heavy stuff like heroin. Anyhow, she was going to appear this night at the Club Algiers, and we were supposed to go on at 8 o'clock. At eleven o'clock they were still trying to find her. And the only reason she couldn't get there was she hadn't had her fix. So after she had her fix she showed up, she made it by about 12 o'clock. And she got up there, and the audience was very sparse. But Charlie was enamored of her! He realized what a magnificent person she was regardless of her little petty condition, which was a life-threatening condition.

Anyhow, she got on the bandstand and I never will forget, She finally started to sing.

DIANNE: *My dad said, when Billie Holliday would take to the stage, he would just go, Woo. It would just get QUIET. You know, just like—QUIET!*

CHARLIE: She started singing a song named "Them There Eyes." And she was singing the song, and she looked back at me and winked. And it was the first time in my life I ever lost the "continuity" of myself. Pardon my French: I peed on myself! Heh, heh. And I said, "What is *this*?" Heh, heh, heh. And so she looked over at me and that was one of the greatest feelings in my life was when I performed in back of Billie.

I went back to her dressing room, and I said to her, I said, "I certainly enjoyed it, and I just wanted to say you're one of my most favorite people in all the world. Thank you for ..." all this and that, and so forth. And she leaned over and kissed me. And her husband, who was a trumpet player and her pimp, was right outside the door, and said, "NOT TOO LOOOOONG!"

I heard her say, "Oops." And she backed off and she looked at my pants, and I had on some light pants and they were a little wet down in the area. And she said, "Oh, you had a little calamity, didn't you darling? What was that from?"

I said, "From you." And I turned around and walked out. And that was my big thing with Billie Holliday. One of the biggest things in my life. I think back now and am thrilled by the fact that I was there on the same stage with Billie Holliday, you know. Because that was one of my big, big, big, big people in all my life.

I had played in a group in Detroit years and years before that where she appeared at a club, I think it was called Club Three Sixes. I played with the house band there but I never really got to meet her and I've always admired and been enamored of, and I love the sound of Billie Holliday. She was *the* singer of those days. And that was the most memorable jazz moment of my life.

One day I heard a piano as I was walking down a street in the neighborhood. And I heard this piano player and I though it was Art Tatum, who was one of the finest pianists, Black or White, to ever perform, you know. I would go by there, and every now and then I heard this piano, and one day I decided to stop. I went up to the door and said, "Excuse me." And I noticed that when I knocked on the door the music, the piano, stopped. And so I said, "Hey. That sure is a nice recording you have of Art Tatum."

She says, "Who?"

I says, "Art Tatum."

She says, "What?"

I says, "Was that Art Tatum's record playing?"

She says, "No, that was *me.*"

"Huh?" And her name was Louise Duncan. The most gentle, fabulous piano player I had ever met in my life, who was just a natural. The good lord gave her a talent, where she didn't have to practice. All she had to do was play. She was a real talent from the time she was three. She started playing in the church when she was three years old! Put her up on telephone directories, in the church, in Lawrence, Kansas. That's where she was from. So I developed a little friendship with her, and I didn't have a chance to play with her then because she was busy playing in the outskirt White joints, in a place in west Denver called the Aviation Club, way out in west Denver. She was there for four, five, or six years. That's why she never got any recognition around because she never played in Five Points—she was not a part of the Five Points congregation that came through at that time. But she still was one of the top piano players that I ever met in Denver.

Later on, she was playing at a place downtown called Al Stromberg's, which was right off of Larimer Square in the basement. And that was one of the most elegant restaurants that I had even been in. By elegant I mean in terms of the ambiance and the food. They had the best rack of lamb. I never had a rack of lamb 'til I had it there. And French onion soup, which was magnificent. So I used to go in there every Tuesday after playing with the Symphony, which was right up the street. I would go in there and play with her until closing. She was also the most elegant lady, in terms of dressing, I'd ever met. Her wardrobe comprised at least 40-50 elegant gowns.

When I first went there and met her she was making, I think, about 30 dollars a night, which was really peanuts, you know. And I talked to Al Stromberg and within a few months she was making a hundred dollars a night. So that became a relationship, there.

After that she went down to the Fairmont Hotel in Denver and started a 10-year stay at the Fairmount. This was beautiful because I used to join her mostly every Sunday for the big brunch they had there. And that was quite a charming thing; it gave me a chance to keep my hand in jazz, and to help Louise gain a financial foothold. Before that, she was making peanuts, but now she had arrived to where she was making a very comfortable salary and playing before good audiences.

Duke Ellington heard Louse Duncan back in the forties, I don't know where it was but he heard her play and he came up and kissed her hand! That was THE Duke Ellington. She had a technique which was just flawless, and she could play in any key. I got a lot of my real broad experience in terms of being a good bass player playing with her, because she wouldn't play in the traditional keys like B-flat, E-flat, and A-flat. She'd play the blues in F-sharp? Or B-natural? And I had to follow her, you know. It was a challenge! And it was a marvelous challenge because it put to use all my experience in practicing scales for all these years. There was some reason, and that was it! Louise Duncan was the thing. She was arthritic and her one finger was bigger than my two fingers, and she played as nimble as you could ever believe.

Chapter 32

One of my most enduring features about Denver was that I was introduced to people of a different nationality, and to ethnic foods which I had never tasted and had always wanted to taste. When I was in Detroit I had never had any ethnic Mexican food, like tamales, tostadas, and I didn't know what refritos were, you know. I had heard about this one thing which always kind of stuck in my craw—I was wondering what that was that was called huevos rancheros. It took me a while to realize that that was eggs, chili, you know.

When I first came to Denver I discovered that there were certain boundaries for certain groups of people. I wasn't shocked, I just came to the realization that this was the boundaries, of where Negroes especially were situated. The Negro area was from Park Avenue West on the west side of town, to Curtis Street on the north side, 22nd Street on the south side, and High Street was the imaginary boundary line on the east side of town. That's where the Negroes congregated, in this particular area. There were a few spotted here and there outside, but not very many.

The Chicano area was, at that time, around Curtis Park, which is Downing and 32nd, 31st, in that area. Their big thing was having their businesses and their big activity on Larimer Street, between I think 30th, 35th, somewhere around there, going all the way down to 18th. That's where they had their businesses and their restaurants, and so forth.

I'd like to speak a little about the rise and still prominent association with one of my good buddies—his name is Ruben Macintosh. I was here in 1949 when his father and his mother had their restaurant on Downing, and they sold food out of their house! Mostly out of the window. Me and my wife were so thrilled to get our first taste of *tamales*, we thought they were the greatest thing in the world—to have good tamales. Another one of our favorites was tostados. I didn't know what a tostada was. But they were beautiful, you know! Consequently, I became good friends with Ruben Macintosh. His father was Irish—Macintosh—and his mother was from Guatemala. I thought that was the most beautiful thing in the world. She was from *Guatemala*, wasn't that marvelous!

Anyhow, they used to sell their food out of the window there on Downing Street. Later, it grew, and with the help of Ruben and his brother they moved a little north on Downing to expand their business. And that's when they called it La Hacienda. A few years after that they moved next door to one of the old Black churches, which is where it is now, on 31st and Downing. Through all of these turmoils and so forth, Ruben and his brother and me became very good friends and have remained friends to this day. He became a real entrepreneur.

I had my first taste of green chili about this time. I had always heard about this. My good friends with our little band in those days, which was comprised of Shelley Rhym, Charlie Sandborn playing saxophone, and Gerald playing piano, we used to have a big time. And our big outing was going down to Larimer Street, which we called the slums—you know how you are in those days—to get some ethnic foods. So they took me down there and I got a big bowl of green chili? And I ate that bowl of chili and before I realized it my head was on fire, and I couldn't figure out what it was. And my friend

Charlie Sandborn was laughing—he couldn't stand himself he was laughing so hard, you know. And I said, Oh, they did a job on me! I think I drank at least four glasses of milk right quick to kinda cool that monster, because it was HOT! I didn't suffer then like I did the *next morning*. Of course, everyone knows what I'm talking about.

I had the pleasure of going on a job to someplace in Kansas where they were having a festival, okay, a Mexican festival, this weekend. And a fellow named Joe Lucero asked me if I would play. Oh, of course. I thought I'd make at least ten dollars a night for Friday, Saturday, and Sunday. So we went down on an old beat up bus, almost like a truck. We went down to this place in Kansas. And we played the weekend. And this weekend was the first time I had a taste of good huevos rancheros. And I think for three days I lived on huevos rancheros. Was the best food I ever had in my life, I think!

On the way back the bus broke down three or four times. We left there Sunday night and got back Tuesday. Maybe Wednesday. We got back, and I'll never forget, Joe Lucero gave me ten dollars. I said, "What's this?"

He said, "Oh, that's good pay! You had food, you had lodging."

"Huh?" I said, Oh, boy. That taught me another vital lesson about don't play with the road. Joe Lucero. I never knew what happened to him.

In those days it was actually an unwritten law that you didn't go much outside the sphere of the Black neighborhood. But I was a little more fortunate because I played music. So I used to work in the joints here and there, and I had one experience which taught me a awful lot about people and life. And that was when I worked on West Colfax, way out near Wadsworth, at a place called Vic Iseno's. This Saturday night I was out there with the band—Shelley Rhym, Roach on piano, and Charlie Sandborn. At intermission I was hungry and I got in my old DeSoto and I went out on Colfax to go down to one of the fast food restaurants where they had hamburgers. (But they made 'em fresh; it was not McDonalds.) And I went down there to get me a hamburger. This is maybe a half a mile or so from Vic Iseno's.

On the way back the police stopped me and they put the old word on me, like, "You look like somebody we been looking for." Oh, really, you know. So they called back, heh-heh, to Vic Iseno's and said, "We have a Black dude here who says he's working out there for you."

And of course Vic didn't know anything about the fact that I went down the street. Vic said, "Oh, no, they're all here; my band is intact." After about ten or fifteen minutes Vic discovered that I wasn't there; this is what Shelley told me. And he called the Police, told 'em, "No, we are missing a bass player. His name is Charlie Burrell." And they let me go. I said, Oh, boy! That taught me a big lesson about, look, don't play games, because they're out to get ya'. It was that way.

Now, this was the middle fifties. It was that way all over town. You didn't go to small towns, unless you were crazy. The race thing was real prevalent in those days.

Chapter 33

When I first went down with the Symphony, in '49, there were three Blacks in the audience. Three Blacks. And that included my first cousin, Laverne Steen, and her son Purnell, and another friend who was Black. The only three that were down there. They sat in the first row. And I used to look up and they would point. "My *cuzzin!*" And there were almost no Chicanos. But as time went on, people like Ruben Macintosh was busy helping to bring kids down to the Symphony on the city busses for the city concerts. And in connection with that, there were other Blacks. One of 'em was Jessie Maxwell, who was the first Black principal, and who was busy helping to expose as many as she could of the Black children down there. So by about 1952 or '53 for the children's concerts we used to have a lot of Mexicans and Blacks. Of course, it was predominantly White, but there was a growing trend that I'm glad to see that has developed into something more positive.

I used to go and give what I call little personal appearances with my bass at the schools. Jessie Maxwell was one of my good friends and only lived a block from me. And she was an advocate—follower of the Symphony, of the arts, and so forth. So I used to go down to her school and give little performances for her class with the bass. She was very appreciative, because she was for the same thing I was for in those days—to help the children as much as you possibly can. In terms of the arts, they really had no outlet. Most Latinos and Blacks didn't have the wealth of records and being exposed to the arts like the average Anglo did, because the Anglos were fortunate in the fact that their moms and dads made sure that they were at least exposed to the opera, ballet, the symphony, and the better jazz, which was the classical jazz. Louis Armstrong and Fats Waller and Duke Ellington. Count Basie. Ella Fitzgerald and all the big people who amounted to something. Made the kids really feel important in terms of social structures. I used to go over with my bass and give little classes for her students, try to broaden their scope in terms of—jazz was not the only thing but it was important, okay. And expose them to the classics.

My ambition in those days was to conjure up—I was still with the Symphony—a hundred people to get memberships for the Symphony. Yearly subscriptions. Within two or three years, I did. I got a hundred people at the jazz clubs and so forth, to become members of the Symphony and buy season tickets. That was my ambition and I succeeded. One hundred people—that was just me, one person. And I think in terms of what could have happened with the Symphony if all the people in there would have dedicated themselves to getting a hundred people for subscriptions. We'd have an overflow audience and a base for helping to finance and support the arts.

PURNELL *I remember sitting in the front row among the Symphony debutantes, the rich you-know-what, the rich girls who ushered. And I was studying the Mendelssohn Violin Concerto, and you told the ushers that I was gonna' sit right front dead center. And here I was with all these rich White gals in their gowns and everything. I remember they passed out the programs, and I was sitting there watching Isaac Stern play the Mendelssohn Violin Concerto that night. And I* *remember Sam Chernyk, my violin teacher, saying when I went to the concert to take my score. He said, "If you see any bowings that Maestro uses, just mark them down." So I was marking down. In a way it was rude. But then, Stern wanted to find out who I was. And do you remember? He went to you and you came and got me and I went back to his dressing room. And he autographed the score—I still have it. I still have that autographed score of the Mendelssohn Violin Concerto with Isaac Stern's notations over the ones that Sam Chernyk wrote. The bowing and the phrasings and all of that stuff.*

I had a few encounters here and there with the Orchestra when it wasn't fashionable in small cities to go out and be treated halfway decent. On one tour, a big tour they had, we got into Roswell, New Mexico. And the Orchestra was supposed to play that night. We went to the hotel where the Orchestra was staying and the clerk pointed to me and said, "He can't stay here." Miss Helen Black, the business manager in those days, was so marvelous. She stood up like a real tiger. Saul Caston treated me like a son, and Miss Black treated me better than a son.

We went to this hotel, and we were all in the foyer congregated, the Symphony. And I went up, the guy called my name, he looked and he saw I was Black, he says, "Well, he'll have to stay out in the back, with the help."

I'll never forget. Helen Black said, "That's IT! Performance cancelled, we're leaving. Bye!"

And I said, "Helen, wait a minute. Let's talk about this, okay. That's not the way to handle it." You know. At that time I had driven my old De Soto on tour, because I had feelings, okay, on that tour. And I said, "I'll go on back to Denver, and I'll meet you in Denver when you get back." Because they had two more weeks on the tour, see. And by that time I was playing with the Al Rose Trio at the old Playboy down there, and that was Tuesday through Saturday, see. And this was just beautiful, because what it meant to me was that I could come back to Denver and play, and still get two weeks' checks from the Symphony, for not playing. Heh. Anyhow, I convinced her right in a hurry that that was not the way to handle it. "Go 'head and play, because the people, the town deserves more than that. And the musicians deserve a better break than that." So she went ahead.

Then they showed me this little room back there in the fuckin' chef's quarters. Fuck you, man. Pardon me. That's pretty much what I said. "Go to hell. I don't need this. Come on, I'm above this, Baby. You don't do that to me." So I went out and slapped my bass in the car and came on back to Denver. And the very next night I started back with the Al Rose Trio, and had no problem, you know, and got four salary checks in two weeks. It was *nice*. Beautiful. Yeah.

𝄞 𝄢 𝄞

I remember in our neighborhood, I was an early riser, so I used to see a fellow who was very light and had good hair—what we called good hair, like White folks' hair—I used to see him walking every morning going downtown. I couldn't figure that out. But when he got downtown he wouldn't speak to you. He walked by you like you didn't exist. Now that was racial. Okay. But when he got back to the neighborhood he would get in his house and that was the end of that—you never saw him. Of course, what he was doing was what we call *passing*.

If a Negro was light, as they called it, *yaller*, real light, had good hair, he could pass. I can't blame those who passed. Hey, you deal with the cards that you have dealt. And they were just doing the best they could with what they had. But the main thing is that I'm glad that most of them did not deny themselves the fact of where they came from. And those silly ones did, but they never really lasted or sustained themselves. I think I have known two or three of 'em and all of 'em went crazy. The pressure, I think, within, from both races. They didn't belong to the Black race and they didn't belong to the White race. I think that pressure kind of stored up and kinda did most of these young men in. That's what happened to a few of the— They were my friends, but only my friends in the neighborhood. As I said before, when they were downtown there was no speaking. They'd pass by you like you didn't exist.

Being a member of the Symphony, I realized that I actually was not accepted by many Blacks because they considered me an elite, an "ickety" Negro who was sucking the butts of the White man—in other words, a big token. And many White people didn't accept me because I was Black. And they played the game with me, I realize now, nicey-nicey, you know, "Some of my best friends are Blacks," and all that sort of thing. But what killed these fellows was they didn't have the outlet that I had—I had a family. I had a good background; my family was here—aunts and uncles. And at that time, my wife, who I was very much in love with. And my two kids. It made it possible for me to have something. But these other fellows that I knew, they didn't have it. And they didn't know how to handle it because they had to live two completely different and dishonest lives. They were separated—they didn't belong to the Blacks and they didn't belong to the Whites. And with the Whites, they had to tread on thin ice to let no one know that they were passing. That was what— the pressure of sustaining that relationship of not letting the White man know that they were Black. One of 'em, the first time they knew that he was Black they fired him. And he went off the deep end, he drank himself to death. But I've known two or three people who've been in that category.

Chapter 34

I had the pleasure of playing with a piano player and arranger, whose brother was one of the most prolific and talented and sought-after arrangers at that time in the country, and his name was Fletcher Henderson. I never met Fletcher, but I had the pleasure of playing with his brother Horace in Denver for quite a few years. Horace also played piano and arranged. And my first encounter with Horace: He took me on a little tour to California. We drove out there in a raggedy ass car. And we played in a joint in Pomona, California. And this is one of the things that made me decide against living in Southern California. At the end of this engagement we left this job on a Saturday night at one o'clock in the morning. Now this was only thirty miles from Los Angeles. We got about 8 or 10 miles up the highway, and there was a 50-car collision. We were there until 8 o'clock that morning, *on the highway*. And I said, I don't think this will ever happen to me. That's one of the reasons why I would never go out on the road, because it was too dangerous.

Anyhow, with Horace Henderson I also went up to Spokane, Washington on one of the little tours. We were up there for two weeks, and it rained night and day for two weeks straight. I was so soggy and wet it took me about a month to dry out after we got back to Denver. That said to me

I don't think the road is the place! Of course, this was all happening on the summertime normally, when the Symphony wasn't doing anything. So it was a help in terms of the financial thing.

I had the pleasure of working with Horace, on and off, down at a club on 17th right across from the Brown Palace Hotel; it was called the Club 400. This was nothin' but a quasi-stripper joint almost. So I worked there with him for a short length of time, and then I said Well, I think that's enough. It had become a conflict with my identity, because I was with the Symphony and what was I doing playing in a stripper's joint? So I got the message in a hurry—well, don't do that. It was a message from the office of the Denver Symphony. They said, "Well, you know, be careful." That's all they had to say. Because Helen Black lived right across the street! Had an apartment—always had—in the Brown Palace Hotel. So I let that go and then started capitalizing on my commitment to the Symphony, and I did.

We worked at a place called Uncle Tom's Cabin, and we worked for a great boxer whose name was Jack Johnson, and today he still owes the whole band money. Two weeks we played, you know, and he was a real scoundrel. He came up the end of the run and said, "Listen, you boys didn't sound so good to me." He wouldn't know a musical note from a boat. "You didn't sound so good to me, so I'm not going to pay you this week." We didn't question it. But I do remember looking back on it: We did put two pounds of sugar in his gas tank, in his Rolls Royce. It didn't mean much to him but it meant a lot to us. 'Cause he had to get another Rolls Royce. The retributions were in terms of—not hating, but getting even.

Chapter 35

A little episode in my life which is very dear to me was what I call the *saga* of living at 2017 Park Place. Now 2017 Park Place was on a one-block street which was between 21st and 22nd Avenue on the north and south, and on the east and west between High Street and Race Street. This was a house that a friend of mine owned; her name was Jeannette Cowan. Between my marriage interims, and so forth, I stayed at her place. Not only did I stay there, but it was a recognized haven for musicians, especially jazz musicians, who came through town and were on their way from Chicago (normally) to L.A. or vice versa. And they always had a place to stop to get a bunk, a bed or something for, you know, a couple nights or a week or so.

Joel Cowan was a guitar player and Jeannette Cowan's younger brother. He had the pleasure of playing with one of the spur groups of the Ink Spots. That was back in the middle fifties. He and my cousin Herman McCoy were with the Ink Spots, and they went to Japan and Fiji Islands, and so forth. They had quite a successful little tour there for two or three years, you know.

That was the first time I ever had a real decent suit, that fit me, and was elegant. And that was a suit that my cousin Herman handed me down, because he'd gotten too fat to fit in the suit. And I never will forget, it was what they called a three-thread gabardine, blue. And if I must say, I had that suit for twenty years and I never had a better piece of cloth in my life. That was the best suit I ever had because you could lie down in that suit and get up and it'd look like you just stepped out of the fashion shop. That was real elegant. Three-strand or three-thread gabardine. And oh, boy, you talk about a hot number! I was pretty sharp in those days. One suit, but boy, that was magnificent.

In this house, 2017 Park Place, there were at one time about seven or eight musicians at any one given time. It was known as the House of Joy by us. 2017. It was quite an interesting house. We had a lot of fun there, I'll tell ya' frankly, lots and lots of fun there. And the people were just people. And we had good food because we'd always chip in, you know, musicians would chip in ten cents here—and that was when money was tight—fifteen, and a quarter there, you know. And Jan would cook up a good pot of pig feet and beans, you know, and neck bones and beans and greens and cornbread. We had a *good* time. It was like a family, a big musical family. Everyone in there loved everyone. We had no problems, *absolutely* no problems whatsoever. Never a fight. 'Cause the musicians were too busy loving. That was a very rewarding part of my life, the fact that I had the pleasure of coming through and knowing these people at that particular time. I needed a family, and that was my family.

Another reason I mention 2017 is the fact that that's where I met my third wife. I know people laugh at me. But anyway, my third wife—her name was Thelma Lightfoot. Her married name was Walker. She was living there, she and her husband, whose name was Harry Walker. Harry went off and left her. Well, he was a handsome son-of-a-gun, but crazy, you know. We used to call him a bon vivant; he didn't know which way to go, you know. He didn't know what to do with his looks. He just thought he was grand. So consequently, he was playing with all the women. And he just left Thelma right there at 2017. He divorced her, and she went through this big emotional thing.

We used to have breakfast quite often; it was like a community house, you know. She would always come down crying and so forth. One day I was just sittin' at the kitchen table, and she was coming down. And I just sat there, eating, and she came down crying, boo-hooing. And I just got sick and tired. I said, "Look, I don't wanta hear any more of that crap. Uuuhm, why don't you shut up that crying and stuff and get on with your life? Harry doesn't want ya'. It's all over." You know. I guess that must have struck her as a positive thing, because we became good friends. After a while we did what two normal people doooo! And so I married her.

One of the most marvelous musicians I ever listened to in my life was a very famous saxophone player with Duke Ellington, Ben Webster. While I was married to Thelma, I invited Ben Webster over the house (they were in Denver) to have a little lunch. And Ben was a real scoundrel—he was a *something else.* Anyhow, I invited him over the house to have lunch. My wife cooked up a nice meal, and he ate the meal. And she was a nice looking lady, okay, very elegant, you know, and classy. And he said, "Oh, by the way. Let me take your wife upstairs and, uh, *do the such and such and such* with her."

I said, "What? I'll tell you what— Wait a second, Ben, okay?" I always kept a little .38 special, so I went back in my stash and pulled out my .38 special and I called him a few names. And he ran through the door, through the screen door. And broke it down, okay. And that was the last encounter I had with Ben Webster, except a few years later, he said, "Oh man, I want to apologize."

I says, "You didn't need to apologize. I had my friends there with me, you know, Smith and Wesson. But you don't ever do that again." I don't think it taught him a lesson, because he was always a scoundrel. One of the most magnificent tenor sax players in all the world. And later I discovered that he could play piano. He played piano way back in 1925. He was just a gifted musician, but a real *dog* as a person. You didn't really want him in your house! You want to leave him outside unless you wanted something violent or vicious to happen because you couldn't trust him. He was the kind that after you got through playing you put him back in the cage. That's what we used to say about musicians of that caliber, musicians like that. A real low-lifer.

Anyway, that was my third wife. And it was a very good relationship until I found out—it's not all her fault—I found out that she had a condition, which was called alcoholism. After I found out about that I didn't think I could make it. Because it was not my nature, you know. I just didn't know how to make it with an alcoholic. I was afraid of 'em, because in the past a few of my friends had gotten burned up, literally, by alcoholic people, because they set the house on fire. And one of my good friends in Denver at that time had burned herself bad from smoking. So I was all on edge. And at that time I said, That isn't gonna' work, either. So what happened was I told her that my music came first, so I divorced her in early '59, before I came out to San Francisco.

Family. Seated are Mary Beth, me, Katie, Joe, and Vada.
Dianne is standing second from the left,
Delores is fourth, and Sharon is all the way on the right.

Part V:

San Francisco

More Barriers Come Down

"A new feeling was growing among people, black and white. Martin Luther King was leading that bus boycott down in Montgomery, Alabama, and all the black people were supporting him. Marian Anderson became the first black person to sing at the Metropolitan Opera. Arthur Mitchell became the first black to dance with a major white dance company, the New York city ballet."

—Miles Davis

Chapter 36

When I lived in Denver, after having gone through two divorces, I met a wonderful lady whose name was Billie Willford. And we became lovers for five or six years, I guess. And because of Billie Willford I was exposed to one of the most beautiful parts of my life. I met her through the Al Rose Trio at the Playboy and we started goin' together. She was a dancer, and she was very important in helping my entire life through my younger days when I was coming through my transition through divorces.

Billie bought a brand new 1959 Mercedes-Benz, a 190 Model, and she gave it to me. So I had it big time. And we went out to San Francisco with that Mercedes. I had the pleasure of goin' through three new Mercedes, which a Black dude *never* had in those days, okay. But because of Billie Willford, you know. She was a very inspiring part of my life. She was at every performance I ever had out there in San Francisco. She was my guiding light. And she could *cooook*! One of the best cooks in the world. So we had a grand time.

She helped me over the humps, and so forth. And we never got married because she was Anglo, and in those times you were very careful of what you did. And then, too, she was on a pension. Her husband had gotten killed; he was a pilot and he had gotten killed. So she wouldn't think about marriage and neither would I because she was getting a good pension from the Government and I wasn't worth a pot to piss in, because I didn't have any money anyhow. So we played the game like we were supposed to play it. I knew her for at least a year before we even did anything; we were just good friends. I knew her before her husband got killed. Then, after her husband got killed, she still came up. She liked to dance; she was a ballroom dancer. She later was one of the owners of Arthur Murray. The old expression was "Arthur Murray taught me dancing in a hurry." Big deal. Anyhow, she had a franchise with one of the Arthur Murray studios in Denver. And that's where we got together. She was a magnificent person, but it was all friendship, too, first. And then nothin' but love.

She became a close friend of the family. She loved my mother and my mother loved her, okay. She did things for my mother, we did, that even my sisters didn't do. That was way back in 1959 and '60, when Billie and I used to drive back to Detroit and spend much of the summer with my mother, taking her around. We used to go to Canada every Saturday with my mother in my Mercedes, okay. Charlie in his Mercedes and his girlfriend, and my mother. She used to like to go over to Canada to pick up fresh fish. Ah, I knew better, 'cause she could get fresh fish in Detroit! The same fish she got in Canada. But she just wanted to get out. Billie did the very best for her, because it was like Mom. It was like her daughter, you know. Of course, my mother was a helluva good cook and so was Billie, so they had a big thing in the kitchen there. That six weeks we'd spend in Detroit was magnificent because we ate the very best food and went to the very best places and got associated with the best night clubs and everything. We were on the top of the heap.

Three Mercedes later, you know, we both came back to Denver in 1965. We decided to kind of call it quits because things crept in. I'll tell ya' about that later. Then she became very ill. She had breast cancer. She finally succumbed to breast cancer. That was the end of a magnificent relationship. I always adored her. She made my life possible.

Because of her, I had one of the best basses that any bass player ever had in his life: Black Beauty. From Alex Horst, Sr. When I got with the San Francisco Symphony, he was so proud of my accomplishment he called me out there and said, "Charlie, you know that bass you like so well?"

I says, "Yeah."

He says, "Well do you think you can get five hundred dollars?"

Oh my God! The bass was worth five thousand, at least, and that was over forty years ago. So I told Billie, I says, "Look, I don't know where I'm gonna get it." And she was the one that bought the bass for me, you know. 'Course, we were sharing everything because I was making good money out in San Francisco, so it was not like I was pimping. No. But we were sharing everything. And because of her generosity I was able to get that magnificent bass. I will always thank her for being a part of my life.

Chapter 37

I headed out to Los Angeles one summer just to take lessons with a renowned teacher whose name was Hermann Rheinshagen. Rheinshagen's big thing was he was an internationally known bass teacher. My good friend Al McKibbon, who was my idol in all of life in terms of bass player, had studied with Rheinshagen also. I had to laugh, because, in studying with Rheinshagen, we first learned that Rheinshagen had a big hang-up, racial hang-up. But he never showed it openly. When we went to study there we both got the same scenario of what he was doing. The first thing he gave us to read was a piece called "Old Black Joe." And that should tell you something about the whole thing! But we overlooked that and we both laughed, me and Al, still laugh today about this thing.

Anyhow, I started taking lessons with him. After a couple weeks, the San Francisco Opera Company and San Francisco Pops came down there. Arthur Fiedler, who used to have the Boston Pops, would play down in Los Angeles with the San Francisco Pops Orchestra. And a bass player named Phil Karp, who was the principal bass player in San Francisco for many a year, was down in LA with him. And Phil got my name from Rheinshagen, that maybe I could fill in as a substitute for the Arthur Fiedler thing. So Phil got in touch with me (I still have the letter) and asked me if I'd be interested in playing with Arthur Fiedler, the summer season up in San Francisco. Of course! Oh, man! I played the summer season without an audition, with Fiedler. Course, it was a temporary job.

I headed from Los Angeles up to San Francisco to start playing with Fiedler. Got in my old raggedy 1949 DeSoto car, which had, at that time, two hundred thousand miles on it. And my bass. And all my belongings, all my earthly things—everything I had in life, you know—were in the car. And I came through a place called Bakersfield. After driving along for several miles I looked and saw all this white stuff. I didn't know what it was. I stopped and discovered that was cotton! I had never seen any cotton! You know. And to me, it was a, a, an eye-opener. I said, That's the most beautiful thing I've ever seen. So I got out and got me a box. I'll never forget, I got me a box, and went out and put a whole bunch of cotton bolls in the box and put 'em in my car. And when I got to San Francisco, I had more bugs than I have ever seen in my life! There was bugs EVERY PLACE in the car! I was fumigatin' that car for about a month gettin' rid o' those cotton boll weevils. Yeah. And every time I'd look up I'd have a cotton boll weevil someplace on me or in the car, you know. But that was an experience. I said, Oh, now I know about why they call it the cotton boll weevil, because they were weaved over everything! That was one of my laughing experiences about the role of cotton in my life! Yep!

Anyhow, I made my way out to San Francisco and played with the Pops Orchestra under Fiedler for that summer. I had a little run-in with Arthur Fiedler, also! Because he made a little remark—those days were not too cool—he gave me a little snide remark and I don't think anyone else in the Orchestra got it but me. He looked at me. He didn't look at the section leader, Phil Karp, and I'm down the other end. He looked at me and made a little remark. I don't remember what it was but it was a little snide remark. And I walked off the stand. That's the first time I'd ever known that I would really stand up and I did stand up to Arthur Fiedler and told him, "Look, you know, you don't play that game with me. Somebody else but not me." And he respected me. We became very good friends, and every now and then we used to have a good slug of Old Forrester 100 Proof Bourbon, good God, you know, at intermission. People couldn't understand what was going on but I'd go back to his dressing room, you know, had a little slug, you know, 'n he would wink his eye. He was a real cool person. He was a demon, but he produced. Real cool person.

At the end of the season Phil Karp asked me if I would be interested in taking an audition with the San Francisco Symphony. That was 1959. And I said yeah! I wanted to leave Denver because after being there for 10 years I was trying to make it to build a little progress in what I was doing, you know, get better and better and better. That was my ambition was to get with a big orchestra. And, of course, the San Francisco was the orchestra.

So I went up to take an audition with the San Francisco Symphony, and in the interim I developed a urinary tract infection. So the day of the audition, which was at 11 or 12 o'clock, I was in the doctor's office at 9 o'clock that morning to see what was going on. The first thing he did was look at me and insult me highly—he says, "Well, what do you got, gonorrhea?" And I let it pass. So he put a "sound" up my penis. If anyone knows what a sound is, it's a big, long, steel tube! Must be four miles long! He put it up there and did his thing without an anesthesia! So after that at about 11 o'clock I went down and had my audition with the Symphony!

Kurt Adler, who was the big man up there with the Opera and the Symphony (he was over all of that musical thing up there) auditioned me, with Phil Karp there. And I guess they saw something in me. 'Cause I was not the world's best bass player. But, you know, I could play "Come to Jesus" a little bit here and there. But they wanted bass players; they didn't want soloists in those days. And they were still looking for decent people.

$$\oint \quad \mathcal{D}: \quad \oint$$

In San Francisco, I was introduced and greeted with open arms. And that's the first time I ever felt like I was accepted because of my ability and not because of a race thing, okay, a token. But I didn't mind, because like Mom taught me about tokenism: "Look, son. Don't forget that the Good Lord was a token. And he was a pretty good man." So I learned from that. I said, Hey, everyone has to be a token someplace.

But in San Francisco, my introduction was quite different from Denver. They were announcing, at the beginning, the new members. And I was the only one, I guess, you know. And they announced, you know, "And the first Black in the history of the San Francisco, and we're proud to have" such and such and such. I wondered who the shit they were talkin' about. Huh? They were talkin' about me. I said, Oh, oh, okay. So I stood up, and they gave me a rousing— I mean, you can't believe that shit. I mean, I was very embarrassed. The ovation. And it was sincere. The best friends in my life I ever acquired were with the San Francisco Symphony, you know. That was my real musical family, you know.

In San Francisco they treated me like a real human being. I couldn't believe this. It was embarrassing they treated me so well; I thought something was wrong. I was expecting the worst, you know, being a Black, but everything was just peaches and cream! I had no idea that it would be so nice. There was absolutely no hate. Everyone wanted to take me out to lunch. I had never been treated that way in my life. Of course, I accepted it gracefully! Mom taught me that, too. How to accept success with grace.

I felt I was very, very fortunate in San Francisco, because everyone wanted my attention. I had more invites than I could stand! For dinners, lunches, breakfasts, bar mitzvahs. I had never had so much attention in my life. And it was all sincere. There was a different kind of mentality out there than there was in Denver, where they looked at you just like, Some of my best friends are Negroes. That crap, you know. But out there in San Francisco it wasn't that way, you know. It was Charlie. They played together out there. They didn't have the fighting out there. Only on the first bass stand! That's the only place where they had this thing going on.

I was treated more royally in San Francisco than I've ever been treated in my life. Humane. And nobody knows any better than me when people are playing a game. That was happening in Denver, but out there it didn't happen at all. They were always helpful. They were like jazz musicians are, they all helped each other. They didn't come to you and criticize you because you made a mistake. They'd say, "We're only human, you know. I made a mistake here. I made one there." You know. Consequently, it made you feel much more comfortable with your playing and your playing ability.

Chapter 38

One of my very best experiences in life was being associated with Phil Karp, who was the principal bass player of the San Francisco Symphony. He made it possible for all my life ambitions to come true, by introducin' me to Arthur Fiedler, and then from that to the Symphony. We were good friends and we would often—at least once or twice a week—have breakfast out on Annie's Tugboat. That was the restaurant out in the bay in San Francisco. And we'd go in there and Phil Karp and she were like lovers, you know. Marvelous people. We'd go in there and eat for two hours, and have everything from soup to nuts for breakfast. Or go in for lunch. Or have a breakfast and a lunch at the same time.

Phil Karp and I would go in there and just tear the place up. And he was about three hundred pounds. Six foot six or seven inches, okay. And he had this, of course, little Volkswagen, with no top on it. And he'd carry his bass in it. That was his status thing. Had a big bass, not the ordinary size—three-quarter—but a seven-eighths sized bass which he would carry in that car. And it was very comical to see this big man and this big bass. The bass would be hanging all out the front. Scroll would be hangin' over the front part, and the rear would be hangin' out the back part, and he'd be sittin' on the side seat over there and you could see the car leaning on one side as it went down the street. It was the most comical thing in the world.

When I started playing with the San Francisco Symphony, the first year, I was on the ninth chair of bassists. That's the last chair! And I worked my ass off for three or four years, and when I finished I was put up to what they called an honorary assistant principal. The reason for that was the fact that the fellow who was assistant principal—whose name was Charlie Siani—and the principal bass player, who was Phil Karp, hadn't spoken in over ten years. So, hate again, you know! It was envy, too. Siani, the assistant principal, was a hell of a bass player but he was a little crazy. His father had played bass in Philadelphia, and Charlie Siani had a big ego condition! He was a superb bass player but cold as an iceberg. Phil was just the other way around. He was warm. Not the best musician but he was likable. Everyone liked him. So Phil was there first. Phil got the job through the one conductor I revered most in life and that was Monteux. Monteux hired Phil Karp.

They wanted to have a little peace in the orchestra so they put me up there as a liaison between these two monsters. They were both my friends, you know. So here I was, like a rose between two thorns up there, you know, keeping the peace. So I was honorary assistant principal, and Charlie Siani had moved down to number three seat. He was happy; he got away from Phil. And Phil was happy because Siani wasn't compatible at all up there with him. I moved, and it was not because I could outplay Siani. Oh, no, I realize that! I was not crazy, I was not that stupid. I know why they put me up there. But that's alright. "Thank you," you know. I'll keep the peace. And I did. I didn't mind. Both of them treated me like a brother. I never made the mistake of talking to both of them at the same time—I always talked to one or the other. I'm like my brother Joe, I got along with people. I didn't have any problem. But that was a big step, because, of course, I was the first Black out there in the San Francisco Symphony, a big major orchestra.

From that I went to the Opera Company. We had 11 weeks in that season for the Opera Company. So that was a God send. Eleven weeks there and 26 weeks with the Symphony; that was a full year's work! It's the first time in my life I didn't have to work three jobs to get along. With the Opera Company, we'd go down to Los Angeles every year for six weeks and come back. To me it was like a vacation, or a home away from home. So I played with the opera out there. Still the only Black out there, you know, after all these years.

And I have to go back and put this into context, and speak about how I got acquainted with opera. In Denver (at a time I was not married), a very close friend of mine—Doris Fleisher—and I struck up a little relationship. (Of course, I had to deal with Gene Carter, her ex-boyfriend, at the Piano Lounge!) Every Saturday I would go over to her house. We were close, obviously. I would go over to her house and we would listen to the Texaco opera broadcast out of the Metropolitan Opera. That was a grand thing in those days. We would listen and she would have the scenario there which was the translation for the performance. And this happened for a period of a year or two. That's how I got introduced to opera, through the relationship with this marvelous person named Doris Fleisher. Later, she became one of the big wigs for Mondale, who ran for president. Doris had moved to Washington. She was a real brain and a marvelous person. And we're still friends to this day. When I got to San Francisco my friend Phil Karp was surprised that I had any knowledge of opera at all.

From the Opera I got to meet big people there. One of them was Marilyn Horne. One of the best singers in the world. Through her I met another good friend, whose name was Henry Lewis, a bass player in the Los Angeles Symphony. Right after I got hired in Denver, he was hired in Los Angeles under Alfred Wallenstein. And I later learned that Wallenstein had contacted Saul Caston to ask him how the Black bass player was working out in Denver. And I guess he got the OK, and from that he hired Lewis to play bass. Lewis was hired on the strength of—"Everything was fine down here with this bass player."—and right after that Lewis's ambition was to do opera. So he married Marilyn Horne. So this was a Black bass player marrying Marilyn Horne. Later on, Henry became the conductor of the New Jersey Symphony for quite a few years. Anyhow, I got to meet some of the most famous people in the world, including Leontyne Price and on and on.

Of course, even though I had these two marvelous jobs, I still played jazz. I got hooked up with a fella' named Earl Fatha Hines, who had one of the big bands in those days. And he was in need of a bass player. So I had the pleasure of playing with him for maybe a year, year and a half, or two years. On Sundays, because we were off from the Symphony on Sunday. I played with Fatha Hines all over the place and had a *good* time! I had the pleasure of meeting the biggest people in the jazz field. It was like a dream come true, really.

Chapter 39

Since I was twelve years old and first heard the San Francisco Symphony on our homemade crystal radio set, my ambition was to play with the San Francisco Symphony and to play under Pierre Monteux, who was one of the greatest French conductors of that time. That was my ambition when I was 12 years old, and by the time I got to be 40, in San Francisco, 28 years later, I had the thrill, pleasure, and everything else of playing under the illustrious Pierre Monteux for two weeks. He was a guest conductor emeritus. He came and conducted and I called my mom, and told her, "Mom, I've arrived. My ambition has been realized in life. I've played under Pierre Monteux." And that was it!

And after that I said, Well, my life is complete! I made it. But I didn't get too complacent. I was just happy that I had made my goal in life, what I had strived for for 28 years. I really didn't think about that difficulty to where it became an obsession. No. But that was what I wanted to do, and when I did it, I'll never forget, I think I went right out and got drunk. I didn't get drunk to the point where I couldn't respond. I went and got me a bottle of cognac, good cigars, and went to my pad, and got sloppy. But no one ever knew it. And I got sloppy through happiness, joy, you know. That was the classical high of my life.

I was practicing at least five hours a day—five, six hours a day on the classical, because anyone that tells you they can play classical on the bass, play all the classical literature, is crazy. You can't do it. Because a lot of it is duplication and replication of the higher string instruments, especially the violin. And there's no way in the world you can play as fast and accurately as a violinist. It's like taking a Mack truck, putting it out on the course with a Volkswagen and saying, "Here, perform!" You can only go so far.

I think I was always my own worst critic. That's why I always practiced, because every day was a new and sensational day, and I didn't take it for granted. And when someone told me how good I was it just made me practice more, because I said, Half the people don't understand what I'm trying to do, and the other half don't really care. So do the best you can. I worked my way up from ninth chair—hard practice, you know, I'm not bragging—to the second stand.

Chapter 40

I have to talk a little about my relationship with my cousin, George Duke. George was probably one of the greatest pianists, I guess, of our time. He was out in Marin County, CA. He's marvelously important in my life; I had the opportunity to help him, tutor him, for five years of his younger life. He was one of the very few people that really respects what I did for him, and he gave credit. He said, "Look, if it hadn't been for Cousin Charlie." I'm not bragging, but I was blessed in the fact that I was there at that time. Make no mistake, I got my good things out of it, because I got meals every Sunday; the best meals in the world. That carried me through the week. Home cooked meal? Oh! My God.

I first met my cousin George when me and my sister Mary Beth went out to San Francisco when she got a new Plymouth in 1950. We went out there and George Duke was 11 years old then. And I didn't see him again until I came back in '59. And when I came back he was playing *good* piano! I said, "Aaaalllright!" So every Sunday we got together—for five years—at least 8 or 10 hours every Sunday. I had the pleasure of helping him—kind of straightening him up. I was a father figure because he didn't have a dad. His mother was my first cousin. She was thankful because she was a very, very ambitious sort of person and she wanted nothing but the best for her son. George wanted to play jazz. I said, "OK, let's do it right."

I would come over there, but there was a twofold reason. The main reason was that his mother and his aunt, Aunt Grace, cooked up good meals on Sunday! That was my salvation—that was like a letter from home every Sunday. Oh, we had the best food in the world! Enough food to last me for the whole week. They cooked greens and beans, and roast—the very best. George and I would be playing all this time and they would be cooking. And we would stop long enough to eat, and go back to playing.

When George was 17 or 18, I had the pleasure of being on the staff at the San Francisco Conservatory of Music. Of course, everyone says, "Token." Look: Everyone was a token at one time. It's not what they call ya', it's what ya' do with it. Anyhow, I had the pleasure of being one of George's teachers at the Conservatory and helping him out with his orchestration and his musical prowess where he had to get this all together.

By the time he was 18 he had written a three-act opera, complete. And I still have it. That was when he was 18 years old. From then, George went on and you see now what he has become. World renowned, because he just took hold of what went on. And I was very, very pleased to have been there to help him in that five years of his first trying to get into the profession. So I felt very fortunate.

VADA: *Our older brother Ruben died young. And his last summer with us, in 1961, my mother called everybody to come home. Charles—I was so impressed—Charles took a leave from the Symphony, and he was my brother Ruben's afternoon nurse, from three to eleven. Seven days, until he died. He took care of him. I had been in nursing school, I was the night nurse. And I got orders from the afternoon nurse, Charlie Brown! And he was givin' orders to the other nurses on the staff at the Henry Ford Hospital. And he did take care of my brother very dutifully and faithfully until he died.*

CHARLIE: My oldest brother Ruben, he was an intellect, really. He got a job, one of the first Blacks, obviously, for a trucking company called Posnik & Co. in Detroit. And he stayed there for quite a few years, and he was such an important factor in the Posnik company that every Christmas he would get a 2-3 hundred dollar bonus and I never could figure that out. Finally one of the fellows that worked for Posnik told me that the reason why he got the bonus was that he saved them 3 to 5 to 10 thousand dollars a year on upkeepin' of their trucks. Because he was the only one that never burnt out a transmission! He told me, "That's simple! I don't use the clutch!" Hm! He had such a phenomenal sense of coordination with mechanical things that he didn't have to use the clutch to shift gears. He saved them. And he was an intellect.

MARY BETH: *My brother Ruben was very philosophical, the wise man. He died prematurely, in his forties, a childhood diabetic. He was very instrumental in our spiritual maturation, even though he was soft-spoken.*

All the Burrells could dance except Ruben.

CHARLIE: Yeah, he could shuffle. We used to call him Shuffle-on Ruben.

MARY BETH: *We always had music going, all the time.*

KATIE: *But Ruben didn't care a thing about dancing.*

CHARLIE: But he was intelligent.

MARY BETH: *Yeah, he was it.*

CHARLIE: He was the real big fellow of the family, you know. We respected him without a doubt. You didn't go against him.

VADA: *Yeah. The ruling person in the house was our oldest brother, Ruben. No one crossed him and he never hit us or anything. But it was, I guess, the way he came across. When he spoke to us he meant what he said and said what he meant, and that was it. No one ever crossed him, including Charles.*

CHARLIE: Definitely. And his other thing was religion. He was a very religious person, one of the very few that really got into church, of the Burrells in that era. And he got in the church proper and became active with the church. He spent most of his time with the church. His big church was the Ebenezer Church in Detroit.

MARY BETH: *He was our spiritual support.*

CHARLIE: Foundation.

VADA: *He was like a father.*

MARY BETH: *He was a real older brother.*

CHARLIE: And we respected him, because we knew he didn't stand for any nonsense.

VADA: *And we always took care of him. We knew how to take good care of him; we always carried something in our pockets in case he went into insulin shock.*

CHARLIE: Something sweet.

VADA: *Something sweet, right. We were told what to do. We knew about orange juice, candy bars, and sugar. And there were many times when he would go into shock. If we missed him too long we would call the hospital and he would be at the Detroit Receivin' Hospital. And they'd bring him around.*

Ruben died in 1961. Complications of diabetes.

When I went back to Detroit for Ruben's funeral, my mother was living in a place she'd just bought which was the first house that she had ever had. And that was a big, glorious thing for her; it was a big accomplishment for her. Anyhow, she spent a lot of her time babysitting for Dianne and Dianne's cousin Carol, who was my brother Joe's daughter. She and Dianne were about the same age.

I went over there one day; it was in the winter time and the radiator was on. And these two little tykes were on the radiator playin', you know. And Dianne couldn't speak very well. But I noticed that every time the music'd come on she would sing right along with the music! And it just happened to be Sarah Vaughn. She was humming right along with it. Impeccable. I said, Whoa, what is this? I heard this little voice, and she couldn't really talk, but she could hum everything she heard on the radio. I told my mother, I said, "Look, um, either one of two things. Either you have a genius or a dunce on your hands! That one's gonna be somethin'. She's got spunk, okay." And then I thought no more about it, until she was about fourteen. I think I had a feeling from the time she was three years old that she was special, but I didn't know how special.

Chapter 41

All in all I had a marvelous time out in San Francisco until one day I looked at my bank account and I had 26 dollars in the bank after five and a half years. I was havin' too much of a good time. I was living high on the hog and having a grand time. And after five years of that I had 26 dollars! Haa-haa-haa!! And that kind of changed my mind to get out of town. I couldn't afford to be out there. I didn't want to pay the dues, you know. If I had stayed there I'd been dead forty years ago, with the good time I was having.

And I felt then that something had to be done. I says to myself, I think I'd better think about going back to Denver where I know I can make good money and save it. I was over 40 years old, and it was time to get my act together. I thought: I think I'd better start thinking seriously about gettin' me a little security in life, you know. The fun was beautiful and I enjoyed every moment of it but it was about time to get back.

Then, on a Sunday afternoon, they had an earthquake out there. I'll never forget, it was 5.7 on the Richter scale. It shook off everything, all the glass, you know. Everything was topsy-turvy. And on Monday morning I went to the Symphony office and started my resignation procedure. I was ready to come back to Denver. I said, I don't need any more of these earthquakes. I cleared everything with the office down there and got my severance pay, and boy, I was almost rich, you know. Then I just came on back to Denver, me and Billie, you know, and started doing my thing with the Denver Symphony again.

Me and Billie had a good time all those years, you know. But I'll let you in on a little secret about what happened in our relationship. The big thing was after all these years she finally broke down and told me that when we were in San Francisco, for a year, she had a private eye checking me out. For a year. I said, "For what?"

She said, "I thought you were running around on me." Because, see, as a Burrell, I got up early. We all got up early. That was our custom. Mom made us get up early, so it lasted all through life. We all still get up early. So I used to get up in the morning and walk downtown in Oakland, which was about three miles, and have coffee and a roll and read the paper and come back. And that's all I ever did! For that year. But she thought I was out playing. But I wasn't. I was true blue! So she told me about that and it did kind of shock me, that she would spend this kind of money on doing that. That's probably why we split apart, but it was all for the better.

Another reason I came back to Denver was that my mother had moved there, you know, and I've always been very close-knit to my mother and the family. I love family. Consequently, I came back to Denver and started working very seriously on getting my roots, and so forth. I had a different outlook on what I had to do in life.

Jammin' with my cousin Purnell.

Melanie and me.

Part VI:

Denver Redux

Professional, Personal, and Political Developments

"Music is nothing separate from me. It is me."

—Ray Charles

"If I believed the world were to end tomorrow, I would still plant a tree today."

—Martin Luther King Jr.

"I hope my mother will be there in that beautiful world on high."

—Negro Spiritual

Chapter 42

I hooked up again with Thelma. I thought maybe we could make it. So we tried again to make it. But it didn't work out, so I got divorced from her again. Now that was the fourth marriage, but the second time to the third person. But I had the good fortune of meeting Melanie White, and we got married a few years later. And that's been over 40 years ago, and I've had a glorious time ever since.

I had just come back from the San Francisco Symphony and rejoined the Denver Symphony. And a fellow named Vladimir Golschmann had been selected to be the conductor here at that time, to replace Saul Caston. So Vladimir Golschmann came in and auditioned people for the orchestra. Melanie was one of the ones that he auditioned. And he learned that Melanie's cello had been used by Toscanini. It was Toscanini's cello. So he, being the kind of person that liked to be a name-dropper, I'm sure he hired Melanie with the stipulation that she play that cello only. And so I met her when she joined the Symphony.

Within the next six months Melanie wanted to learn how to do pizzicato, plucking the strings. She was kind of enamored of the way I pizzicatoed and she wanted to learn a little about jazz. She knew all the classics up one side and down the other; she had been with them all of her life. But never jazz, and she loved jazz (but only good jazz). She was carried away with the fact that I could do pretty good pizzicato, so she became one of my students. And for I think a year and a half she just studied with me. And that was all there was to it. She had the wealth of (I'm not bragging, but) being taught the jazz way of pizzicatoing, which was a very, very pronounced and heavy way of pizzicato, contrary to the way that most classical players thought of pizzicato. They thought that pizzicato was demeaning and downgrading, and they fluffed it off. But Melanie didn't. She learned, and she had the best pizzicato. That's primarily how we got together. One favorite song which we will never forget was "Blues in the Closet," written by Oscar Pettiford. That's where that relationship began, a relationship that is still going strong!

What first attracted me to her was her intellect; she was a brain. She went to Vassar! And she was just nice people, which was very rare in those days, believe me. She was sincerely nice. There was no (as they say) bullshit. I mean she was for *real*, alright. And being White, in those days, that was quite an accomplishment, but to her it meant nothing; that's just the way she was. And that's what I'm sure attracted me. Plus the fact that she was such an outstanding cellist. I had never heard a tone like that, and such intonation. She taught me how to develop a pure ear for music. Before that I could hear well, but I wasn't really tuned into the finest clarification of sounds that she was. But after being married to her and listening to her practice, I think I developed something that she didn't know about—something she had—a natural ability. Plus, she had studied with some of the best cello teachers, probably, in the world—back in New York—and was blessed that when she went to Vassar, a very renowned teacher in those days was, put on the staff. So she had the advantage of studying with him at Vassar all the years that she was there.

In hindsight I look back and I think that if I had really known beforehand that she was a Vassar graduate, cum laude, I think it would've scared me to death! Hey! In those days when someone said Vassar the men shook their heads and said, "Oh, noooo. We don't touch that!" You know, that's a different breed. But it didn't mean much to me after that, you know. I just admired and respected her for her ability as a musician and as a person.

George Rhodes, who had hired me way back in the '40's and was now the leader of the Sammy Davis show, led to Melanie's introduction into the hierarchy of jazz. Sammy Davis was in Denver with his show, and came with his orchestra, which was about 12-14 pieces. But he added strings. They needed a cello, and they automatically picked Melanie because of me. She was the only one in the orchestra who actually could cut it.

In the band was none other than my favorite bass player of all times—Al McKibbon. So Melanie had the pleasure of playing cello next to Al McKibbon. And, instrumentally speaking, it was an immediate love affair, because Al McKibbon had one of the best basses, and still does, in the world, which was called a Steiner. And Melanie had one of the best cellos in the world, which was called a Testori, the same instrument that belonged to Toscanini. It was initialed by Toscanini on the underside of it. It was a crude-looking instrument but one of the best-sounding cellos I had ever heard. Of course, she'd been hearing me, but Al McKibbon was her favorite bass player in all the world, because he had a sound that was truly magnificent—one of the best bass sounds I've ever heard.

So Melanie and I got closer and closer. And that led to a marvelous affair with two *families*, one Black and one White. She had four kids and I had four kids, by a previous marriage.

Consequently, we developed a relationship with the children which has been marvelous integration of the truest nature. Her family and my family were like one. And we *never* had any racial problems in the family—absolutely none.

That was the beginning of a beautiful relationship in terms of how I learned to get along with *people*, and to keep everything sane and going forward. In terms of surviving, this country has to get a correlation of the races together to learn that we, as a Black culture, have one thing, and they, as an Anglo culture, have another thing. So what you do is learn from each other and learn to accept people as just people. And that's what happened in the relationship between me and my wife.

Our relationship was destined to last six months—that was the prognosis in those days when we got married. "Six months on the outside, because Charlie's such a scoundrel, a bon vivant." So we did trick all of them!

Chapter 43

When I came back to Denver I went to Denver University to get my degree and also to get a teaching certificate. That was my ace in the hole, because I didn't want to be doin' that 9 to 5 routine the rest of my adult days. It didn't appeal to me. So that was why, you know.

I'd been takin' a class or two at a time for years, because that's all I could afford to. I was workin' three jobs, you know, through the fifties. I took what I had to do to make the requirements for the degree. In about 1957 I was so busy I didn't go. And then I came back in 1965 from San Francisco and quickly got my degree. So it took 25, 30 years for me to get my degree, but in the meantime I was still workin' on all of that. As my mom would say, "Always have an ace in the hole."

I had the pleasure, one summer, of teaching Ray Brown. We only had one lesson, but it lasted five hours! He wanted to learn to bow. He was the most famous bass player then, period. But he had a little—I'll say it this way: He was lacking in how to bow. I had twenty years of bowing experience by that time, so I had a couple things to say to him, you know, teach him how to get more out of the bass than he was. In those days musicians helped *other* musicians. You didn't knock 'em, you helped 'em if you could. And you took the best of what they had and incorporated it into what you wanted to do. And that's where Ray Brown really started to learn how to bow the bass. And he did very well!

I hung out with him, in Denver, and gave him that one lesson. I had to laugh, because he gave me a hundred dollars. I said, "What's this for?"

He said, "Man, you know, that's for my lesson."

I said, "Well, hold on..... okaaaaay!" So I went right out and bought cigars and cognac. That was the thrill of knowing people like Ray Brown. We've always been friends since then.

I just heard a story about Zoot Sims, the fine tenor sax player. He was out in Hollywood, at this club, and the bass player didn't show up. And the owner said, "Can you get a bass player?" And it just so happened that Ray Brown was hangin' around, you know? And Ray Brown started playing. And the owner kept coming to Zoot and saying, "Hey, Zoot! Do you know? That's *Ray Brown!* That's *Ray Brown!* That's *Ray Brown!*" And Zoot says, "Yeah, Baby, that's all I could get, man." That killed me. In those days musicians were down to earth!

When I got back to Denver I was with the Symphony, and I had the desire to make a little more money. And one of my friends, who happened to be a skycap out at Stapleton Airport said, "I think they might be hiring." So I went out there and had an interview at Continental Airlines and I got hired as a skycap. I didn't know until later on that the vice-president out there, Mr. Kelly, his wife was on the board of the Symphony. So there was a big connection there, and I didn't realize that until maybe a year or two later.

Skycap for Continental Airlines was the best job I ever had in my life. It scared me to death, because I was making so much money I couldn't stand it. I think it was the first time in thirty years I hadn't worked *three* jobs to support myself. A skycap in those days was making up to $150 a day cold cash without declaring. That was before the IRS stepped in to say that you had to declare it. When they started that, that's when I quit.

I spent five marvelous years as a skycap, and I met all kinds of fine people like you can't believe. One of my most memorable times was when Jerry Lewis was there. The big Jerry Lewis was getting ready to go out on a plane and they were rushing him down to the plane to get him on there in time. When he got to the plane he said he wanted a strawberry malt. And the guy said, "Well, we don't have time." And they were haggling and all that shit. When they started haggling I ran back to the terminal and went to the shop there and got him a strawberry malt. Came back out there and I had it before they put him on the plane. He looked at me. I'll never forget. He gave me the biggest tip I ever had in my life, an enormous tip. And, heh, heh, I have to laugh because all the skycaps said, "How'd you do that!"

I said, "Just being people." You know. That was one of my big things out there.

Dick Gibson, who used to put on the big jazz shows in Denver at the Paramount, who was one of the very influential men who brought in all the big-time names, came to the airport once with his Model A to pick up a bass player. I was the skycap in charge there—I had charge of putting this bass in Gibson's Model A Ford. Well, I had done that before in my youth! So I knew exactly how to do it—nobody else could do it. So I was delegated and relegated to go ahead and put this bass in the car for one of the performances here.

I remember meeting Carl Fontana, a trombone player who lives in Las Vegas. Carl Fontana came in town, and he was supposed to play up in Vail at the Gibson jazz party, and he missed his connection someplace. He got here about 4 o'clock in the afternoon. The other boys had come in in the morning, and he was going around the airport like a cat about to have kittens, because he didn't know what he was going to do and how he was going to do it. At that time I had my brand new 1965 Chrysler Newport and I was eager to get on the road. So I told the fellow who as in charge at Continental, I said, "Look, we have a good chance here to make a big score by helping this situation out!" And I explained to him.

He said, "Go ahead Charlie."

What I did—now this is a 110-mile drive—I told Fontana, I said, "Look Baby, get in! I'll take you up!" Now, he thought it was just 2, 3 miles or 5 miles, you know. After we'd driven for about a half an hour he says, "How far is this?"

I said, "Oh, not very far, about 100 miles up the road." Carl Fontana and I became good friends; when I got there and Gibson had discovered what I had done, it was open season for me for anything I wanted!

Carl didn't know I played bass. When I got there Dick Gibson enlightened him. He said, "Do you know who this is?"

"No."

"That's Charlie Burrell with the Denver Symphony. A bass player!"

Carl said, "What?!" Then Major Holly, Mule, told him, "Yeah, that was my first teacher!"

I had the pleasure of meeting all the big names in the jazz field. I had an open ticket because of what I had done for Carl Fontana, and we're still friends. We still talk about that little episode of when he almost missed the party—we just crack up laughing about what he didn't know about me. It wasn't any big deal with me, you know.

I had some outstanding times with Continental airlines. One day there was a little episode where United was having a big problem and they didn't know how to handle it. They had a little Black dude from Nigeria who was coming in on their plane. And they couldn't talk to him. He hadn't eaten anything since he left Nigeria, and they were really upset because he spoke only French. Consequently, when he got to the airport in Denver, they were going crazy out there at United Airlines. They happened to ask, "Does anyone over here at any other airline speak a little French? We have a problem here."

I said, "Well, I speak a little French!" So I went out there and went to the boy and I greeted him in French. He looked at me, and I knew he was hungry. What I did was I took him by the hand and we went to the hot dog stand and got three hot dogs. And that broke the bind, and he was straight. And I talked to him—he was en route to Salt Lake City, Utah. He was supposed to meet his mother in Salt Lake. I made sure that he got on the plane properly. From that came a letter of commendation from my airlines for meritorious service above and beyond. I got that and I got a week or two vacation. And a little money on the side. Yeah, I had a marvelous stay out there with the skycaps.

Also when I was at Continental I had the pleasure of going to Europe I think nine times in the course of that five years. You had to pay a surcharge, so I had to pay fifteen dollars to go to Europe. I also used to fly to New York on the weekend for five dollars. It was cheaper to fly to New York and have dinner and stay overnight and get on the red-eye and come back to Denver than to spend a weekend in Denver! So I think I must have gone there at least 25, 30 times just to have dinner at one of my favorite places, the Carnegie Deli. I would fly to New York just to get a Carnegie Deli sandwich, you know, corned beef sandwich, and call it a day, and just be happy as if I had good sense!

At the same time I was out at Continental Airlines, there was a drummer friend of mine whose name was Kelly Martin, who was then a skycap for one of the airlines in New York City. I told you about Kelly Martin, he was one of the first drummers I ever heard that I respected as a superb drummer. He and Al McKibbon played at a joint right around the corner from me in 1938 and '39, at Frog's After Hours Club in Detroit. He was one of the finest drummers I ever heard, and he dressed elegantly. He was the sharpest dresser I had ever seen. Plus he was cute. Plus he knew how to handle women, you know. So he had all the qualities that I thought I'd like to have!

Kelly's big thing was he played with Erroll Garner for quite a long spell, and a lot of the other big boys. And in the sixties he was a skycap in New York City. I just wanted to mention that because that was, to me, a very astounding thing to learn that some of my brothers were in the same position. But in his case, he didn't have a chance to get out, because that was all he could do. Mine, I had the Symphony, so I was more or less well-blessed in terms of where I could go and where I couldn't go.

And my most discouraging moment: I had set up out there with the Black skycaps (there was nothin' but Blacks, anyhow)—all the skycaps from the four or five different airlines that came there, United, Frontier, Braniff, and so forth—I had formed a little club which I called the Skycaps Social Club. It was designed to put in money for a year and then invest it and make some money. This little club was designed to help the Black skycaps get a foothold financially. What I did was set up this organization. I'm not bragging, but I set up the organization and I think I had 40 skycaps at that time, and I said to them, "Look, here's the way we go." We set up a corporation, the whole legal thing with the lawyers and so forth, and got it set up right. And it was running along smoothly. My stipulation was you put in five dollars a week and at the end of the year we gonna' invest this in the stock market, okay.

We started that, and I was the head of that crud. And it was going along smoothly; I kept the minutes, and everything was straight. And I invested the money in the bank in the name of The Skycaps Social Club, Incorporated.

Now, with forty men, five dollars a week, that's $200, you know, $800 a month, and you look up and it's quite a sizable chunk. But then and I discovered one of the failings of my race, the fact that they never stuck together business-wise, and this was a classic example. In four or five months, after these skycaps, which were all Black, began to see what they had in there, they got a little nervous and they started pullin' their money out. Said, "I need money. I can spend it now," and all that sort of thing. All kind of excuses. They didn't foresee the future of what this could mean in terms of making money. After a little while I just said OK, and I returned all of their money, but I kept my chunk of the Skycap Club and I still put in my thing there, and by the time I got through I think I had—from the Club and from investments—about 8 or 10 thousand dollars. Which was not *baaaad* in those days, okay?

All of 'em looked at me like, You cheated us! No, I didn't cheat ya', you cheated yourself. That was my one disastrous experience with my race. Traditionally, over the years, that has been our big failing with the Blacks. They never stuck together, and that has been a condemning factor. And I said from then on they won't do that again to me, okay. So I cut that loose.

Chapter 44

MARY BETH: *When the civil right law was passed in '64, I had put in for a promotion. And the promotion was to be a PBX supervisor. It wasn't a big job. Basically, you trained PBX people. You were out all the time; we had to go to different businesses to train supervisors. So he told me he didn't feel the time was propitious for Blacks to be doing that kind of job. And I really wanted it; that's the only job I could say I really wanted at the telephone company, because I liked the idea of the freedom.*

Jim Reynolds was with the Colorado Civil Rights Commission. I mentioned to him what was going on. He says, "You should file a charge. They can't take your life."

I said, "Oh. Yeah." So I filed the first civil rights charge from the telephone company. It was very interesting. They had no way of dealing with this. They didn't know what to do.

There was a young man from the Commission, Jim Warren, who was a big guy, real dark skin. And he weighed about 300 pounds. Like a gentle giant. Basically, very kind person. And I was working, and I saw him come into the office, going into my supervisor's office. When my supervisor looked up and saw him, he turned a very deep, deep, deep, deep red. He was so red. And I found out later that he was so frightened he didn't know what to do.

I did get that job, and I stayed in that type of work, really, until I retired. But in the interim, it was not easy. I was filing charges forever. It got to the point: People said, "What do you do for the telephone company?"

I said, "Well, my vocation is filing charges. The avocation is I'm a PBX supervisor." And I was just talking to Ruth Steiner the other day, she's a young woman who works for the Civil Rights Commission. They still use my information. But that was the first charge, and every time when there's anything going on, I've had to file charges.

But, see, this all comes back from your childhood. I told you that my mother told us we must always fight back. That was the story of my life at the telephone company, on up to the time I got ready to retire. I mean, and maybe a three-year period when I didn't have to deal with all of this stuff.

$$\oint \; \mathcal{I}: \; \oint$$

The big thing was centered around the inequity between the White and the Black race in those years. My philosophy about the whole thing is: I love Martin Luther King and what he did, but we must face the reality that before Martin Luther King came thousands and thousands of Black people—mothers, especially—were out scrubbing on their knees to make it possible for us and for the next generation to have a better shot at a better life. And that, to me, was very important.

Actually, before Martin Luther King's big speech of "I Have a Dream," there were thousands upon thousands of Negroes who had the same dream. And that started way back in slavery days. And they helped to set the stage to make it possible for Martin Luther King to come up. There were hundreds of thousands of us who were Martin Luther Kings, but we were doing it one on one. So when Martin Luther King came through the time was just right for the uprising. And when he made his speech everything did change; there was more outward acceptance of Negroes as people. And it changed not only in the South but in the North and everyplace else. In other words, you didn't have to be quite as reticent about what you were saying in terms of equality and so forth.

As you notice with my younger sister, Mary Beth, when she gave her little dissertation on what happened with her with the telephone company, this was an extension of that time—they had the right to pursue. We had the right, and the law, on our side, which we had never had before. And that helped change the tonality completely for being accepted in terms of being Black.

From that came the "slyness" (I call it) of the White man's activity. They were no longer up front with their racial slurs and their racial things. They began to tone them down. And they began to use discretionary tones in terms of how to handle race things. One of my biggest things in the world was when people would say to me, make a certain statement, which used to inside infuriate me but I handled it. When they used to say, "Oh, yes, you know, some of my best friends—" Ooouuugh! Boy, that used to get to me. Because it let me know, right off the bat that this person is condescending, okay, and they're not for real.

Caucasians were prone to find something, they thought, that would make you feel comfortable, in terms of them, to put them apart from being a racist—to let you know that they were not really racist, okay? But the average Black, when a person said that, knew right off the bat what was going on. That was an open door. That was a red light for them to know that you were full of crap, okay. You were nothin' but a—not a real racist but you had the thing in you, Baby. The streak.

After that they began to change their language a little bit because they realized that that was not the right thing to say. What happened after that was White society was a little more aware of the feelings of the Negroes. But, make no mistake, that did not end all racial prejudice, and we still have it today. You look around and you see how it's permeating the society. The White man is still in charge, and he's supposed to be! But only up to a point. Make no mistake: Give the other minorities a decent chance and don't condemn and ostracize them just because of color. And so they're coming around little by little. Slowly, not too swiftly.

The average Negro doesn't give any credit to Anglos for what they did. But if it hadn't been for the trials and tribulations of many Anglos, and especially the big people in the entertainment field such as Peter, Paul, & Mary—these people helped tremendously to make this thing go. These people, Peter, Paul, & Mary, were in the march, okay, the '63 march. And that was not a small thing; that was a big thing. And they're still carrying on in terms of integration and making more respectability for the minorities. These, to me, were important assets to add.

I've never had a chance to say how I felt about my niece Sharon. We have a pretty close relationship, quiet as it's kept. We both came through the school of hard knocks. And I'd like to say she is truly one of my great unsung heroes, because she came through more things in a month of her lifetime than I did normally in a year of my lifetime. I was so proud of the fact that she came out of real poverty, in terms of being a person. She came through from nothing, from scratch, to gettin' to the top of the heap. Compliments are only falling short in terms of what I feel for how she has done and her contribution. Inadvertently, she helped me along my way. No one else has a closer relationship in terms of coping with life than me and Sharon.

SHARON: *I started out at Northeastern Junior College up in Sterling. And I couldn't stand that, 'cause they put me in jail every five minutes. They told me I was mischievous and I was a trouble-maker. Because I went to the theater and they were gonna make me and my girlfriend sit upstairs. And I asked them why.*

That was just '64. So they told me because we were Black. That wasn't acceptable! I'm not goin' up there, I'm gonna sit down here with anybody else. Even though I preferred to sit upstairs; I can see better. And I would have gone up there if they hadn't said anything. So, they called the school and told them I was causin' problems.

My girlfriend and I go downtown—downtown Sterling, now—to buy some personals. We shoppin' right, in catalog stores. Sears and Wards. So we went in there to buy some personal things, and they accused us of stealin'. Why would I have to steal? I have a pocketful of money, and credit cards. So they took me to jail. Heh, heh.

And in the dorm, they had four of us in one room, which only is supposed to accommodate two. So the White girls had two in a room, and the four Blacks were in one room, in bunk beds. And our roommate Mary was this big! Huge! So she couldn't sleep on the top bunk! We were scared of that.

Somebody defaced the bible in the lounging area—turning the ash trays upside, or whatever they did. Here comes the dorm mother; that's what they called her. She said I did it. And I'm tryin' to explain to her that I didn't do that. Why would I do something like that? Well, she says, "We're going to dorm you for the weekend."

I said, "I'll tell you what, if you dorm me you're gonna dorm every goddamn person in this dorm. I'm not stayin' here by myself. 'Cause I didn't do anything." I mean, I raised all kinda scenes. I started a little riot, that's what they said. Girls were all riled up, you know—if Sharon stays, we're gonna stay. Finally, the little White girl came forth and said she did it.

I used to work for the Civil Rights Commission. I resigned from the Civil Rights Commission because it was like 24/7; there was a lot of pressure. Political pressure. My son was young, and we moved to Colorado Springs. I said, I'll take the position in Colorado Springs, it'd give us a chance to be a little bit away from family. But they treated us so bad down there. They called me, the school—they were gonna bomb the school my son was in.

I rented an apartment, and had a state car. I was parked, you know, within the lines, or whatever. I came out one day and there's four Coors bottles, a Coors bottle under each tire. Coors meaning, we had the biggest lawsuit against Coors that they've ever had. So they were tellin' me somethin'. Next night I parked. I went out to get my car the next morning—they towed it, because they said I was across the yellow line. In a private parking lot.

I got to be friendly with the police chief. And it got to the point, because of bein' with the Civil Rights Commission and the kinds of issues that were comin' up down there, that my son literally had to be escorted from school to home. The police department arranged for a cab to pick him up, same cab every day. On the weekends, I would have to pick him up and drive back into Denver. Colorado Springs cops would follow me to Castle Rock (about half way), because of all the racial stuff.

Then I started driving alone, and the Castle Rock Police, before they knew who I was, would pull me over, wantin' to know what am I doin' with this state car. I had a state car, myself and my son, and a big black dog. They put all three of us in jail. Me, the dog, and my son. Heh. Until they could figure out what I was doin' drivin'. What was this Black woman— "We not used to a Black woman drivin' a state car." That's what they told me. I'm like, Lord, have mercy!

$$\text{𝄞 𝄢 𝄞}$$

PURNELL *Being one of the first Black folks in the oil business was treacherous! I felt the same loneliness that Charles felt throughout his life because everybody, the good ol' boys, hated me. There was an employee who deliberately tried to sabotage everything I did. She was a clerk, and she mis-trained me and I thought back to what you, Charles, said about being mis-trained by your bass teacher. This lady was supposed to train me on the use of these forms and so forth, and she deliberately mis-trained me to see if she could get me fired.*

And she got her comeuppance because the next year, during National Secretary's Week, I drew the short straw and I had to take her out for lunch! She was from Oklahoma, and she'd only had this one job with the oil company, and she sounded just like a old Okie. I remember taking her to Trader Vic's in the Cosmopolitan Hotel. The whole department paid for me to take her out for lunch. And I bought her a drink called a "suffering bastard." She was a suffering bitch! It was a beautiful drink—it came in a conch shell, it had a lotus blossom in it, and it was made out of four different kinds of rum and all sorts of fruit juice. She had one of those, and then I ordered another one for her! And she went, "Oooooh, howdy!!" She had never missed a day of work—she had perfect attendance—until she met me! I poured her into a taxi—I staggered her over to the Brown Palace and sent her home.

DIANNE: *There were examples that the family set, the things that I had to pick from, from all of 'em, because they all dealt with it in different, unique ways. But at the core, it was always that we are family, we love each other in spite of our differences, and, "Be for who's for you!" That's somethin' I heard all my life, you know. In other words, people are accepting of you, you could be for them as well. And vice versa. It helped me to understand that it is the content of people's character that you look for first and foremost. And if that is something that you understand and you can work with, and at its core for me, you know, a humanitarian spirit, then you can do that.*

Chapter 45

MELANIE: *I'm Melanie Burrell, and I'm Charlie Burrell's wife. I grew up in upper New York State, in a family that was poor but educated. Had one brother. My father, William Marquet, had always been in newspaper work and was working with the Newspaper Guild, which was a new union. And he was black-listed along the eastern seaboard for his union work. This was a quite, quite unpopular kind of activity. My mother was a schoolteacher and was also active in the cooperative movement in general. So I came from a liberal background, and a very politically active background.*

Anyway, enough of that early stuff. But I think the significance of my upbringing was that there was a belief and a persistence in your learning to do something well. And that gives you a background that shoves you to the point where you cannot quit. You have to accomplish. And in part, it created too much pressure, I think, because eventually my brother and I both had heart attacks as we got old. But I think that the pressure that was put on us by family is pressure that we put on ourselves, too, as we grew older. And so maybe your accomplishment in one field or another is interesting to other people, but it does often take a toll.

CHARLIE: Her father and I got to be very, very dear friends over the few years that he had left in his life. I understood him. Before we got married, she went to him, I think for advice, was it?

MELANIE: *Not for advice. He told me, when he came to visit me—and I had already been divorced and I had four little children—he told me that my children would be better off if I died rather than marry Charlie.*

CHARLIE: Hee, hee. Commit suicide! That's the first time I saw Melanie laugh like I couldn't believe.

MELANIE: *It was a very, very, heavy kind of situation! I could hardly believe he would say that but he did. He believed that I would be ruining their lives if I married Charlie. Because Charlie was Black, and the influence of a Black second father was, to my father, unbelievable.*

CHARLIE: It would be devastating for kids, unacceptable.

MELANIE: *There's no way that he could accept the idea that the children's second father would be Black. Or Japanese, or anything. But I think Black was probably worse. And there's a little anecdote about Charlie's visiting us. Courting me, but visiting us, as a family. Charlie loves to swim. And so my youngest daughter, Jennifer, went swimming with Charlie—Charlie invited her. They went swimming together, and when Jennifer got back she said, "Oh, he has a real good tan!" Ha ha ha!*

CHARLIE: Hee, hee. She was about nine.

MELANIE: *Probably. So you can see that my father was not that influential in terms of my children's thought! But that's just a little anecdote about Charlie's relationship with the kids. It was really warm. Warm.*

𝄞 𝄢 𝄞

MELANIE: *I kept practicing cello. The kids would go in for naps; I would practice cello. The kids would go in for bedtime, and I would practice cello. But I was not a professional cellist while my children were infants. I did play all over Denver as principal cellist of amateur orchestras, and chamber music, and little productions. But I decided that I would become professional if I could get into the Denver Symphony by the time I was thirty. That was my goal. So I did do that. The Denver*

Symphony had just moved to a new conductor. An older man from Paris, Vladimir Golschmann, had been well-known in this country because he conducted the St. Louis Symphony. But then he came to Denver, and the Denver benefactors of the Symphony felt that this was the beginning of a new life for the Symphony. Unfortunately, in some ways, Golschmann thought of Denver as the hinterland. He came from much more sophisticated circumstances. When we went on tour to mountain towns, he sometimes left out a whole movement from a symphony, because he wanted to get it over with! It was just more than he could stand.

But Golschmann was very popular with the audience, because when he spoke to them or when he went to fundraising events he was a very, very charming French gentleman. He was very popular, not so much with the musicians but certainly with the audience people.

Charlie and I met for the first time, my first year in the Symphony, which was 1965, the same year that Charlie came back to the Denver Symphony from the San Francisco Symphony and Opera. I learned about Charlie's expertise in jazz, and I knew basically nothing about jazz. But what I did know is that I wanted to learn the technique of pizzicato. And Charlie was one of the best! So the thing to do would be to study with Charlie.

Charlie is not always gracious with other people. He decides for himself whether you're worth something, whether he likes you, whether you like him, truly, or whether you're just putting on an act in front of an African-American person. And Charlie liked the idea that he was special, because he had just come back from a bigger, better, symphony. But he did say that I could study with him, and I went to his house with my cello and he started teaching me how to produce some sound with fingers on strings. It was a special technique that was probably better than most string players could produce. The sound, you know, just rang out, if you could learn how to do this.

So I used to take my cello up to the mountains, to a little mountain cabin. And I practiced. And I practiced pizzicato 'til it was coming out of my head. I practically forgot what a bow was for. And my kids that would go off hiking in the hills would say, "Oh! We could hear your pizz way up there, Mom!" So I knew I was making some progress.

So that's how Charlie and I met. And he was a tough teacher. Once in a while he would demonstrate, maybe with bow, a rapid technique of Strauss or something, or he would demonstrate a technique of pizzicato coming from a Tchaikovsky symphony. He was really showing off, but he was so good that he could get away with that. He loved to show people what he could do. That was his existence, that was the important part of his being, to be able to play so well that other people had to sit back and admire.

In fact, we went to Durango one time with the French conductor Vladimir Golschmann. And Charlie's special friend, pianist Al Rose, played in the bar. Al Rose and Charlie decided that they would play in the bar that night. And all of the Symphony came into the bar, because they knew that Charlie was supposed to be really so good. And the French conductor came. Not only was it sensational—they were both marvelous entertainers and players—but Golschmann had never heard a jazz bass player do what Charlie could do. And he never forgot that this Charlie Burrell was so special. I think Golschmann would have let Charlie do anything. If Charlie wanted to walk off stage I think that Golschmann wouldn't have minded. Golschmann considered Charlie to be the most spectacular player he had ever seen or heard. And that was a fun part of our tours, when somebody could get together and play. But it was rare that you had anybody as good as Al Rose because he was a marvelous, wonderful, wonderful pianist.

CHARLIE: When we were at that hotel, the Hotel Strater, in Durango, we were given by the owner, for our wedding present, the Bridal Suite! Which was hilarious, you know.

MELANIE: *The other Symphony players, I think, were nonplussed. They couldn't believe— See, they normally didn't have an opportunity to hear Charlie do something different from the classical music that we all played together. So he wasn't considered any different from any other string player in the string group. If you get into a symphony and stay in the symphony without getting fired, you're usually pretty good anyway. It's just accepted that we were all talented together. But the players had* *never heard anything special like that. They thought Charlie was magnificent, they loved it. I think everybody stayed until lights out. And Charlie was loving it. Really eating this up.*

CHARLIE: I enjoyed it. I was glad they enjoyed it. I think for the first time they accepted me as Charlie, the bass player. And I felt pretty good about it! Wasn't bad, you know.

MELANIE: *I always felt that Charlie wanted to be known as a symphony bass player. I mean, that was the huge accomplishment in his life at that time. And he really did not want people to think of him just as a magnificent jazz player. He wanted it to be more than that. He wanted it to be the more unusual event of being a Black, bass, classical player. And that was the accomplishment that meant so much to Charlie, that the Symphony players came to admire him—for whatever reason initially they admired him—simply put him back into balance with the Symphony players, classically. That was very, very, important.*

CHARLIE: The reason why I loved the classics was because it was a challenge and it made me better on the instrument. And that was my ambition all my life. And I still say that if I had put one fiftieth into jazz that I put in the classics, I probably could have been the best in the universe. You know, I'm not bragging, because that's the way it was. Jazz to me was a big, fun thing. And jazz helped me to survive in the world of the classics, because I could make a few extra dollars on the side. But make no mistake, I never practiced jazz. *Never* practiced jazz. And the classics—it must be two hundred thousand hours at least. I still do. That was always the big challenge to me, and it helped me to develop a good technique for jazz, you know. One art form gratified the other art form and made it possible. If it hadn't been for jazz, I couldn't have played the classics because I couldn't have made any money. And if it hadn't been for the classics I couldn't have gotten where I've gotten today—I'd still be in the joints. That's how simple that was.

MELANIE: *And the technique part of playing classical music really, really, made Charlie's bass playing for jazz special, because he is so superb with the bow, and that's what most jazz bass players can't do. In fact, Charlie taught Ray Brown, and yet when I heard Ray Brown try to use the bow, I said, "Charlie, what did you teach him?" He played a sol-do kind of thing at the end of a piece with the bow and he had absolutely no bow technique. That means that if you have somebody that good and he hasn't ever learned to used the bow, then Charlie's expertise in using the bow and mixing up the pizzicato and the technique of playing a song with the bow made Charlie extra, extra special. And that came from classical technique. That's why I wanted to learn the jazz technique, to add to my classical technique, because they can so, so enhance one another.*

And Charlie spent some time—it was very funny—teaching me to play "Blues in the Closet." Ha! I was truly out of my element. I loved it, but—

CHARLIE: It was hilarious! Ha-ha. I used to crack up every time when she'd leave, I would crack up! Boy, she'd sit there and count. One, two. No, I said, you don't have to do that—

MELANIE: *Now, Charlie, don't exaggerate, now.*

CHARLIE: Well, I mean something almost like that, you know! But she was a hell of a good student! Like I told her, she turned out to be one of the best pizzicato-ists, put it that way, on the cello, besides the famous Rostropovich. I've never heard sound like that out of any of the cello players except my wife, okay.

MELANIE: *Hah, hah! We had fun. We had fun. Charlie was tough, he was very tough.*

CHARLIE: Well I was tough on myself. That was the whole thing, I never let up on myself, all my life. Because, hey, if someone come up to me and said, "Oh, you play so marvelously. That was beautiful." I looked at 'em and went back home and practiced not only an hour but two hours, you know! I said, Ah, they're full of crap. They don't know what they're talking about. That didn't get to my head. Never did, never did then, and never does, now. No, no, no, no.

But the big thing is that I've always enjoyed playing. And that's one of the reasons why me and Melanie got along so well, because she enjoyed playing. She never knew it, but she was feeding my musical attempts to play the bass like a cello, with sound. That's where I got a lot of the sound, from her. I listened to her practice, okay. And I said, oh, that's the way it's supposed to go. Because she was a natural. And I was an un-natural. That's the way I used to figure it, okay. I said, Now that's the sound that I like. In other words, she gave me, and I gave her the pizzicato technique. So we had an even trade there. And still today, she's one of the finest cellists I think I've ever met.

MELANIE: *Charlie and I were lucky in that we could go to the same job, we had the same conveyance; Charlie drove us, another violin player and me, down. We had to have big cars, because we were often taking cello and bass in the car, plus a violinist friend. We had the same time off. That's why, I think together, the idea came to us that our time off should be and could be time apart. It was alright to have time apart. Because we worked exactly the same job, the same hours, the same everything. We were even in the string pool together. It's not as if he played flute and I played cello. We learned that on vacation time I could go alone with my cello and a couple of dogs, to the little mountain cabin. And I'd go and practice and paint. I mean paint wall, paint windows, not paint pictures. And Charlie would stay home and take care of things there, and he'd practice and he had lots of friends here. Very gregarious.*

We had a house in Denver that we added a large music room to. And Charlie practiced in the music room and I practiced in the dining room. We practiced at the same time very often, with the kids running around in between. But the kids knew they would never bother us. I could hear Charlie practice, and I could hear when he became impatient with himself.

And then he could hear the endless repetition that I would do over little tiny, tiny phrases, and the long, long, moves to make something silken in sound. So I'm sure that we did affect each other. We could hear each other, but we could also blot out each other. We had our own little music school going.

The house. In Cherry Creek—

MELANIE: *—a beautiful, predominantly White area.*

CHARLIE: How we got in that place, I'll have to tell you about that, that's funny. We were married then, weren't we?

MELANIE: *Just before we were married.*

CHARLIE: Just before we were married, we were house-hunting, okay. And Melanie found this cute little farm house, a wooden farm house in the front and one in the back. With lots of foliage between the two houses.

MELANIE: *Charlie found that farm house. It was just beautiful. And then he sent me to look at it.*

CHARLIE: Yeah, I guess that's what it was. Because I knew better. You being Black, you don't make any inquiries, you know. So she went and she fell in love with it. And lo and behold, she looked up and she had bought the place, you know. She went ahead with the settlement that she had received from her ex-husband, heh heh. She bought the place outright and paid cash for it. That was 1967. If I remember correctly we paid $13,500 for it.

The next day after she had bought the place we went down to Colorado Springs and got married by a justice of the peace down there. At a Chinese restaurant we had our first real, legal, meal together, heh.

Anyhow, we came back to Denver and immediately I began to feel the pressure of being where I really wasn't wanted. The family next door to us, the Larsons, had the corner lot, which was about two lots. A nice little home, spacious garage, a Winnebago, the whole routine. And when Melanie bought the place, the Larsons, who were Anglo, were thrilled. And when she said, "This is my husband," BLEEEEAHH!! Mrs. Larson—I don't think she spoke to me for the first year without looking at me with that raised eyebrow. It took me damn near a year to get them to even speak to me civilized. Mr. Larson wasn't quite that apprehensive; he was a little more civilized, you know, about the situation. And after that everything came along pretty well. But they always had that race thing in there, and I knew that.

Melanie started planning to have a place for us and to have a place for her four children. Right off the bat she designed a music room between the front house and the back house, connecting all this. So we had a passageway like a passageway to India, you know, from the front house all the way back to the back house. The front house was designed for me and Melanie, and it was designed not to have the kids up in that section of the house. Connected to that Melanie designed the music room, which was about 20 by 35, maybe 40. A nice, spacious music room, with high ceilings, wood beams, a fireplace. In back of that we connected what we called the girls' rumpus room, which was a wild room back there for three young daughters. Plus Gary, who was the one boy. And we had his room immediately adjacent to the music room—his sleeping room. That was all he was allowed because he was a little strange individual. He had been spoiled rotten all his life, so he wasn't the nicest fellow in the world for a while.

We had a marvelous fireplace, which I had always wanted. That was one of my dreams. That was where I spent most of my idle time was in the music room, either practicing or sitting before the fireplace with my cigar with the windows wide open.

In our back house we had that so designed to where the three girls lived back there, and they were a riot. You can imagine three girls going through their sub-teens and teens. And I laugh because Melanie never knew what was going on back there but I did. Being from the neighborhood where I grew up, we learned how to keep our eyes and ears open for the siblings. We realized, hey, they're only siblings and they're going to do certain things. And they did certain things. But I was always there. They used to call me Herr dictator. I'd laugh. I wasn't a dictator; I just loved them madly but I didn't let them get away with any crap, okay. Kept 'em halfway straight.

Before we got out of there we had my two youngest children there with us for a while. Charles Jr. and Andrea. We had them. That was a real, whew! It was six kids in there, and that was something else. But we held together, through the years.

MELANIE: *Race didn't really make any difference before I met Charlie, probably because of our profession, where there are gay people in ballet and symphony orchestras, and to be different didn't mean that you would be ostracized. So I suppose once I was in the orchestra I just heard a wonderful player, a marvelous musician. And it didn't really dawn on me that in 1967—it should have dawned on me—that this was not the best time—*

CHARLIE: Not the most kosher thing in the world!

MELANIE: *—to have an interracial marriage. It did dawn on me when we went on tour periodically. We went to Oklahoma, and Charlie and I were walking down the street, I think hand in hand.*

CHARLIE: We stopped at the bus stop.

MELANIE: *Right. An older Black lady was standing there.*

CHARLIE: Mumbling and grumbling.

MELANIE: *We walked by. She said something to Charlie that I didn't understand. Charlie knew what she was saying, but he had to indicate to me that she was very unhappy that he was with a White —*

CHARLIE: She grumbled, and I heard her, "You can't find any Black women to marry? They got all kinda fine, good Black women, you gotta get that White woman?" And she didn't hear it. I did, and I told her that's what happens. And she became a little aware, like, "Huh??"

MELANIE: *We toured in Texas. Before I knew Charlie the Symphony went to New Mexico and Charlie was sent home because they didn't have a place for a Black person to stay.*

CHARLIE: No accommodations.

MELANIE: *I didn't meet one of Charlie's aunts for quite a long time. And I found out from Charlie that she said, "What's the matter, a Black girl is not good enough for you?" And then when we did meet, the fact that we liked each other and we sat, drank, and smoked together, she thought I was fine! Ha! Ha! It took that to get through that barrier.*

I think race became much more clear to me, that race was a very basic factor in our lives. I will never forget: In Cherry Creek, Charlie every morning used to go out and jog, and one day he was picked up by the police. "What are you doing here?" He had, of course, his license. "I live here!" That was one case that made me furious. Livid.

Then we were on tour in western Colorado; I can't remember where. But Charlie went out jogging. And Charlie got picked up by the state patrol. Who are you and what are you doing here?

CHARLIE: And that was in the seventies.

MELANIE: *Then we were in Wyoming, and one of the cellists—we were up by Lander, northern Wyoming—one of the cellists wore fairly long hair, 'bout down to here. And he got accosted by some Wyoming boys, who objected. "We don't want your kind here!" You know. So there was other kinds of discrimination. And that was a White cellist. But I learned a big lesson, I think, after I married Charlie.*

CHARLIE: To me it was second nature.

MELANIE: *And to me it was certainly not second nature.*

CHARLIE: I'd been there before, you know, done that and that sort of thing. I laughed at it because I realized how far they could go. Only, I was very careful not to get caught outside of the big cities. In the small cities, they could put you in jail and no one would ever hear from you again. And that was even up as far as the seventies and eighties, they were still doing that. So I knew all about that. With her it took a little time, 'cause she had no reason to think—why should she, you know?—about the race relationships. But gradually she learned. She got a different view of this thing called race. I'm sure she did. Because to me it was a little more prevalent then, you know. They would speak behind my back, you know, and Sam Gill's, and all the Blacks.

I guess one of the worst things that happened to me in terms of race relationships was when we had a violist there named Patterson. You remember him? He was Black.

MELANIE: *Oh, yes.*

CHARLIE: Yes, okay. He was Black. And there was one morning rehearsal, for this concert. It was on Wednesday morning, now. And they had been rehearsing this viola concerto I think for a week or two before that, with the principal violist. And this Patterson was assistant principal. So the morning before the concert they called Patterson and said, "You'll have to play this concerto," because the principal was not going to play it. And the principal violist was not sick, I found that out later. He was just doing it, okay, out of spite. They had this poor little Black dude play that concerto and he did a magnificent job at rehearsal, okay. He learned it in one day. And he played this concerto, and this will always set in my mind: After he played at rehearsal, flawlessly, *no one* in the orchestra applauded, or rubbed their feet, or anything. And Marin (Marin Alsop, the conductor) didn't give him any kind of, "That was well done," or *nothing.* And that to me, hurt.

As a matter of fact, he almost committed suicide. Remember, I told ya'? For a day and a half I had to take him around by the hand to keep him from committing suicide. And then I told him the facts of life. I said, "Listen, Dahling (what I used to call him), here's the way it happens, okay. Now, if these people in the Colorado Symphony had shuffled their feet and said bravo for you, and all that sort of thing, that would have meant one thing, that you weren't worth *shit!*" That's just the way I told it to him, okay. I said, "But because they didn't, that meant that you were on your way up. That you were gonna' be a real professional, and they *resent it*. In other words, that was a big plus." And it took me a day and a half to explain it to him. And his brother still calls me every now and then and thanks me. Patterson got out of the Symphony and started playing with quartets. But that hurt me. See, I could take it, but he couldn't. He didn't know that there were two worlds, you know. But I had been through that story for fifty years before he even got here, you know.

MELANIE: *But, you know, there's a parallel, Charlie. And you know this, 'cause you were in San Francisco. Orchestra conductors were as treacherous and mean as, in this case, the orchestra was to that young soloist. And there have been suicides among symphony players that have been on the hot seat, maybe a first bassoon or first trombone, where they are required to play solo position. And if the conductor bugs you enough, makes it so uncomfortable that you never can please him, then that's when sometimes we've had trouble in the past.*

CHARLIE: In San Francisco, there were two suicides while I was there. One was Ross Taylor, who was a fine, fine, French horn player. And the other was a trombone player. The pressure got to be unbearable for them. And every other person there had ulcers. Now, I was determined not to have ulcers.

Like that little incident that happened just before I got with the San Francisco Symphony, when I was playing the summer season with Arthur Fiedler. I was the first Black player to play with Arthur Fiedler, okay. So I'm playing with Arthur Fiedler, my first big thing with a big orchestra, okay. And he made some disparaging remark about Blacks or some crap, you know, up there. And I walked off the stand. I walked off the stand. And I told him to his face, and I cussed him out! Arthur Fiedler. I said, "You go to hell."

MELANIE: *He was a nasty man.*

CHARLIE: He was a real nasty man. I said, "You go to hell. Who do you think you are!" And all that kind— And people in the orchestra said, "Oh, you shouldn't do that!" But he grew to be my friend. He used to invite me back to the room to have Old Forrester, a hundred proof, you know, at intermissions. But that was the thing.

MELANIE: *He didn't go on stage until he had that in his room. He had to have a bottle in his room.*

There's a lighter aspect of this race thing that I like to think of. Jennifer is my youngest daughter. And Charlie and Jennifer have always been very close. She has admired jazz, and Charlie's taught her a lot about jazz. When she was seventeen she had long blond hair, and she was in high school. She loved jazz, and was it Count Basie's orchestra that came to Aurora?

CHARLIE: Yeah.

MELANIE: *Someplace in Aurora, to perform. And Jennifer went by herself, I think, to the front of the stage at the end.*

CHARLIE: And says to Marshall Royal, "Do you know Charlie Burrell?" And he says, "Yeah!" She says, "I'm his daughter!" And he turned around, and she said throughout the orchestra they were crackin' up. And in the back, a guy said, "AAAAAAAGH!!!" Ha, ha, ha. And they loved her. And that was her first light encounter, which is a nice thing for this girl, and for them. 'Cause they still kid me. The bass player there was Jones. He talked to me all through the years about, "Hey, man, how's your daughter?"

Another reason I respect Melanie was because she took the initiative going into an organization which was called

ICSOM, International Conference of Symphony and Opera Musicians. Nationwide. She was with a small group of dedicated people responsible for the big orchestras and all the orchestras in this country now making the kind of salaries that they're making. It took them five or six years to put in line the process of getting the musician's unions lined up to get behind these orchestras and to support them. Plus, working with the NEA in New York to get decent salaries. When she and that organization came in, that was her first year in the Orchestra, which was '65. She got on that organization and was in there first of all as the secretary. And then in 3 or 4 years they put her up to treasurer. And then three or four years after that she was the first woman to have the position of being the C.O. for ICSOM. The very first woman to have been appointed C.O. In the meantime, it took its toll on her physically and emotionally. She fought so hard. It was nothin' for her to leave here on Sunday afternoon after the matinee performance, and be on a six o'clock flight back to New York, Philadelphia, Pittsburgh, Los Angeles, San Francisco, all the big cities. And come back Monday night and be there for rehearsal on Tuesday.

Chapter 46

I decided to run for the musician's union board of directors. I wanted to make a difference and be an inside influence for the betterment of the Symphony musicians. So that's what I did. And I got on the union board. No one got any more votes—I'm not bragging—maybe 'cause I was so popular. I was always out on the streets, you know. Everyone knew me, you know, Charlie. Didn't know whether I was bad, good, or indifferent, but they knew the name! So I got on the board of directors and I spent seventeen years on the board. And the reason I did was to salvage and save the Denver Symphony Orchestra, because they were having big problems in terms of discipline within the orchestra, and also tryin' to get funds from corporations, and little things that were not conducive to the building of a good orchestra.

On the board of directors were a bunch of good fellows who had the interest of the musicians at heart. They were not afraid to speak up, but they were all what we call jobbers—they just played all gigs, and I was the only one on the board from the Symphony for all those years. Consequently, I had a good hand in helping to keep things straight with the Symphony.

I spent most of my time being a real pain in the sides of the people down at the union; every time a question about the Symphony would come up I would be loud and vociferous. I would tell them, "Look, first thing—you fella's are full of shit." Heh heh. And they'd be in a bit of shock. I said, "Look, it doesn't go that way, see." I'd jump up and I would have things to say. And they got so sick and tired of me talking—when I got up I would get a little irate and a little vulgar with the language. And they said, "OK, Charlie, what do you want this time?" So I would tell 'em. Actually, that was very, very, very important.

One of my pitfalls was that being from the quasi-ghetto, I did learn a few cuss words, and some people had earmarked me because I used a few indiscriminately. But I used them not viciously—I used the words to get through. But I wasn't out of control. I chose my words very carefully. I wanted to get the point across. I had to because that was something that had been festering since I first started playing, since I got my first lesson from Brohan when he told me about, "I will teach you if you promise not to try to play the classics." Well, see, that was when I was only in my teens. Now I was about 50. In other words, I had all those years of building up this little animosity within me. But I handled it fairly well.

And I was lucky and fortunate to have good friends on the board of directors. And we made a lot of things possible in the Symphony in terms of getting more money from the Symphony and getting better working conditions.

Being on the inside track of the Symphony, I was allowed to wear two hats. I could make a case against someone, a charge, from the Orchestra, and after they were sent before the board of directors for the union, I would be on the board of directors! Heh, heh. It was a no-win situation. And I'll never forget, we had one outstanding case, there. This is not to belittle a guy, but they were having big problems with Jurgen de Lemos. He was the principal cellist, okay. And he was a real sore spot. As they say in the vernacular, *he was a asshole*. He was on everyone's case. And the reason why we had to bring him before the board of directors was that he was screwing around with the cello section. He wanted to fire half the cello section. He was just running crazy over all the musicians, you know. A real tyrant. He had that old German ACH NEIN thing. Yeah, we're the master race and all that sort of crap. So it got to be a little harrowing, okay?

He was playing around with the cello section, and my wife Melanie was in the cello section. Jurgen de Lemos made the mistake of harassing one of the cellists there, so (being in the Orchestra I could do this) I put in a letter of reprimand through the union and had him brought up before the board of directors. And that was unreal—he could not believe this, that a Negro could do this to him, you know! How could you do this thing?

Anyhow, we brought him before the board of directors and I had to laugh because on the board of directors we had all kinds of marvelous fellows there, and most of 'em were good guys. And it was all White except me. We went and brought these charges against Jurgen. And he came there with a long list of things and he thought he was gonna make a big impression with the board. And he gave an hour or so of what he was doing and how great he was and where he'd been and all that sort of thing. The board asked him, "Well in light of that, this suit is about your action and reaction with another member of the union. We will deliberate and let you know." So we deliberated five minutes and we came back and our president said, "Mr. de Lemos, here's the decision the board has made. You either straighten up your act and stop harassing people in the orchestra, or we will pull your card. And what that means is this: You can play with the Orchestra, but the Orchestra can't play with *you*. Because they're all union."

That was what we told him the alternative was if he didn't straighten up. And he didn't get the significance of that for a little while—he had the nerve to try to come back with a counter. And they said, "There's no counter, here. You did wrong." It was because of some of his foul actions; he was a demon when he first came to Denver. As a matter of fact, he was such a demon—I can put it out like it was. He was just, then, an unpleasant person. He would say, "Oh, you got a fine ass," and all this sort of thing. These things were uncalled for.

Of course, I had a little encounter with Jurgen after that because he played a little nasty game with my wife; he was being a real prick with my wife. And she was getting emotionally upset. She didn't realize I knew this was going on. So I went to Jurgen as a person to person, and I had to tell him. I had to give him the ghetto reading, like, "Look, now if you don't lay up off my wife I'm gonna' crack your ribs and break your legs." And so forth. "As a matter of fact, I'm gonna' have my clan come down from Five Points. I think I have twenty cats from Five Points who'll come down here and work you over! Am I getting through to you?" And it scared him to death because in those days when you said Five Points it was like, "Oh my God," you know. That was like the *jungle*. This was all a big act, but he didn't know it! I was playing a big game, but I got through. He stopped. And he's been pretty clean ever since, you know. We've had no problems with Mr. de Lemos! Who is a good friend of mine, okay? Very dear friend of mine, and I value his friendship. But that just goes to show you what's happening in those days.

Chapter 47

VADA: *My brother Allen, the talented one, loved to dance. He could sing. Recite Shakespeare. He was a choreographer. He did a little of everything. Just an all-around fellow, very, very, entertaining. Unfortunately, he was the one that got on drugs. That was a very new thing for us because we didn't know about symptoms or what to look for. By the time we found out that Allen was on drugs, it was perhaps a little late. But on the other hand, my mother tried everything she could. She got a psychiatrist to talk to Allen. Finally, the psychiatrist told her that Allen was givin' him therapy, and he wasn't helping Allen! Allen was a talker. And a great, great talent. He could sing, dance, anything you want. He was a real character. And he met his demise in 1973. He was murdered in Detroit. That was a sad time in our lives. And he was the youngest brother.*

CHARLIE: What happed with Allen and his demise: This came through the grapevine; because we knew everything that was happening in the ghetto, okay. It came down, the Mafia (in those days which had control of the dope, prostitution and everything else that was illegal) came out with the edict that if a person was a peddler and a user, they had to be eliminated. And he was a peddler and a user. They hired someone. We all know, that's common knowledge. They hired someone to do him in. This happened on a big, wide street in Detroit named Warren Avenue. Allen was walking on one side of the street, and a police car was on the other side of the street. And a fellow walked up in back of Allen and blew him away. The police said they didn't see anything. And we all knew what had happened. That's what happened to Allen, okay. And the same fellow was out on bail, I think for another murder or something, during that same time. He went back to jail and he was killed right after that, I think.

Chapter 48

Before Melanie and I got married we only had two stipulations. One was mine, that we'd have no TV dinners in the house, and we never had. And the other was hers, that she didn't do breakfast, and she didn't, for quite a long spell there. And I didn't mind because in those days we were so flush I was eating breakfast at the Brown Palace, ha ha ha, heh heh heh, livin' the life of joy. So it was no big deal. But we never had any questions about race. And to my knowledge we never had any friction between the kids. Never. They were always just kids—they got along.

My mother and Melanie were just as close as could be, and Melanie's mother and me were close. We had the best mothers-in-law in the world, between me and Melanie. Her father wasn't worth much, but we got along, you know, after this episode of him suggesting to her that the way to get out of this dilemma before we got married was to commit suicide. After we laughed about that, he became one of my friends. He was an alcoholic, and I knew how to get to alcoholics: You, you know, put the bottle in their hand. That's what I did. Every time I'd see 'im up in Montclair, New Jersey, you know, I'd bring him a little taste. Ha ha ha ha! Sneak in a bottle. And he would just love it. So he finally came around.

I had a good relationship with Melanie's children. The girls were marvelous. As along as they played the game according to my rules and regulations, and got their education, that was as good as I wanted.

Melanie was a magnificent person, but she was never much of a mother. Melanie was a loner, I realize now. And so am I, but I knew how to, I think, bring up a family right. Anyhow, we had this little episode with her son Gary. He was always taunting his mother, and putting her down. And I said, well, somewhere along the line this will reach a conclusion where I might have a chance to straighten him out. And I did.

It happened one day at the dinner table—because we always ate together. That was one of the prerequisites I had: If you don't eat at the table, you don't eat! That came down from my mother. Anyhow, this particular time Gary was sitting at the table with one of these very slimy appetizers. It was a salad. He loaded it down with ranch dressing. He must've poured a half a bottle of ranch dressing on his salad. And I kept watching him. He had a ruler in his hand, a three-foot ruler in his hand. And he kept inching this ruler over toward the—I knew what he was up to—edge of the table. And I said, OK, let's get prepared. So at his opportune moment, he pushed it off on the floor. Well, this was a real no-no in my house. So I politely got up. I wasn't angry. But I got up. We had three houses there, connected. So I did the fatherly thing: I grabbed him by the back of his collar and drug him down to his room, which was back of the music room, and sat there with him for an hour, and gave him the word of thou shalt not do these things to thy mother. Of course, he was very belligerent, you know. I had realized before that they believed I was insane. And that was good, because it put the fear in him.

But he stood his ground and said, "I'm not afraid of you."

"You're not supposed to be afraid of me," I said. "But I'll tell you what. I'll break both of your arms and both of your legs. This is the way I perform. We'll have none of that in this household, as long as you're here." After that, he kind of straightened up.

I was a little incensed at the way he related to his father. He never called him Dad or Father. He always called him Al. (That was his father's name, Alan White.) Well, his father went all out to make it possible for him to become a lawyer. His father paid for all of his education, and bought him a car. Everything that Gary wanted he paid for.

Gary did finally manage to get his act together; when he was younger he joined the Moonies and got married at one of those big ceremonies that the Reverend Moon had at Madison Square Garden in New York where they had four, five hundred people married. And that lasted quite a long spell. He had two children by that marriage. He was a part of the Moonies, and he sold flowers, which I never could understand, but that was him.

After some years he finally distanced himself from the Moonies, and he now is in Houston Texas and has a little law firm. To my knowledge, he has 8 or 10 people working in his office. So Gary has made it.

One thing that has always stuck in my mind as to how appreciative he was—one day probably ten years ago, he called me and he said, and I'll never forget because it almost brought tears to my eyes, he said, "Hey, Dad." What? He called me Dad. "Hey Dad, this is Gary." Whew! I was struck! I almost cried because of the emotional thing it put on me. Called *me* Dad? In other words, he's coming along. He's come a long way.

One big problem was that my son, who was somewhere around 16 then— I had always preached to him that you are what you associate with, okay. If you hang out with fellows that do illegal things, you're gonna be put in that same category. Well, I don't think he believed me until one fair day or fair evening when the police called me and told me they had my son down at detention home. And the boy across the street was down there also. They were up in the park, right north of where we lived, and they had been apprehended. And Nat Cooper, who was the young fellow, 14 or somewhere around there, had had a little box of marijuana, okay, and they were smoking marijuana, my son and Nat.

The police took them both down to the juvenile. And they called me and I went down there, and I had learned how to handle this through my mother. I learned a lot from my mother. I went in there and saw what was happening. And I've always had a good rapport with the authorities, no big deal. They respected me. I guess because I was with the Symphony and so forth, they thought this was very special, which I guess it was.

Anyhow, I talked to the detectives down there. He asked me, "Are you going to sign for your boy to come out of jail?"

I said, "No. Let 'im stay in jail this night." That's the best thing that ever happened in his life.

I'll never forget, when I left there he was crying: "Daddy! Daddy!" I just wanted to say, Yeah, I'll see ya' later, Baby! What he didn't know is that when I got home, that's the only night in my life I've been awake *all night*. I think I smoked my way through that night in front of the fireplace; I felt for my son, but I knew that that was the thing that had to happen.

The next morning I went down there. "Hey, you think you learned your lesson, Baby!"

Boy, my son was so happy to get out of there. He cried! "Dad! Dad! I'll never—" and he hasn't looked back. Now, that's been 1967 or 1970, somewhere around there, and he hasn't looked back. He learned his lesson and he learned it well. That was called waking up to real life.

Chapter 49

I gotta tell you a little about a very dear friend of mine and marvelous musician whose name was William Alonso Anderson, alias Cat Anderson. I had heard Cat for many a year with different bands, and always respected his musicianship because of his ability to play extremely high notes accurately and with much musical taste.

I had the pleasure of presenting Cat at one of my classes which I taught quite a few years ago, about 1977, down at Metro State College, called "Jazz Music Appreciation." Of course, they got me because of one factor: there was no one else there who knew anything about jazz. They knew about what they called the standard jazz, which was not really jazz. So they got me. Of course, they always knew me as a jazz musician and not a classical musician, which I resented. But I didn't make a big issue out of it—it was not that big a deal to me.

So I contacted Cat (he was traveling through) and asked him if he would allow me to—interrogate him, I call it, you know—before the class. And he said, "OK, fine, I'd love to, Charlie!" He was such a nice guy.

Speaking about Cat Anderson, to me one of his most famous moments was when he played the last note on this Alfred Hitchcock movie, called *Anatomy of a Murder*. This, to me, was the most thrilling second of my life when at the very end of this movie I listened and I heard something: Whhht! And I thought it was a whistle! I later discovered it was Cat Anderson playing one octave over altissimo C on that trumpet! I got the record of that and I think I played it a thousand times, just to hear him. They used to call him the Whistler, in endearing terms, because he was the greatest whistler in the world. They had another fellow who whistled up there, Maynard Ferguson, but not with such marvelous control. Ferguson was magnificent up there, but he didn't have the control that Cat Anderson had. That's why they called him the Whistler.

So Cat came there this one day, and I started to interview him. And of course, the kids were all asking him why did he play so high. And I was surprised, too, because I didn't know. Cat said, "I tell you what. In high school I was a little pudgy and I didn't look too good—I wasn't the most attractive person around. And I was playing in a band, and the girls didn't notice me. So I had to do something to make them notice me." He says, "Now, I hit a high note on that trumpet, and I've had girls ever since." And I had to laugh. He says, "And that's the way I got started playing high notes on the trumpet."

I said, "Oooooh, good!" So we played a couple of selections there, just bass and trumpet, and he gave them a good musical understanding for jazz! That was probably one of my most memorable times, because this great musician was there and he did his part for helping kids understanding what jazz was all about.

When I started teaching this class I was convinced that I was gonna let these people know how beautiful jazz was. So we started from scratch. I mean, most of 'em had never heard of Count Basie, or Duke Ellington, you know, and Louis Armstrong, and Art Tatum, and Erroll Garner. So I got these records together—I had a good library. They were all Black, but that was the name of the game because it was a Black man's legacy. So we had to do it like it was. It was a class of 23, 25, I guess. I said to the class, "Look, we're gonna' learn about what it means to react to jazz music." I says, "There are two facets to jazz music. One is the musician, and the other, the most important, is the audience. And then I would play records by Duke Ellington and I would play records by Count Basie. This was the big test, OK, because these were two extremely different sounds of music.

Most of them didn't know the difference between Count Basie and Duke Ellington. And I said, "I'll tell you what. We're gonna' have for the final exam—I'm gonna' tell you now—to tell the difference between Duke Ellington's band and Count Basie's band. Now that's a part of the examination. Plus, we'll have a surprise for ya' on the examination."

I got them accustomed to what they called "touch dancing." It was funny; we've been doing that for centuries, you know. I said, "What is this touch dance? When we came up that was all we did was touch! You had to touch, you know, or else you weren't dancin'. It was not gyrating like they do, two, three feet apart for two or three hours and then go home and don't even remember what the person's name was that you were gyrating *with*, you know!"

Anyhow, I discovered that most of them couldn't even dance. I said, "Aaaawww, we'll work on that!" What I would do when we played the records, I would have them—one at a time—come up with me, girls and boys, and we would do the time step. Okay? Now, that was funny, because most of 'em had no sense of rhythm whatsoever. I said, "Look, this is the way you count such and such and such." Through the course of that semester it was surprising how much they had learned. Everyone would come by. One of the professors came by. "Look," he says, "you're having too much fun there."

I said, "So?" And I looked at him.

For the final examination we were in there for two hours. I played the records and asked them about the difference between Count Basie and Duke Ellington. And the people outside said, "Boy, that's rocking!" They couldn't believe it, us having so much fun in there. As a matter of fact, one of the teachers came up the door and tried to get in. I says, "Not now, later. We'll let you know." You know.

And I had to laugh; out of all those students, every single one of them, except one, could tell the difference. I later questioned him after the class, I said, "You didn'?"

He said, "No, Mr. Burrell, I knew the difference. I was just playing with ya'."

I said, "I'm glad you were, because I wasn't gonna play with you if you didn't know the difference between Count Basie and Duke Ellington!"

I had to laugh, because one of the teachers said, "Well, how'd they do in their examinations?"

I said, "They all passed, with A-plus."

They said, "What do you mean?"

I said, "Well, all of them knew the difference between Duke Ellington and Count Basie. And they knew where jazz came from, and they all now know how to touch dance!" And they looked at me like I was crazy. But I wasn't crazy. I think I gave them a good lesson in what it means to be a participant in the whole sphere called music, because without the people, music is nothing. So that was that little deal there! That was my big encounter down there with the College. I had a marvelous time doing it.

Count Basie was probably the smartest musician I've ever known, because he was the only piano player that played as few notes as possible, but they were oh, so important. He could make a rhythm section swing because he knew how to play as little as possible and contribute. Most of the piano players play too much and they overpower the feeling of what the other instruments are for. And Count Basie didn't. And if anyone wants to hear a real beginning of the truest rhythm section in all the world get an old recording of Count Basie and that will enable you to hear what the real, the best rhythm section (in my estimation) in all the world ever was.

Chapter 50

I had my own trio for a long time, and we had a few little adventures. This was up in the eighties when this happened, and it happened at the Denver Art Museum when Louise Duncan and I, and Lee Arrelano, were playing there: We went to the front door to unload, and some jackass, I don't know who he was, came out and said, "You can't unload here, you have to go to the loading dock."

And, of course, I gave him a little reading, and I told him, "You tell the big boss in there that Mr. Burrell and his group will not be performing today because you wouldn't let us in!" And I gave Louise and Lee a hundred dollars apiece, I said, "Here's your money." I always paid in cash. That's why they loved me, because Charlie always paid up front in cash!

And we started walking out. And *boooy*, you talk about shit hittin' the fan! Three people came running out, "Charlie, Charlie, Mr. Burrell, such and such and such!" Apologizin'. We walked in the front door.

There was another episode where that happened in the Fairmont Hotel, too. This was funny because I think the only musicians who went in the front door were Louise Duncan, and me, and Billy Ekstine, and his piano player, whose name was Bob Tucker. These were the only people. Now listen to this: All the musicians who were White had to go in the back door. Hah, hah, hah! That was the funniest thing in the world!

CHARLIE: We had to move from our house in Cherry Creek: The big thing that happened was that after the Larsons had passed away, the realtors got a hold of that place on the corner and turned it into townhouses.

MELANIE: *A big, three-story—*

CHARLIE: I think it was about two and a half lots there, maybe three. They turned it into a great monstrosity of a townhouse, with four units, I think, in there. And the one unit was five feet from our property line, and 50-something feet up in the air. Looked right down on our patio, and on our music room. So that was one of the main reasons Melanie said, "Look, that's it. We have to go."

MELANIE: *And we loved that farm house.*

CHARLIE: We loved it. It was our house, you know. The angel house. But the real thing that put the cap on it was the fact that near the end there I went out one morning, and we had three cars out in front. All three cars had punctured tires.

MELANIE: All *tires.*

CHARLIE: All three of 'em.

MELANIE: *All four tires.*

CHARLIE: With ice picks on the side, which meant you had to buy new tires. That was 12 tires right there in one fell swoop. And I bought tires for all those cars right quick, you know. And two or three weeks later we had more, and I counted up actually we had punctured 23 tires. And I'd report it to the police and they gave me the song and dance. But I knew what it was. It was either real estate people wanting to get us out, or the race. We never found out. I said to Melanie, "I think it's really time for us to move." Within myself I knew that it was either me getting a shotgun and killing somebody, or move. So I said this is not worth that. And that's why we moved out of that neighborhood and haven't looked back.

MELANIE: *That was '94. I was still recuperating from the first heart surgery when we moved out. I remember the kids came—all three girls came to pack up the house. It was big, sprawled from the front to the back of the lot.*

CHARLIE: Three houses connected.

MELANIE: *And they packed everything but the garbage! Heh, heh, heh.*

Chapter 51

My first physical encounter since I had been an adult happened at Morrie Bernstein's, the Piano Lounge downtown in Denver around 1957. And it was over a female, of course. This female in question was the same female I was indebted to for life for introducin' me to opera, Doris Fleischer. And I was sitting there talkin' at intermission; she was sitting at the booth there and I was sitting there talking with her. And this fellow came up, Gene Carter, okay. And he was a little drunk, and he started talking to her very, very rudely, you know, what he was gonna do to her and all this sort of thing. And he made the mistake of saying after cussing her out, he reached over to me and he said in my face, "And next I'm going to—" and when he did that I grabbed him around his neck. And it took four or five of 'em to get me off 'im. They said I must've given him fifty-five punches to the head, okay. The next day I look up and he was like you couldn't believe it. He was like a deformed person in the head. But he came by and apologized. We've always been friends since then, you know.

That was an encounter, but the one after that was the big one, which I had with the personnel manager of the Denver Symphony. That was not an encounter, it was like a knock-down-drag-out, you know. He provoked me because of eighteen years of what I call waiting to get even with him for what he did to me. Let me set the stage:

273

When I came back from San Francisco, Mrs. Black, who was the C.O. of the Symphony then, asked me if I would be interested in being principal bass. I said, oh, no. Because John Van Buskirk had been my teacher and my friend, so I wouldn't do that. And Mrs. Black asked me if I wanted to be assistant principal. I turned it down, because Alex Horst was my dear friend—he had given me the bass of my life. And I couldn't do that, I said; we don't do that to friends. So I sat third man down.

When the shit hit the fan was when Alex Horst, Sr., the assistant principal bass player, decided to retire, about 1970 or '71. And it was funny—I have to look back now and tell you these little things. He was never a smoker, okay, and they gave him a gold-plated cigarette lighter! Haaaaa! I cracked up. I said, What kinda people are these, you know! Anyhow, the personnel manager, whose name was Harry Safstrom, had the audacity to come up and sit himself as assistant principal, without an *audition*, okay? In other words, carte blanche he just went up there, because he was the personnel manager. Okay. And I thought that was pretty low, but it didn't get to me. And I didn't bring charges or anything. I said, I'll get him. And then over the years it aggravated itself.

When Brian Priestman came to Denver, that was in '78, around there, he made the mistake too of pullin' the same race movement on me. What happened was we were doing one of the Strauss tone poems which had a four-part bass divisi—that means four different parts for the bass. And I was, of course, the fourth man. Because there was Harry Safstrom, who was at that time the assistant principal, and Harry was third and I was fourth. And Brian Priestman was gonna conduct this thing. At rehearsal, they got to the thing and I heard some commotion and they called an intermission. I didn't know what it was all about. And all of a sudden Harry comes back and says, "Well, they're gonna pick John Arnesen to play your part." Now, John Arnesen was White, and he had had, I think, three weeks of experience in the Chicago Lyric Opera, playing. I had had years of experience, plus being acting assistant principal in San Francisco. And I couldn't play that part? You know. And I went out, and I'll tell ya' frankly, I did cuss Priestman out, yeah. I cussed him like he didn't have good sense. I used words I had never used before, you know. Language right from the old ghetto. But, out of that came a good friendship. Because he knew that he was wrong. And we're still friends. And his daughter, we're still friends, you know; Kelli calls me Uncle Charlie. That was the big encounter, okay, that happened then.

But the maximum thing was when I had to go up against Mr. Safstrom. I hated to do it but it had to be done. After that it was a relief that you can't believe. And that's why so many people have ulcers and things, because they don't let their frustrations come out. You have to harbor them so long and so far, and then you have to let mother nature take its course. That's how simple that was.

This happened at Boettcher Hall. It was the early part of the nineties, I guess it was. And we were playing a concert. And at that time we had instituted a plan for the bass players to have risers, because we were sitting at an angle where four bass players were sitting in back of the two in the front, and it was very difficult to see over them, so you had to have risers. Well, I was sitting in the back at this particular time. And for the first part of the concert I couldn't see. And I went to Harry Safstrom, and I asked him like a gentleman, I said, "Harry, I need a riser because I can't see."

But, to preface all this crap, what happened was this: Whenever anybody else would go to him (I found this clique crap out, okay)—whenever anyone else would go to him, a White person, he would *do*. Right now. He wouldn't forget. Everything was done, and he especially catered to all the principals, because he knew that his job— He was not the best bass player in the world, I mean this is just speaking like it was, okay. Plus he had a condition, a physical condition— he smelled. Okay. And I mean he smelled to high heaven. That's where I got this idea of standing back off the stand for about three feet, to read what I called long distance, because that was getting away from that smell.

Anyhow, the thing that happened was I asked for this riser, at the beginning of intermission, like a gentleman. And I came back at the end of intermission, and it wasn't there. I wasn't angry. I politely took my bass up and carried it off and put in a locker—I was gettin' ready to go home, you know. And Harry came fuming out there, you know, and his race streak caught him, okay. So he made the fatal mistake of grabbing me and he swung me around. He said, "You son of a bitch!" Well, I was smart, because someone always told me if ever any altercation comes like that, make sure you have a witness as to who started it. And it was my fortune to look out of the corner of my eye and see the fellow who was the head of the auditorium. I forget his name. Max somebody. He was the big man of the auditorium. He saw what had happened, okay.

So when Harry grabbed me I whirled around and cracked three or four of his ribs, I guess. I learned in the ghetto that you don't disfigure 'em in the face because that's a tell-tale. You pump the mid-section, okay. In other words, I got the good training in the ghetto! So I did his ribs in. I was all over his ass like white on rice, as they say. Shit, I said Hey Baby, that's a golden opportunity I've been waitin' for for all these years, thank you!

The office called me in—this is what really upset my cart. The office called me in and wrote me a letter, okay. The C.O. was gonna read me the riot act about this. And I listened, listened, and I said, "By the way, did you send Harry Safstrom a letter?"

"No."

And I went berserk on his ass, okay. I did another one of those classic cuss-you-out jobs, you know. And I said, "Look, man. You want a fight? I got material," I says. "I got a good lawyer, here." That's what I told him. "I got a *good* lawyer, here. And he happens to be Jewish." Heh, heh!! (His name was Tom Blumenthal; his father played bass trombone earlier with the Symphony and was one of my best friends.) And it scared the living crap out of him, you know. I says, "And we *will* fight. Okay, now you do what you have to do." And that was what happened there. And nothing ever happened. Of course nothing happened. But that's how they tried to cover that crap up. You know, like Harry was right and I was wrong. But I had all the evidence there, so it wasn't no big deal. You know. But that was the only time I ever really had a real encounter, physical encounter at the Symphony.

In the Symphony, this wasn't all milk, cream, and honey, and all that sort of thing, you know. It was a little more than that, and it was still the race thing, okay. And that's been recently. And that's one of the main reasons why I resigned from the Symphony—I quit. When someone says, "When did you retire?" I didn't retire, I quit. And there's a difference. And I quit on my terms, before they got to me. But I held the upper hand on 'em, thank God. I'm not bragging, but I learned how, like my brother Joe says, to learn the white man's way! Through the books. Through the law, the letter of the law. And I did that nicely, but they always accused me of being a troublemaker.

My mother taught me, "Sticks and stones will break your bones but names will never hurt you." And that's fine, you know! But there comes a point.... And all of us in my family are like that. Don't touch us, because that's a cardinal rule, especially with the ghetto, you don't touch. I'd never start a fight. And I was lucky because in my youth I never had a fight.

Because I never put myself in the position to fight. And I was not a sissy, by no means. But, hey, I was busy with my bass, and that was my most important thing. As I say, we never, never, never, to my knowledge, caused fights, but we wouldn't let you step over us. Mom taught us that, too! Back up against the wall. And if they hit ya', come out fightin'. Because she would! With all kind of humility, with all kind of respect for people, but by the same token, you have to know how far to be pushed.

JOE: *When I had my trucking company, a policeman stopped me. And when you're with the Fire Department the police wouldn't give you a ticket, ordinarily. This policeman stopped me one day; I was hauling dirt from the expressway there. And when he found out I was a fireman, oh, we bullshitted for about fifteen or twenty minutes! And when we got through, he gave me three tickets! And I sent the commissioner a letter, commending him on his professionalism! And the commissioner got a hold of me, took me out to lunch, and says, "Goddamn, no one has ever got three tickets and thanked the person for it!" And I ate lunch with the commissioner. This was in the sixties. I don't let anybody— I don't retaliate with anger. I'm positive and I will write a grievance and report you in a minute for being negative with me. Also, I have commended people—police that have given me tickets and different things—for their professionalism. You'll smile at me, I'll thank you for your smiling. But when you shit on me, you'll know it. That's the way I handle it. To me, it's rewarding and makes me feel good.*

CHARLIE: I realize now that back in those days when you were a little vocal and you were Black you were a troublemaker. That was the phrase they used, you know, to suggest how you were as a person. "Oh, he's alright, but he's a *troublemaker!*" And I'm kind of glad I was because if I hadn't been I'd have been *dead*, from ulcers and everything else from holding it in. I'd treat you fair if you treated me fair, but if you didn't we had problems.

I'm not angry at these people. I'm just telling it like it was, okay, and like it *is*. Because so many people want to put glossy coating over this, like everything is peaches and cream. It wasn't peaches and cream, Dahling. It just wasn't. And ya' have to tell the truth. By the same token, I went on and did my job and I enjoyed every second of it. I wouldn't trade one moment of playing with the Symphony for a million dollars, because that was my big thrill, and always has been my big thrill. To play with a team. Big teamwork, you know. I have no ill-feelings. Never had time, you know. Me and Mr. Safstrom were still friends. We developed a good friendship. We had no axe to grind; he realized that he was wrong, and I realized that I was wrong. And we shook hands and went on from there.

Chapter 52

When Dianne Reeves was maybe about 14, I had the pleasure and thrill of hearing her up at Central City, doing one of those little things they called a pre-program, little jazz program, for the Central City Opera Company. And she was singing with a little junior high school group. And I heard her sing and I realized, hey, this was a big talent. She was about 14. So I talked to her mother, took it upon me to try to groom her, not only in terms of being a singer but in terms of being a person. Before that, she was a little roustabout, we used to call her, a rowdy. I think every other week her mother was up to the school tryin' to smooth over what Dianne had done. She was whipping all the girls, you know, and most of the boys in the school, so Vada had a big job on her hands. But then I took Dianne under my wing—you know, not bragging—but took her under my wing and taught her, tried to teach her how to become responsible as a person. And how to get along, and get an education, which was primary. And how to be exposed to the White man's culture. She came up in a time when the expression was "Black is Beautiful." Well, I had to get her out of that notion that black was beautiful and get her into the notion that education, in the head, was beautiful. And it took quite a bit of doing, because she was kind of steeped only in the Black culture, which was not—in my way of thinking—

the best thing. It was a ruination of most of the Black kids because it taught them the wrong philosophy of what was important in life.

My mother talked to me about that, and I knew what we were saying was the truth. She would say, "Look, son, black or white or blue or yellow is not beautiful. Intelligence is beautiful. Inside." She says, "Don't ever make that mistake." But Dianne got involved in that with her aunt and her mother. And it took quite a bit to kinda help bring Dianne out of that.

If it hadn't been for my mother, Dianne would never have made it. When Dianne wasn't even a year old, my mother started babysitting her more than she babysat all the rest of her family. And she did that up 'til the time when Dianne was almost seventeen years old. And my lovable sister Vada was busy playing. She didn't have that kind of ability to be a real mother to a child. Consequently, my mother took over and helped raise Dianne and her sister Sharon. Another big pillar of progress in the family.

SHARON: *When I was little, staying with my grandmother at that time, he would always come in, talkin' about his music, playin'. My other uncle would come in, who was a fireman, talkin' about his job. Actually, they came over there to eat. 'Cause Gramma would cook some hellacious dishes for them, in which usually were beans. And I couldn't stand them. So I knew when they would come, I'd say, aaaahhh, Gramma's cookin' beans. That means Charlie Brown and Joe are comin' over. And Charlie Brown would kinda make me eat these beans. Told me, "You'd better eat— you're not gonna get anything else to eat." And I'm sayin' to myself, I'll bet, you wait and see. I'm not eatin' no beans! And to this day, I don't eat beans. Never have liked 'em. But, you know, we always joked back and forth.*

CHARLIE: I get emotional when I go in sometimes and start cookin' a pot of beans. That means something, because it means I'm able to do that, I'm able to enjoy that. A pot of beans means something to me because in the early days to have a pot of beans meant that you were not hungry. And in the old philosophy of the ghetto thing we didn't say hungry, we said *hongry*, which was not even in the language. But that meant that, baby, you needed something when you were *hongry*.

SHARON: *He was stern. And committed to whatever it was he said. I was very proud of him 'cause he stuck to his guns. If he got into an argument—or disagreement, I'll put it like that—with any of his siblings, he held his ground.*

I decided I was gonna play flute. I was very frustrated, 'cause I could not get a sound outa that flute. Remember? I couldn't get a sound. I mean, I blew and blew for at least three, four days. Nothin' would come out. Charlie Brown was just laughin' at me. Finally he said, "Blow in it like you blowin' into a Coke bottle." Which is what we used to do all the time.

I said, "Ah, okay." Sure enough, the sound came out. I was gone! I had it flat goin' on. I carried that on up to the first year of college. So I went on to do first chair in concert orchestra and I had first chair in marching band.

But during that time, Charlie Brown said, "You have to practice." Da-da-da-da number of hours a day. I'm not doin' that! I got over here to East High School. I was in the concert orchestra. He says, "C'mon, get your flute little girl, let's go out here to the park." For what? Charlie Brown had me out there at City Park, standin' under a tree, him playin' his bass and me playin' flute, for three hours. I was so mad at him. I went back and told my teacher what he did, because he wanted to know how I mastered this song as quickly as I did, and that was because of Charlie Brown's efforts. But I always appreciated Charlie Brown for his indulgence and for having that discipline to practice.

Dianne wanted to be a singer. So I started working with her when she was about 14, and exposing her to the better things in life and the better people. Let her know there's a different way of life, and so forth. I would take Dianne to places like the Brown Palace, and expose her to these cultures. I'd take her to lectures, I took her to the Symphony. I think I took her to everything that was uplifting. And she finally graduated with good grades, after all that, and went down to CU, I think, for a couple of years to the university downtown here in Denver. And that's where she really started to blossom and get herself together. And right after that she started singing around town here and there.

I think her first real job was with my trio, playing for a party, and I think she was maybe sixteen. Dianne played with me, with Louise Duncan on piano, and Lee Arrelano on drums. And I think it was her first big job. I gave her a hundred dollars, okay. And that was *biiig*, *biig*, money in those days.

DIANNE: *Because of Uncle Charlie I never was afraid. I came up at a time where there were still jam sessions, and I was never afraid to go. I remember when Blue Mitchell was livin' here in Denver. I found out he was livin' here 'cause I was readin' the back of the records like Uncle Charlie told me to. And I said, Wow, Blue Mitchell's here! So I went and I said, "Hi, my name is Dianne." And he was lookin' at me like How old are you? You know. "And I can sing 'On a Clear Day' in F and we can do the blues." And I would sing one of the blues my Aunt Kay would teach me. But I never had any inhibitions because he was takin' me to gigs early on. And just sayin', Do it. Sing.*

I remember when I moved to Los Angeles. They had the famous Parisian Room. And I went there and I wanted to sit in and sing. You had to put your name on a list. My name was at the end of the list, so the evening ended before they got to my name. And so every week I was determined because, you know, that's what you do, you know! You want people to hear you. I was determined. And I went and they said that the jam session started at eight, so I got there at six. And I put my name on as soon as the lady walked down. I said, "I want my name on the top of the list; I want to sit in and sing." And she was like, um, Who is this girl? You know. And once again, not even old enough to be in there but knew how to carry myself.

When I got up there, you know, it was just like, Gotta let 'em know. Always, you gotta let 'em know. And I was just never afraid, 'cause I was in an atmosphere where no one told me You should be afraid. And that's what I'm sayin', you know, like, for them it was either you do it or you don't. There was no maybe. Maybe was created after they created a world for me to live in. But I was still goin' on the premise of, you do it.

CHARLIE: Dianne kept feeling her way. Her big thing was this: She was only about 17, and I arranged to have her do a jazz performance with the Denver Symphony. At that time, they were bringing in Clark Terry, my friend from the old Navy days. So I talked with him, and he had faith enough in me to believe that she could perform, and so she did. She performed with Clark Terry as a special guest and Ellen Rucker was playing piano. I had to laugh, because Ellen Rucker said, "Charlie, I can't play." She was so nervous.

I said, "Ellen, just play!" And she did. She played in back of Dianne. And I don't know whether I accompanied Dianne or whether somebody else did on bass. But anyhow, that was her first big opening, because Clark Terry heard her then. Clark also heard her again at one of the school concerts, I think it was in Kansas, someplace. I don't know whether it was Topeka or where it was. But Clark heard her sing there, and he took an interest in her and helped her along her career. And that was the beginning of her real career, was when she was exposed to Clark Terry, who had faith in her.

I must say that Clark Terry was also instrumental in helping her realize her position in terms of her relationship to musicians. As the story goes, Clark told me that Dianne had the nerve, the audacity, to come up to him and tell him that This wasn't right, and such and such and such. And that's when, as they say in the old vernacular, Clark put the reading on Dianne, okay. He told her, "Look, this is not your show, this is my show. We do it my way. You don't know shit." In other words, "You listen to Clark and I'll tell ya'." And that, I think, helped to straighten Dianne out in terms of the relationship of singer and musician.

She started her own groups, and they went from here to there. As she grew, she realized that (which I had told her before) you're only as good a singer as the musicians you have backing you. And that, I think, stuck in her craw; little by little she learned to upgrade her musicians in back of her. Dianne has now reached the pinnacle of her entire life by having the best musicians with her. I have ever heard behind a singer. She has won four Grammy Awards.

DIANNE: *I've always referred to him, over the years, even when I left home. Still would want him to come and see my bands. You know, some of the music he wasn't really crazy about; he'd go, "Yeah, yeah." And it wasn't until really recent years that it was like, "Now THAT'S what I'm talkin' about." I had to find my thing, you know, and settle into it. Once that happened—*

The biggest thing that really moved me, in a way that no other experience with my uncle was when I performed in 2002 with the Colorado Symphony. He was at the show. And I didn't hear from him for about two or three days. And everybody liked it, but there was only one person I wanted to hear from. And finally he called. And he told me how much he liked it and what he thought of it! And the reason that he couldn't call was 'cause he was so full of emotion. It was the thing that really made me see a side of him that I'd experienced but not as openly as that. Even though it was over the phone. And he spoke in a way that I knew, once again, that his confidence in me made me stronger. There was just really, really, nothin' I didn't think I could do, because he was the measuring stick. If he said that it was really wonderful, then I believed that. You know, you listen to a lot of other people, but there are very few people that you really respect their opinion like that. And I waited for his. And I waited and I kept sayin', "Mom, I haven't heard from Charlie Brown."

She said, "He loved it, he was cryin'." But that's his sister, and she's just gonna tell it, you know. But I wanted to hear it from him. And when I did, it really warmed my heart. It brought tears to my eyes, because it was like, uh, full circle.

His heart was open, totally open. His words were always real but they weren't covered in anything. They were just straight from the heart to the mouth to my ear. They were emotional and they were spiritually lifted, and they were words that said more than the things that he told me. Before there were things that he wanted from me. But this time it was like, "You got it."

PURNELL The night I got your vote of confidence was when we were playing up at Arthur's on the Avenue, and I told you I had this gig, a Friday and Saturday night gig. And you came in after the Symphony the first night. You heard us play, and you didn't say anything. You didn't crack a smile. And I thought, uh, oh, I screwed up again. Heh-heh. And you said, "Hey, Couz, when are you playing again?" I said, "Tomorrow night." That Friday night you sat in front of the stage, you had your cigar lit, and I told them to give you the best cognac in the house. You had this wonderful snifter of cognac and you sat there looking like the Buddha, and you stared me down, and I got scared. I kept looking at you and you kept staring at me. You had this plume of smoking going in front of you. And then you said, "Do you mind if I play with you tomorrow night? You're ready." That was the finest night of my life! I had your endorsement and I knew that I would never let you down, from the way you taught me and from the standards you set.

Chapter 53

I did not retire from the Symphony. I quit. On my terms. And I never felt better. And it's been years and every day has been like Christmas. I miss the music but I don't miss the people.

It was not all bad. It was 99% good. Every day I enjoyed it; every single day. And I didn't miss a rehearsal in 45 years, because I enjoyed it thoroughly. It was a salvation for me, and it was a salvation for other Negroes, too, to help them realize their potentials, what they could do in terms of music, especially the classical side of music.

It was a marvelous experience. And it couldn't have been more fruitful in terms of making my life what it was and what it is today. Every time I played was like a new experience, and I was there for forty-five years. And the few little pitfalls I had didn't mean a thing compared to the marvelous experience that I had received. And also the marvelous opportunity it brought forth for minorities, especially the Blacks, to know that they could be accepted in this elite realm of music, rather than just playing in the corner joints and so forth. I looked at my Black musicians in those days and I realized that 99% of them couldn't go anyplace but the corner bars. It was a little devastating. The main objective was that I was stimulated to try to make it better for the Blacks to get in. And I did. And I was happy. And in the interim I didn't lose myself. Over my entire life my stimulant has always been music. And I love music and love to play music and that's been my stimulant—classical or jazz. Just as long as it's good music.

The people in the Denver Symphony were by and large very excellent people. We had no big problems, and I still say glory to the conductor, Saul Caston, who was the pioneer in engineering the amalgamation of minorities into the classical sphere. My hat always goes off to Saul Caston and the people around him, especially Miss Black, who made all of my life as a musician (and with the Symphony) profitable and bearable.

San Francisco was a major orchestra; that was one of the major six orchestras in the country then. In San Francisco, I was looked up to like I had never been looked up to in my life. It kind of frightened me, on one hand. But then I said, Oh, okay, this is just the way it is. But I was happy and delighted to know that the average Anglo—all the Anglos, as a matter of fact—in the Symphony were just sincerely gracious to me, and it was not a put-on. Because I'm probably one of the first people in the world that can tell when a person is phony or not. And the people in San Francisco were genuine. And that made all my career worthwhile, to realize that I was accepted for me as a person, and my ability, and nothing else. That was important.

MELANIE: *Recently, I've focused entirely differently, on dressage driving, and horses. And I had to make a decision, what I would do about cello. If I wasn't going to play professionally, would I practice every day? In order to stay good you have to practice every day. And I decided that I would rather give up the cello, which was like cutting off my hands, and learn something about training horses.*

So I don't play cello. I had two cellos, and one was a superb Italian cello. And a string repairman and maker took it and did some repair and sold it. This was really like selling a child; it was a gorgeous Testori cello. It was made in 1742. Beautiful sound, just a round, golden sound. And I had made up my mind that I'd better make up my mind! Otherwise I would end up just sitting in the rocker doing nothing. He sold it and he called me and asked me if I wanted to see it after he restored it. And I said no. Go. And I have another one that I used in orchestra a lot. And it's a good cello, but it didn't have the kind of quality that the Italian cello had. I have a couple of bows that are really nice, that are still sitting around somewhere.

I felt that if I came here—Longmont, for instance, has a little symphony—I was gonna be tapped, and was gonna be tapped into a situation that I really didn't enjoy. So I felt that I would be tapped for chamber music and such things. I thought I'd better just leave it alone. It was a hard decision.

If you're retired, you really better think about what you're gonna do. Otherwise, you'll do nothing and kind of just wither on the vine. So if you have something that can really be a challenge, it gives you life, it really does.

CHARLIE: We're having the best part of our lives, because she's doing what she wants to do, which is with her miniature horses, and still studying. And by the way, in connection with the miniature horses, she was so astute that she won most of the blue ribbons for almost ten years. And we now have a garage full of blue ribbons like you can't believe. I think the last time I counted it was something like sixty. Now she's kinda cut back because she's had a reoccurrence, a spillover of what she had from her heart conditions. But she's still doing her lessons three times a week with her trainer up there. And I'm still here smokin' my cigars and having a nice time.

The bass has always been my mistress. And what the bass entailed, which was music, has been my mistress from the time I was 12, and nothing got in my way. And the people along the way helped me. The important people, my wives, my children, and a few important people who helped me in the neighborhood and out of the neighborhood to make it all possible. But the main thing: I *never, never* thought about quitting music. I don't even think about it now! And I'm a hundred years old, almost. I'm still tryin' to play a little blues and having a good time doing it. That's the nature of what I do. That was how simple it was. There was *never*, absolutely never, any possibility of quitting music. I didn't think about it, but I would rather give up my life than give up music because that is my life. And the people who have been around me have realized that my best feature is playing. They love to see me play, because I have so much fun. I enjoy every second of it. When I'm in the jazz scene, no one has more fun than Old Charlie.

The big thing is that I've always had fun playing. God, it's always thrilled the shit out of me. I couldn't believe it, you know, like I'm doin' this. Oh, boy! But make no mistake, there were hundreds of thousands of hours behind that, which made that possible. But I don't object to it. I look at it and say Thank you for me being able to be physically and mentally equipped to do this. There are so many of my friends in the classical field and also in the jazz field that have fallen by the wayside because they didn't have enough determination to stick with what they were doing. They were not patient enough in terms of what they were doing. And they didn't realize that this whole thing called life is nothin' but a matter of enjoying the surroundings, the trees, the birds, the bees, the people, the ups, the downs, the ins, and the outs. And just living. And make every day count a little bit. Don't go into it like ho hum, what can this world do for me. As I say like Kennedy said, think what I can do for this world. And respect people and yourself. And that's the simplicity of it.

Epilogue

"It all comes from my dear mother."

It all comes from my dear mother. She was a monster. I didn't realize that until I got older, and Dianne realized it when she got a little older, that Mom was saying something that you couldn't buy in books. She was giving me a foundation for life. To be ready for life and to accept life. As a matter of fact, she, on her death bed, got me ready for death. Which I wasn't before. That was 1979,

March the 1ˢᵗ. She used to say, "Chunky, when you go through, be thankful. Always realize that everyone has to go." She said, "And don't fight it. Just let it come." And she did that.

DIANNE: *I used to love my grandmother to come to my concerts. I remember one time I made her this dress—I cannot to this day believe she wore it, because, ooh, the seams were terrible. But it was my creation and my idea of what I wanted to see her in. I bought her a blouse to go underneath it. And it was a green dress and it went to the floor and it was velvet. And she wore it with such pride, because it was not just the dress, it was a gift that she accepted from my heart, being totally supportive of what it was that I was doin'.*

SHARON: *I think the other saving grace is we're a happy family. We have parties. As a matter of fact we had Mary Beth's 75ᵗʰ. That was a big party, wasn't it? I mean, we turned out. Purnell played. And I had a comedian. And a bartender. And all those people were in here, must've been fifty people in here. I don't know how I did it but I did. But anyway, we always stay positive. There was always somebody to catch you. If I had a real serious problem or concern and wanted to talk, I called Charlie Brown. "What are you doing?" "Why don't you come by." Or he'll call me. Or he'll just drop by to see how I'm doin'. And we have a chance to share, not only what's goin' on in your personal lives but what's goin' on within the family.*

DIANNE: *They're forward thinkers. Forward everything. What has happened in the past—it's like you can't unring the bell. Just keep movin' forward. And they have a lot of energy and they really, really, look forward to havin' a new day. I know my mother always said, and I'm sure my Uncle Charles, all of 'em are like this—my mother would say, "I'm NEVER bored." And none of 'em are ever bored. They're just full of life. They believe in communicating, helping one another. Growin' up as kids, it was just really important to stay together. And they always have been like that.*

The interesting thing with me, is that my uncle and my mother and all of them, they only had two answers to a question, yes or no. They also gave me choices. So I think that more than anything, being aware of the past, being aware of the struggles, I was already armed with a lot of information. My greatest struggle was that there was a lot open to me and how do I choose. That was what I dealt with more than anything, and how do I keep my integrity, how do I protect my voice, how do I maneuver through all of this, music industry especially, that is an industry that now is, like, everybody's makin' tons of money. But I hear somethin' a certain way—how do I do that? So more than anything it was relating to, you follow your heart. You follow your road. You follow your passion. You follow what it is that you love. Basically, what happens is, the more you love yourself, the more people will start to love you.

Charles had an understanding of his music early in his life that made him passionate and made him really, really, want to do whatever it took to master this music. Once again, that's how they all are. It was something that he just had a love for, and there was nothing that was going to deter him from getting to his goals.

CHARLIE: I'll be frank with ya': I had a good time, marvelous time. It was a hard road but it was an honest road. And I never had any problems with drugs, alcohol, or jail. So I can consider myself very lucky. And I tried along the way not to hurt people but to make people happy. And I think I did a pretty good job.

I was out there in no man's land. And Mom taught me a lesson like, "Look. It doesn't matter where you are, just be yourself." And that was how simple that was. Be yourself, you know. And from that everything else will take it's place. And of course you're going to have trials and tribulations. We all have had them and will have them. Until you get to where I am now. I don't have any trials, because I'm just about ready to check over to the other side. But that's okay, because I've been there.

About the Authors

Charlie Burrell

A Denver legend and a pioneer in breaking down color barriers, Charlie is loved and revered by generations of both jazz and classical music devotees.

In 1949 Charlie joined the Denver Symphony as the first person of color under contract with a major orchestra.

In 1959 he moved to San Francisco to become the first person of color in the San Francisco Orchestra. In Charlie's 60-plus years as a professional musician, he played for conductors including Arthur Fiedler and Pierre Monteux.

He has also worked with the who's who of jazz greats—appearing on stage with the likes of Billie Holiday, Charlie Parker, and Lionel Hampton.

About the Authors

Mitch Handelsman

Mitch is an award-winning Psychology professor at the University of Colorado Denver. When Mitch is not in class or writing papers and books on ethics, he plays jazz trumpet in the Denver area—appearing on stage with the likes of Charlie Burrell.

Dianne Reeves (foreword):

A four-time Grammy-winning jazz singer, Dianne has performed with Wynton Marsalis, Clark Terry, and countless others. She was featured in the hit 2005 motion picture and soundtrack, *Good Night, and Good Luck.* She grew up in Denver and is the niece and protégé of Charlie Burrell.

Photo Credits:

Reccommended Reading:

African American Music: An Introduction by Mellonee V. Burnim and Portia K. Maultsby
ISBN: 0415941385

I Never Had It Made: An Autobiography of Jackie Robinson by Jackie Robinson and Alfred Duckett
ISBN: 0060555971

Having Our Say: The Delany Sisters' First 100 Years by Sarah L. Delany, A. Elizabeth Delany and Amy Hill Hearth
ISBN: 0440220424

On My Own at 107: Reflections on Life Without Bessie by Sarah L. Delany, Amy Hill Hearth and Brian M. Kotsky
ISBN: 0062514865

Soaring On The Wings Of A Dream: The Untold Story of America's First Black Astronaut Candidate by Ed Dwight
ISBN: 0883783053

The Scalpel and the Silver Bear: The First Navajo Woman Surgeon Combines Western Medicine and Traditional Healing... by Lori Alvord and Elizabeth Cohen Van Pelt
ISBN: 0553378007

Miles: The Autobiography (Picador Books) by Miles Davis and Quincy Troupe
ISBN: 0330313827

Buck: A Memoir by M.K. Asante
ISBN: 0812983629

Freedom Flyers: The Tuskegee Airmen of World War II (Oxford Oral History Series) by J. Todd Moye
ISBN: 0199896550

Classical Music in America: A History by Joseph Horowitz
ISBN: 0393330559

If you liked

The Life of
Charlie Burrell

Breaking the
Color Barrier
in Classical Music

please leave a reveiw on Amazon.com